To
Davi

GW00580192

SUMMER HATES CHRISTMAS

Thanks for supporting
Children in Read

RACHEL DOVE

Happy Christmas &
Birthday!

December 2023

love from

Rachel Dove

B

Boldwood

First published in Great Britain in 2023 by Boldwood Books Ltd.

Copyright © Rachel Dove, 2023

Cover Design by Alexandra Allden

Cover Photography: Shutterstock

The moral right of Rachel Dove to be identified as the author of this work has been asserted in accordance with the Copyright, Designs and Patents Act 1988.

All rights reserved. No part of this book may be reproduced in any form or by any electronic or mechanical means, including information storage and retrieval systems, without written permission from the author, except for the use of brief quotations in a book review.

This book is a work of fiction and, except in the case of historical fact, any resemblance to actual persons, living or dead, is purely coincidental.

Every effort has been made to obtain the necessary permissions with reference to copyright material, both illustrative and quoted. We apologise for any omissions in this respect and will be pleased to make the appropriate acknowledgements in any future edition.

A CIP catalogue record for this book is available from the British Library.

Paperback ISBN 978-1-80483-626-2

Large Print ISBN 978-1-80483-625-5

Hardback ISBN 978-1-80483-627-9

Ebook ISBN 978-1-80483-624-8

Kindle ISBN 978-1-80483-623-1

Audio CD ISBN 978-1-80483-632-3

MP3 CD ISBN 978-1-80483-631-6

Digital audio download ISBN 978-1-80483-630-9

Boldwood Books Ltd
23 Bowerdean Street
London SW6 3TN
www.boldwoodbooks.com

Dedicated to the dear departed June Rosamunde Milne
Dreamer, poet, carer, and much-loved auntie.

All the lonely people
Where do they all come from? All the lonely people
Where do they all belong?

— 'ELEANOR RIGBY' BY LENNON & MCCARTNEY

1

Summer Hastings walked along the front of Bridlington beach, right alongside the harbour, flip flops dangling from her fingers, bright-pink toenails flashing in and out of the shallow sea water as she walked along. Her maxi dress ruffled up in one hand, her handbag slung across her shoulders. Oversized shades on her tanned nose, brows sculpted and bright, summery nails on her fingers, she was feeling great. It was mid September, and the weather was amazing. She loved living here year round, but these months were her absolute favourite. Work was busy, people constantly in and out, changing money, booking last-minute deals, coming to iron out last-minute niggles. It was perfect, and she wouldn't change a thing about it. Except perhaps, her ability to leave once in a while. So many times, her finger had hovered over her keyboard, just poised to grab a last-minute deal and see the world. She never pressed the button though. She couldn't quite bring herself to do it, not with how things were at home. Instead, she just grinned and nodded when her customers came back to gush about their dream travels. She smiled and laughed along with them over their holiday snaps, all the while wishing it was her that had the tale to tell. Just once, why couldn't it be her? Still, she took solace in the present. Simple pleasures. The sun, the walk on the beach every morning. The sheer joy and pleasure to be gained from a nice summer's day.

That's how she remembered feeling that fateful morning. She would declare it later to be BC. Before Christmas. Eugh. Now that was something she did hate, even more than her wheels being grounded. The mere tinkle of a seasonal bell had her coming out in a cold sweat. When the first Christmas carols were played on the radio, she would hit the gin and start painting 'The End Is Nigh' sandwich boards. How could *anyone* like Christmas? It was expensive, noisy, freezing, and tacky. Everyone cramming their cupboards with food and drink, forced to spend time with their so-called loved ones? No, thank you. She would choose a hot beach and a cold cocktail any day of the week. Summer was salads and cold, crisp wine, BBQs and Pimms, Wimbledon, strawberries and cream. Bridlington lived for summer, and so did she. The fact that they were having an Indian summer, a late heat wave, was all the better. She didn't even want to think about Christmas, and she had no intention of starting now, when it still seemed so far away. When it did swing around again, she would deal with it then. In her usual way: totally avoiding it altogether. She smiled to herself through her dusty-pink lip gloss, enjoying once more the feel of the sand under her feet as she walked her usual coastal path to her travel agency, Summer Loving. She loved walking down past the shops, the cute cupcake bakery, the chocolate shop, the surf shack. Seeing the same customers, the same shop owners day in and day out, living their lives. Having their routines played out in front of her. Life was pretty good here at times. Times like this, when the air of opportunity and promise seemed so fresh and ripe, there for the taking. She loved the scent of delusion in the morning.

Then she turned the corner to where her travel agency stood and heard the slap of her flip flop soles hitting the pavement. She had dropped them as she stood there, glued to the spot with shock. *What the hell?* She blinked rapidly, as though the movement would dislodge the offensive vision from her sight.

There was a green tree, right outside her shop doorway. A large, green, fir tree, complete with red, gold, and silver decorations. It looked like Santa had thrown up on it, and against the backdrop of the palm tree decals in the shop window, it looked even worse. Summer walked across to her shop quickly, not taking her eyes off the tree. Was it a joke? Had someone realised that she hated Christmas and decided to mess with her? Whatever it was, her morning was ruined now. She got close enough to touch it when a hand seemingly appeared from nowhere, and the tree was yanked to the right, away from her grasp.

'Hey!' Summer shouted, lunging for the branches as it passed her. 'What the holy hell are you doing?'

'Eh?' A gruff confused voice replied. From behind the tree came a man who did look decidedly confused. 'What's the matter?'

'What's the matter?' Summer echoed, feeling her face get hotter and hotter. 'Why the hell is there a Christmas tree outside my shop?'

The man smiled then, and straightening up he offered his hand. 'Sorry, I was just moving it into my place. The truck had to leave, so I dumped out what I could. I'm Noel Pritchett, I just took the lease next door.' He smiled again, a full one this time, showing off the whites of his perfect teeth and the dimples in his cheeks. He had shaggy, black, curly hair, like Aidan Turner off the telly. Summer scowled, looking at his outstretched hand. This inconsiderate arse-hole had just ruined *Poldark* for her.

She folded her arms against her chest and his smile faded a

little, lips twitching. He left his hand out there a beat longer, before tucking it under his opposite underarm.

'Summer. Hastings. What exactly are you selling next door?'

Noel pointed to the tree, as though he was holding a big elephant, not a tatty looking travesty. 'Er, Christmas?' he said, 'my shop is called Forever Festive.'

Summer's eyes bulged, and she felt her left eyelid twitch. It always did that when she was stressed, or overtired, or over caffeinated. She could feel it twitching rapidly, but she couldn't move. This was her worst nightmare! How the hell could she get rid of him? This was a disaster, all wrapped up in a ridiculously good-looking tinsel tat bow. She had a flashback to the old days, when her dad would come home, his van laden with the latest craze. Crazy frog toys, the latest band T-shirt. Tat and crap that people lapped up. 'Gullible punters', he called them.

'Hello? You there?' Christmas Poldark was waving his hand in front of her face now, getting only a glazed expression in return. She looked like a hot mannequin challenge. 'Hello? Summer?'

She came to at the sound of her name being called. Her eyes slowly focused again and narrowed when they spotted him.

'You okay? Where did you go?' He looked genuinely concerned now, shepherding her towards his shop, his corded forearm resting under her wrist. 'Come and get a drink; I've unpacked the kettle thankfully.'

Summer was nearly through the door when she came to her senses. She pulled her arm away from his, backing away from him. It felt like the ghost of her father was walking with them, and she could feel it happening again. The panicky feelings of loss and anger, all balled up in the pit of her stomach. It always made her feet tingle. She looked down at them, and back across at her unwanted new companion. Noel looked like he half expected her to cross her fingers to ward him off. He made no attempt to follow her; he just crossed his arms and leant on the door frame of his shop. The tree stood between them, a big, spiky, green bystander to their first meeting.

'I don't need help, thank you. What I need is for you to keep your bullshit tat the hell away from my shop.'

Noel raised his brows. 'Wow, you really don't like decorations, do you?' She growled in response, and he raised his palms in surrender. 'Listen, I'm almost moved in. I will get it done as quick as possible, and keep things out of your way, okay? I'm sorry. Would you let me buy you dinner, apologise properly?' He gave her a big grin, and she ignored the jolt of unexpected electricity that passed through her. *Not on my watch*, her mother's voice said in her head. *Men like him never end well, my girl. Keep walking.*

'No, I don't think so,' she said flatly. 'I'm not interested.' He folded his arms tighter, and she saw the muscles in his arm twitch. The mother in her head tutted loudly, snapping her out of her body lust stupor. She stood to attention, banging her left foot on the floor to get herself moving again. 'This isn't Cornwall, you know! We don't have need for your kind round here! I just want you to keep your festive fuckery away from me!' She turned on her heel, giving the tree a swift kick with all the venom she could muster. The tree keeled over onto its side with the tinkle of broken glass, but she heard no movement from Noel. She didn't wait to see his reaction either. She fumbled for her shop key, and didn't draw breath till she was locked in and sat on the floor of the back store room, trembling amongst the brochures.

Noel looked at the tree, crumpled on its side, the ornaments on it askew, with some smashed to bits. A solitary bauble with Santa's smiling face splashed across it rolled to the edge of the pavement, smashing as it fell into the road.

'What the heck has Cornwall got to do with anything?' he asked aloud. 'I'm from Leeds.'

* * *

'Jean, that's hardly the point, is it? It hasn't been closed that long, anyway.'

Jean took a stack of brochures down from a shelf and sprayed it with glass cleaner, her vigorous cleaning movements making her many bracelets rattle. 'It has though love, and it made your shop look less attractive, being next to an empty shop. Especially with all the fly-posters sticking up their gaudy adverts all over the place. Sticks in my craw, it does. I broke three nails the other week. Sharon my nail lady, wasn't best pleased, I can tell you!' Jean raised her hand, looking at her now perfect long nails, today painted with pictures of pencils, apples and rulers. She called them her 'Back to School' nails. She had indeed gone back to study. Jean did a new course every September, and was now a whizz at flowers, cakes and pottery. She could open up a hell of a gift shop, but she was happy to be a cleaner for the local shops in Bridlington instead, tending her garden, doing her crafts with her cat for company. Jean could often be seen walking on the beach in the early mornings before the crowds gathered. Another happy habitant. This year, she was doing sugar craft, and so she often had little crystals of sugar on her clothing, and a lovely, sweet smell to her. Rather more appealing than the year before when she was learning pottery. Some of the bits of clay she had shed back then were still welded to the carpet in the back room, Summer was sure of it. And the mug Jean had made her had leaked, unfortunately pouring hot coffee onto a customer's scrotum. He never did book that round the world trip.

'Fair enough, the empty shop might have been a little annoying, but having a bloody tat shop won't be any better, will it? I'm trying to entice people away for Christmas, make them yearn for palm trees and pina coladas, and before they even get to the doors, bloody Bing Crosby is there, banging his bloomin' 'White Christmas' drum! We'll have to report him to the tourist committee and the council. The landlord has to be told to kick him out.'

Jean placed the brochures back in the rack neatly, brushing a feather duster over the already dust-free shelf. 'You can't do that! You know Reg needs the rent, come on, Summer! Not all men are horrible idiots, you know; some are actually rather normal. Nice, even.'

'Reg can rent it to someone else! Bridlington is a tourist hotspot, he'll soon fill it up, and if it's so easy to find nice men, why doesn't every woman have one? I get enough people in here shopping for lone trips to realise that not everyone needs company, or to alter for some bloke.'

Jean stood up slowly, rubbing her knee.

'Jean, are you okay? Do you need to go home?'

The look Jean shot her had her hunching her neck into her shoulders like a startled turtle.

'Okay, I'm only asking.' *Stubborn as ever.*

'No woman is an island, Summer. Everyone needs someone at some point in their lives. And for the record, I'm getting old, not dying. My knee twinges. Your ankle clicks; does that mean you're knocking on the door of death?'

Summer rolled her eyes. 'Okay, okay. Fair point.'

'You can't expect Reg to have to find a tenant this close to Christmas. Not with the season winding down. He needs the cash, and with his heart, he doesn't need the stress. I think you're being a little bit selfish, and a little unfair to the poor lad next door. He's running a business all on his own. Sound familiar?'

Summer's jaw dropped wide open. 'Me! Selfish? No, I'm only thinking of the community, my business. Hell, everyone's business.

That thing,' Summer jabbed at the wall dividing them, as though the gates of hell had literally opened up next door, 'that thing is gross. It's not in keeping with Bridlington at all; it's about Christmas, not the beach!'

Jean frowned, moving to the next shelf. 'Blackpool illuminations has thousands of people flocking for the weekend, for Christmas trips, getaways, Christmas parties. So do we. People buy things here, souvenirs, why wouldn't they pick up something for their tree at home? Besides, we're locals, we shop here too. People need Christmas things, hon. And I imagine he'll be on his way in January anyway.'

'Why?' Summer demanded. 'What have you heard? Have you spoken to him?' *He was leaving! That was good, right?* The mother voice in her head stayed silent. Great, now she shuts up.

'No, I only saw the shop this morning, same as you, but how many shops selling seasonal goods stay open all year? I bet it's one of those pop-up shop thingies. Surely you can just get along with him for four or five months, let Reg enjoy his recuperation in peace?'

Summer sat back in her seat, crossing her arms but saying nothing. Reginald Andrews used to have the shop next door, selling old fashioned sweets, newspapers, souvenirs. He had been open for years, a stalwart of the local community, but the recession and a bad ticker had taken its toll, and he had reluctantly retired. The shop was his, lock, stock and barrel, but with the property market being in the toilet, Reg had decided to rent it out for a while. Jean thought he wasn't ready to let go completely. Summer knew where he was coming from. She loved her business. It was her baby, which was why she felt like a mama bear ready to rip her new neighbour apart with her bare claws. She couldn't cause Reg any hassle, though; he had always been amazing to her, like the grandfather she never had, so adding to his stress now was not an option.

She would just ignore Noel, freeze him out. Soon, like Jean said, she would be on a beach, and Christmas Nightmare and his little shop of horrors would be a distant, shuddering nightmare. If she could pull the beach thing off, of course. She had a business to run, and a long, devastatingly depressing winter to prepare for. She would just ignore him. That was it. She would just ignore him completely, and hopefully he would stay out of her way. After all, he had just moved in. Perhaps it was just bad timing this morning. She fired up her computer and, opening up her email, she got to work. Holidays wouldn't book themselves, and she had plenty of regular clients emailing her to book their annual holidays, with the best deals she could get. Before too long, she was immersed in her work.

* * *

An hour or two had passed and Summer had not stopped. Dealing with drop-ins, regulars, online queries and emails, she was positively buzzing at how busy she was. This really was a brilliant month, even with the unwelcome interruption this morning. The phone rang, and she picked it up.

'Good morning, Summer Loving, Summer speaking?'

'Where did you get to this morning?' the voice asked. 'I wanted to make you breakfast, but your room was empty.'

Summer puffed the air out into her cheeks. 'Sorry Mum, I wanted to get an early start and have a walk on the beach.'

'You could have told me; I had planned to make breakfast. I really wish you would be more considerate.'

Summer sighed, sitting back in her chair. 'Mum, I've told you so many times, I'm a grown woman. You don't have to make me breakfast any more; I can do it myself. I often do. It's only on your good days that I even see you at all!'

There was a small silence. 'Oh, and I suppose you can do your own laundry, too?'

Summer opened up a new email and began to reply, putting the headset plug into her phone and gently replacing the receiver. 'Well, yes Mum, I do my own washing when you don't.' She resisted the urge to add, *when you aren't in a dark mood*. 'I really can't talk about this now, I need to work.'

Her mother huffed down the line, and Summer looked out of the window at the people passing. Something caught her eye, just off to one side. A young girl, standing across the road, looking right into the shop. She was wearing a pale-pink hoodie, large, black-rimmed glasses filling much of her face. Summer waved at her, being friendly, but the girl turned and ran off. Weird. Must be a tourist. Her mother was still talking away, telling her about how she sometimes did her laundry because she was always at work, and never there to do her chores. Summer was used to it by now, and she let her mother get it out of her system. Chores were a joke, given the state of the house most weeks.

Summer could see her other line ringing, the light buzzing at her and the phone line beeping in her ear. 'Mum,' she tried, looking at yet another blinking light. She knew she should hire some seasonal staff, but money was tight, with the shop, the bills and looking after Mum. She had to be careful with the holiday summer season coming to an end.

'Mum,' she tried again, interrupting her in full flow. 'I really have to go. I'll see you tonight, okay?' Her mother kept going, but she just trilled, 'Love you!' down the phone and hung up. 'Good afternoon, Summer Loving?' she said, not missing a beat. She really did need to speak to her mother when she got home. She had to get her out of the house, to integrate in life again. A weekly trip to the shops was not a social life, but she wouldn't be told, or even try to venture out. She needed to get things sorted, once and for all. Tell her that things had to change. It would be a start. A trip to the shops, it was a step. Something.

She dealt with her client, dealing with the booking then and there, inputting it all into the computer. She was on her fifth call when she saw she had scribbled the words, *nothing ever changes* on her notepad. Her subconscious had a point, she thought to herself.

2

Noel Pritchett loved Christmas. Most people liked Christmas to be fair, or part of it at least. There was normally some kind of element of the festive season that had people smiling, whether it was the food, the family time, or just the excuse to day drink for the best part of a fortnight and do what the hell you wanted. How many people have said, 'Oh sod it, it's Christmas!' to justify the extra glass of wine/mince pie/drunken fumble? It was a good time of year, no matter how Scrooge-like you claimed to be. Noel luurvved Christmas. He was full on Santa-loving, Christmas-adoring, head over heels for the festive season. He loved everything about it and couldn't really understand anyone *not* loving it. How could you not?

Since he left university, he had pretty much been all around the world, but he was never away for Christmas. It just wasn't Christmas to him if he wasn't back in the UK, praying for snow and checking out the Queen's speech. He couldn't for the life of him remember a time when he hadn't had a good time at Christmas. Although after this morning's encounter with the prickly pear next door, he had a nagging doubt in his mind that perhaps, this year, it might just be a little bit harder to coast through the December month. The look on her face when she saw the tree had said it all. He might as well have left a naked cardboard cut-out of Donald Trump outside her door, for the reaction it had produced.

For a travel agent, a person who got to send people off around the world to chase the sun, she was decidedly frosty. Maybe it had just been a bad morning, though. Not everyone was a morning person like him. It took people a while, he got that. His mother was always telling him.

'Noel,' she would say. 'Not everyone was born with a rod of sunshine up their arse, remember that.' His mother, with her typical northern, tell-it-like-it-is candour. She did have a point, though.

He was sat in the back room, going through his invoices and ticking off the goods he'd just had delivered that morning. Thankfully, he had been all but finished by the time Summer had rocked up. That was a blessing in itself. She might have karate chopped his boxes into oblivion, had she seen them. He couldn't help but smile to himself when he thought of her. She seemed to be a firecracker, to say the least. He wouldn't mind getting to know her better while he was here.

He stood up, his long legs protesting at being sat down for too long, and headed to one of the unopened boxes. He took out the box cutter from the back of his skinny jeans and cut the tape on the box. Opening it up, he grinned to himself. He bloody loved doing the pop-up shop. Pulling out one of the items inside, he put in on his desk for later. Maybe he would take it around to Summer, apologise for their unfortunate first meeting. After all, they were going to be neighbours; it would be nice to have someone to chat to. Maybe she could put him on to his next adventure once January came along and the pop-up shop was done.

He went to flick the kettle on and was just heading to the front of the shop when he saw a little face at the window. She was tucked into the doorway, furtively looking through his window and into next door. A young girl, large glasses sitting snug on the bridge of her nose. He went to open the door, to ask her if she needed something, when she spotted him and ran off up the street, towards the beach along the front. She was only wearing a thin, pink, hooded jacket, with a small backpack in between her skinny shoulders. It was a week day; she must have been on her lunch break. No uniform though, he remembered. School holidays were over. Poor kid was probably just bored. Hiding from her parents and playing hooky, skint from a busy day at the arcades. He frowned and headed back to the kitchen to finish making his drink. He wanted to get the shop open by the end of the week, and it wasn't going to sort itself out.

* * *

Summer's stomach was rumbling so loudly, she felt sure that the customer would be able to hear it through the headset. In fact, their pauses in conversation were often timed with the grumbles and groans of her empty tummy. She finished the call as quickly as she could, taking the available button off her headset to stop another call coming through. When the customer finally agreed on where they wanted to go with their wife, she rang off, promising to email the details that afternoon. She processed it at lightning speed and grabbed her bag. Jean was already gone for the day, heading to one of her classes, and Summer hadn't had the foresight to pick up lunch on the way in, feeling unusually frazzled. She flipped the sign on the shop to closed, setting the time for re-opening on the plastic clock attached, and went to head to the local shop that stocked meal deals. As she locked her shop door, she noticed that Noel had started to make a display case for outside the shop. It looked like he was going to have bargain bins outside the front window. Summer could feel the empty pit of her stomach start to fizz with anger, and it gurgled again, like the roar of a lion. She kicked at the nearest metal leg and was satisfied when it moved away from her front with a squeak.

Trash. That's what his shop was. Tat and trash. Everyone knew that the coast had its cheesy parts, of course. Donkey rides, kiss me quick hats, ornamental Bridlington souvenirs and booby postcards saying, *Wish you were here*. That was all good; it was part of the English Northern coast experience, but this! No. It was like the anti-Christ of her business. As soon as Christmas was done, what do people do? They go and book a holiday. They book that two-week adventure in the sun, that trip of a lifetime. Turkey and stuffing is out, bikini in Turkey is in. To have the two shops together looked ridiculous. Like having a baby wear shop next to a funeral parlour. Cradle to grave, no waiting. It was going to kill her summer vibe and she couldn't stand it. Why did people still even bother with Christmas? Not everyone was religious, so why did they insist on spending a week trapped with their families and hiding from the credit card bill come January? It just didn't appeal to Summer. Passport stamps over seasonal Santa stamps any day. She was about to push the metal racking a bit more when someone walked out of the shop.

'Hey,' a voice said, and she turned away, pretending to be locking her already locked door.

'Hello,' she retorted, with enough ice to freeze his arse off if he got too close. Just like one of his tacky snowmen. He could be the biggest one of them all in his stupid window display. Mr Frosty Pants himself.

'Leaving early?'

She turned to face the voice, irritation exuding from her pores. 'No, of course not. I'm going for lunch. Not that it's anyone's business. I was busy looking after customers.' Summer threw her keys into her handbag, zipping it closed with a flourish.

'You know, I don't mean you any harm. I'm actually a nice guy.'

Summer turned to face him and fixed him with one of her meanest stares. The one she saved for people who littered on the beach, for those who laughed at the one-legged seagull that hung around the front of the shop. Her deathly, 'I despise you' look.

'I'm sure that's the case, Mr Christmas, but some shops are just not meant to be. I think the sooner you realise that, the better for all of us. The last thing we need around here is some dodgy new bloke, selling his bargain-basement fluff and scarpering. It's not you that has to pick the pieces up Noel, just remember that.' She turned her nose up at the racks and flounced off, her stomach growling loudly. To Noel, it sounded like the low, rumbling drums of war. A shiver ran down his spine, and he headed back indoors. He couldn't help but think there was more to that girl than her bright clothes and deep, dark soul. *Men like him*, she'd spouted. He wondered who had been stupid enough to upset her. His fist tensed at the thought.

3

Summer walked along the cul-de-sac of her street and sighed when she saw the house sat tucked into the corner. There were no lights on again, and the curtains upstairs were closed in the front window. She knew her mother would be in, but she couldn't help but wish that she had finally decided to go out somewhere. She walked up the drive, closing the gate behind her and scooping the post out of the letterbox at the bottom. Her mother hadn't even walked down the drive, let alone past it and out into the world. She knew already where she was; she was in bed. That would be her for the night now, and she would be up before the lark and making breakfast. It meant another night alone for Summer, shuffling around the house like a ghost so she didn't wake her mother. The patterns changed, they got worse, sometimes they felt a little better. All of it was bad, really. She knew it deep down; she just didn't verbalise it. If the thought didn't leave her head, it wasn't out there. She didn't have to deal with it.

She was almost at the door, key in hand, post in the other, her bag on her shoulder, when she felt a sense of something heavy on her chest. It took her breath for a moment, and she sat on the front step, tucking the post behind the ornamental hedgehog her mother had bought years ago for removing the mud from people's boots. It was still pristine, given that no-one ever came, though the porch was dusty and unkempt. Hell, even the postman didn't enter the front gate. The poor hedgehog was still wrapped in bloody plastic, a relic of normal life suspended forever.

Summer had learned a long time ago to get anything she wanted delivered to work, rather than risk her mother not answering the door and it being returned. One Mother's Day, she had arranged for flowers to be sent to her mother, but with Summer going into work unexpectedly for an hour, the florist rang her to apologise. They had tried to deliver them, but there was no answer. The delivery girl had even seen her mother at the window, but she had hidden and not come to the door. Summer ended up collecting them herself. Her mother denied all knowledge, saying that she had been deadheading in the garden, but they both knew that she hadn't been out there. It was always the same.

Since then, she never asked people to the house for any reason, and she had lost track of how long it was since she had seen her mother outside the house. It was far too long, she knew that. She looked at the key on the bunch in her hand and shook her head to herself. She couldn't do it; she just couldn't go in and spend the whole night alone. Not again.

Summer was up off the step and walking out of the gate before she even thought of where she was going. She needed to blow off some steam, she knew that. Now was the time to do something for her. She would text her mother when she got there, just so she wouldn't panic if she woke up. Knowing her though, she was in the arms of a sleeping tablet, and wouldn't hear a rhino knocking on the wall next to her.

Walking out of her neat housing estate and onto the main road, she saw a taxi heading to the beach front. She flagged it down, and the driver looked at her expectantly.

'Just the front please, near the bars.' He nodded once and pulled away, leaving Summer alone with her thoughts in the back of the cab. She looked again at her keys and tucked them away into her bag. Time to get a life, if only for a few hours.

* * *

Noel was just draining his glass when he saw her walking into the bar. He felt her presence from across the room. He was sitting at a bar stool at the quiet, empty bar, having polished off a pie and chips for his tea with a pint for pudding. His legs were tired from all the dashing about, and the muscles of his back sang from time to time to let him know that they had had their workout for the day.

At first, he thought he was imagining her. Like he had conjured her image up from his thoughts. She had been running through his mind all day since their earlier encounters. He had been about to leave but when the barman went to take his glass, silently asking him a question, he said yes, and the barman went off to refill his drink. He could have another. He only had a B&B to go home to, after all. Cheap and no frills, just how he liked them.

She paused at the door, her head darting from side to side as though she was looking for someone. He glanced around, but saw no-one that looked as though they might be waiting. She was clutching her handbag to her like a life jacket, and she slowly walked across the room to sit at the bar. She didn't see him at first, keeping her head focused on the seat she was aiming for, and he noticed that she was still wearing the clothes from that day. It was some time since the travel agents had closed; what had she been doing?

She was almost at the stools when her gaze finally flicked up, and Noel flinched at her reaction. Her eyes narrowed and she looked as if she wanted to kill him. *What was her deal?*

'Hi,' he said, flashing her a friendly smile.

She stopped walking, gripping her bag even tighter. So much tighter that Noel could see her fingers blanch white on the handles of her bag.

'Hi,' she replied, rather reluctantly. She looked pale, drawn. 'I was just...' She looked back to the door.

'Sit down,' he said softly. 'You look like you need a drink.'

She turned back to look at him, at the bar, the door, and then as though deciding something for herself, she sat down wearily on the stool next to him.

'What would you like?' he asked kindly, motioning to get the barman's attention.

'Er, gin and tonic please. I'll get my own, though.' She started to rummage in her handbag but Noel placed his hand gently, just one touch, a brush, on her arm.

'I'll get it, to apologise for this morning. And this afternoon.' He turned to the barman. 'Gin and tonic please, mate.'

She looked like she wanted to argue, but then the fight seemed to leave her. She sagged down onto the stool, throwing her bag down by her feet. 'Thanks,' she said, reaching for a straw from a black container on the walnut wood bar.

The barman brought her drink, and she took it with a polite, 'Thank you.' Sticking the straw into her drink, making the ice tinkle, she took a long pull. 'Oh, that's good. I bloody needed that.'

'Bad day?' Noel asked, taking a swig of his own beer.

'Yep,' she said, draining more of her drink with her straw. 'Preceded by about a decade of equally crappy years.'

'Really,' he drawled. 'That bad? Earlier, it did seem like you were upset.'

She drained the rest of her drink, her straw making a noisy

slurping sound as it hit air. 'Yep, it is,' she looked at the barman and nodded when he pointed to her glass. 'Yes, please.'

'Well, can I help?'

Summer turned in her seat slightly, looking at the rather gangly man who was draped over the stool next to her. What was this man about, that she actually found herself wanting to tell him? She'd been here before, trusting people. It didn't end well.

'Can you help with what?'

Noel pursed his lips, and turned his head to one side, making his dark curls bounce. He looked as though he was contemplating something. He looked almost comical. She bit down the random urge she felt to tell him. She needed to get it off her chest. Why not test it out with a stranger? A flash of her mother's panicked face hit her thought process. It wouldn't work.

'Sorry, question too hard?' It slipped out of her mouth before she could stop it, and she wanted to bite her tongue off for being short with him for the second time in a day. She just couldn't keep it back. To his credit, he didn't show any sign of being offended, just flicking his gaze to her and giving her a tiny little smile.

'No,' he said softly. 'I just know that you haven't had an easy day, and I don't want to upset you any more, or leave you to suffer on your own. Can I help? What is it, man trouble?'

Summer, thanking the bartender and throwing a note onto the bar, erupted into spontaneous laughter. 'Man trouble would be a welcome problem at this point, believe me!' *Shut up, Summer! Poldark doesn't need to know this!* She swapped the straw into her new drink, suddenly very interested in the bottom of her glass. 'No, no man trouble.' Not any more anyway. Life was just one big ripple effect now. She felt like she was adrift on them most days, clinging to the remnants of once calm and still waters.

'Okay, so work then?'

Summer smiled when she thought of her actual working hours. 'No, work's great, I love it.'

Noel grinned then, a real smile, and she tried not to stare at him. He was quite pretty, handsome even. His white teeth flashed behind his pretty, pink lips. She found herself watching his mouth and wondering why this specimen had rocked into her day, her life.

'That's nice to hear. I always think it's really important to do what you want in life. You have to work a long time; if you're not happy, what's the point, eh?' He took a pull of his own pint and she waited for him to say more, but he didn't. He looked as though he wanted to though, and she wondered whether he was as happy as he appeared.

'You have a point,' she said, wanting to shake him out of his sudden fug.

He frowned and tapped his left index finger against his closed lips.

'So, no relationship or work problems, what's left?' He looked at her in enquiry.

I'm not going to tell him. It's nothing to do with him.

'My mother,' she uttered, before putting her fingers to her lips to shush herself.

Noel's face fell. 'Oh no, is she...?'

'No, no, she's fine. Healthy as a horse.' *Although, with her never leaving the house, what could happen to her?*

'Ah ok, so...?'

'It doesn't matter. Forget about it. Did you have a good day?'

Noel's eyebrows shot up to his hairline, and Summer laughed. Must be the alcohol. It came out like a girlish giggle. 'I'm not all bad, you know.'

He grinned. 'Well, I did have a good day actually. My stock arrived, and I enjoyed setting the shop up. It seems nice here.'

'Where did you move from?' she asked, realising that she couldn't really place his accent.

'I was in Bali this summer, and I rented a long-term room in a B&B nearby.'

'Bali, where?'

'Ubud, and a few months in Depansar. It's pretty spectacular over there. You been?'

Summer shook her head. 'No, it's on my list.'

'Oh, it's definitely worth going. I was even thinking of going back next summer. They have a fair few charities over there, let you help out in exchange for food and lodgings. Makes travelling cheaper, and it's nice to feel like you're helping.'

Summer nodded, feeling like she had a slab of concrete on her chest. *Nice to feel helpful*. Apart from work, Summer hadn't felt like she was helping anyone for a long time.

'Have you been away this summer?' Noel was still talking away to her, and she realised she had spaced out a little. She nodded her head, but it felt awkward, like her head was perched numbly on her neck.

'Cool, where?' *Sheesh, life story much? What am I supposed to say now? Lie?*

'Nowhere special,' she tried to be nonchalant. 'I should go.'

Her mother would no doubt still be asleep, but she needed to get back to make sure everything was organised for the morning.

Noel didn't say anything, just stood and started to pull on his jacket. Summer looked at him in question. 'Where are you going?'

Noel shrugged. 'I thought I would see you out, you off for a taxi?'

Summer picked up her bag and waved him away. 'Yes, I got here fine, and I can leave fine.' There it was again: her nasty, snake-like tongue! *Don't be rude!*

Noel flicked up the collar on his coat and said goodbye to the

barman. 'No problem, goodnight then.' He walked around her and
headed for the door. The barman raised his eyebrows at her, obviously not impressed with her behaviour either.

'I know, I know,' she said begrudgingly, throwing her bag over
her shoulder and walking out of the pub. It was really quiet for
Bridlington this time of night, and Summer found herself taking a
huge gulp of sea air. The gins had done their job, and she felt better,
but the thought of going home still didn't appeal to her. She looked
at the taxi rank and went to walk the other way.

'Hey, you not getting a taxi?' Noel's voice came from behind her,
and she turned to face him.

'No, I thought I'd get a bite to eat.' She pursed her lips. 'You've
eaten, right?'

Noel nodded. 'I have, but I could eat again.'

Summer giggled despite herself, and Noel grinned, rubbing his
non-existent tummy. 'What can I say, I have to keep my strength up.
Where did you have in mind?'

* * *

Jean was sitting in front of the television with her knitting on her
lap, her cat Benny (after Benedict Cumberbatch) licking his butt
near the fireplace, and the TV on. It was showing the latest
murderous plot on the soap operas she had tired of, but couldn't
quite bring herself to give up. Her detached, four-bedroom house
was as neat and clean as always, and she had a little tot of sherry on
the side table. She was wearing her nightie, thick dressing gown
and comfy slippers, and was bedded in for the evening. Until the
doorbell rang. Benny took his tongue away from his anus just long
enough to look at her in question. She looked right back, shocked
herself.

'Who the bloody hell can that be, Benny?' she said, more to

herself than her beloved black cat, as he was already back to his bathing. She put her knitting into the wicker basket by her chair and padded over to the front door through the hallway. She could see the shadow of someone tall and thin through the frosted glass, the glare from her porch light shining down on to their shoulders.

'Hello?' she asked through the door.

'Hello,' a friendly, male voice said. Of course, axe murderers who turned up at your door could be friendly, so she didn't immediately open the door.

'Who is it?' she asked.

'I'm Jim, Jim Mullaly. I just moved in next door. I just wondered, possibly, if I could borrow some water, and perhaps a cup of milk?'

'Milk and water?' she echoed, wondering at the randomness of it all.

'Yes, please. The plumber said the water needs to be off till morning, and I'm gasping for a cuppa.'

Jean didn't answer, biting the inside of her mouth as she weighed up whether she could slip the liquids through the letterbox.

'Err, listen, I don't want to put you out. I can go to the shop, I just wanted to avoid it. Good evening.' The figure shifted from the doorway, and she realised how ridiculous she was being. Burglars and axe murderers didn't tend to want water or milk, did they?

She opened the door.

'Jim?' He turned to look at her, and she saw how handsome he looked, how normal. His hands were thankfully axe-free too. She belatedly realised that she was wearing her dressing gown, and stepped back away from the door.

'Sorry, I just didn't expect anyone. Please, come in and I'll get what you need.'

She left the door ajar and wandered into the kitchen. She spun around the corner and checked herself out quickly in the mirror on the kitchen wall.

'Oh Jesus, Jean, what's going on here?' She quickly flicked her hand through her hair and, grabbing her lip gloss, slicked on a little bit before half running across to the fridge. She pulled out a four-pint carton of milk and placed it on the worktop just as Jim walked into the kitchen. Benedict came wandering through from the lounge, looking very put out at the intrusion. He stopped in the doorway and glared at Jim.

'Thanks for this,' he said, looking around the kitchen. 'Nice place you have here.'

'Thanks, I like it.' She went to the pantry and got a couple of large bottles of water out.

'I save water, just in case. Here you go.' She passed the water to him and he took it with a smile.

'Great, thank you. I'll buy you some back tomorrow.'

Jean waved him off. 'No problem at all, call it a moving in present. Your building work going okay?'

He nodded and ran his hand down his face. She noticed he had a day's worth of stubble, and he looked really tired. 'It's going okay, it's a bit more work than I expected, but I'll get there.'

Jean nodded. She remembered Mrs Willis next door was a bit of a hoarder, and never saw a bit of Bridlington tourist memorabilia that she didn't like. She had recently moved to Florida, her health failing a little, her house too big and too outdated to keep up. Her son and his wife had finally got their wish of having her live with them, and from her recent letter, she was loving every single minute. No doubt shopping for lots of souvenirs too, given the fact that she had sent her a fridge magnet featuring the image of a half-naked, well oiled, muscle man.

'I can imagine. Trudy had that place on her own for years after her son left home and her husband passed. She couldn't keep up to it, bless her.'

He nodded, a little smile crossing his features that made his blue eyes sparkle. 'She did have a certain taste, that's for sure. I need things to be sorted as soon as possible so it's certainly been an adventure. Thanks again, I'd better go.'

'Have you eaten?' Jean asked, before she could stop herself. 'I have some leftover chilli. I could reheat it?'

Jim went to shake his head, but then seemed to sag a bit further. 'I am starving, to be honest. That would be lovely. I have a bottle of wine back at mine; I got it for a housewarming present. I could go get that?'

Jean thought of her lonely sherry and the solitary basket of knitting in the lounge. 'Sure, that'd be great.'

Jim went to take his water and milk and get the wine, and Jean saw him out, running upstairs to throw some clothes on before he got back. Benny was now sitting on the bed, watching her dress.

'What?' she said to him, feigning innocence. 'Missing a bit of Coronation Street won't kill us, will it?'

Benny was decidedly not amused.

* * *

'What is that sweet smell?' Jim asked, dipping a buttered slice of white bloomer bread into his chilli and covering it with the bright, spicy sauce.

Jean's fork stopped halfway to her mouth. 'Sweet smell?' She sniffed the air herself, and recognition lit up her features. 'Ooh, it's my cake, for class. I was practising earlier. We have to present a design for a special occasion tomorrow.'

Jim took a bite of his chilli and bread and closed his eyes momentarily. Jean watched him, wondering to herself when was the last time that a person was actually in her kitchen. Or even her house, for that matter. Here she was, sitting and enjoying a meal with a man. A man who was obviously starving.

'Did you not eat today?'

'So, what did you make?'

They both spoke together and laughed awkwardly.

'Sorry, you first,' he said, forking another mound of chilli into his mouth.

'It was nothing really, I just wondered if you had eaten today. You must eat, moving and house alterations is no easy thing to take on.'

Jim pulled an apologetic face. 'I did grab a soft drink and a packet of crisps from the petrol station earlier, but other than that, I just got busy. I need this house to be done as fast as possible. I have my grandchildren waiting.'

'Grandchildren! That's lovely,' Jean said, suddenly picturing children playing on the front lawn, them giggling in the garden in the summer time. It would bring a bit of life to the street. Everyone here was pretty quiet, even for a residential area. People liked to keep themselves to themselves here, away from the touristy areas of the town. The residents were mostly young families or elderly couples. Having children so close would be a lot of fun. 'They going to be staying weekends?'

Jim put his fork down then and looked a bit uncomfortable. 'Well, no, actually, they're coming to live with me full time.'

Jean said nothing, just continued to eat. She figured he would tell her if he wanted to. He hadn't pried into her life, or asked why she was rattling around in a large house on her own, so she decided to show him the same courtesy.

Jim looked at her, as though waiting for her to speak. 'Doesn't that bother you?'

Jean felt her head snap back in surprise. 'Bother? Me? Why

would it bother me?'

Jim bit his lip. 'I have three grandchildren, two boys and a girl. They will be living here, next door, with me. Aren't you worried about the noise? The estate agent said it was ideal for a family here, away from the fuss, but I've noticed over the last few days it is very quiet.'

Jean waved her hand. 'Listen, people aren't here much; they work full time or are off travelling the world, or a bit of both. As long as you keep your garden tidy and put your bins back in, you're good. As for me, well I think it'll be lovely. I only work part time and other than my classes, I'm home a lot. Be nice to have a little entertainment.'

Jim sagged down onto the stool, into himself. It was like he was being held up by a rod, and someone just whipped it away. 'I'm so glad to hear you say that. I was a bit worried I had bought the wrong house.'

Jean smiled at him, glad she had relieved his fears a little. 'No, it'll be lovely, don't worry. Although, I was serious about the bins. Mr Hart from number six had actual fisticuffs with Roy from number eight. Moody old bugger was furious about him leaving out his recycling bins. Poor Roy. He'd forgotten to ask me to pull it back in. He'd just got back from a long weekend away in Mallorca. I thought Mr Hart was going to murder him, and then use the bin to hide his body. Roy ended up doinking him on the head with his novelty donkey. The police were not amused. I thought it was bloody hilarious.'

Jim's face dropped and Jean couldn't help but laugh. 'Sorry, I've freaked you out, haven't I!' She poured wine into both their glasses. 'Honestly, you won't have any problems. As long as things are kept neat and tidy, no one will care that you have children living here. Everyone's pretty easy going.'

Jim took a swig of his wine, sitting back on his seat. 'Thanks, that's a relief. I'm really glad I met you, Jean. So, what cake did you make?'

Jean blushed. 'Finish your supper, and I'll show you, but no laughing!'

* * *

Angie tried Summer's phone again, but for the fiftieth time, it went straight to voicemail, and her daughter's ever-chirpy voice washed over her. *Where the hell was she?*

She resisted the urge to leave a message. She never left messages, fearful of who would hear them. Who listened to them anyway? She never listened to them on the house phone. She never answered the house phone, come to that. Summer always rang twice and then rang back, so she would know it was her. Their little code, whenever they needed to speak. The shop phone was safe because she would only get her or Jean anyway. Jean, she could cope with. She liked Jean, trusted her. They'd been good friends, even. Once upon a time.

Angie wasn't the type to trust people easily, not any more. Not since he left. The hole he had ripped through their lives was too terrible to contemplate at first, too awful to be true. Angie had gone from being a vibrant, happy, working wife and mother to someone who considered walking to the post box on the corner a day out. She didn't even do that now. She didn't send any letters really; Summer dealt with all that. She just rattled around in the house, waiting for Summer to come home.

Tonight though, she had no idea what was going on. She'd just disappeared, and now she wasn't answering her phone either. It wasn't like her, and Angie didn't like it one bit. She felt totally out of control, and she would be telling Summer just what she thought when her daughter finally deigned to drag her sorry behind in, that was for sure. Making her own poor mother worry like that. She had raised her to know better.

Angie turned and sat on the bottom step, glaring at the front door and the hall phone in turn, willing one of them to give her an answer. She wouldn't rest till she came through the door, and Summer knew it. Pretty selfish of her, to be fair.

Angie took herself upstairs to try to sleep, but after an hour, she was back at the hall table, dialling her number again.

* * *

Summer was really enjoying herself, despite the fact that the man at the opposite end of the table was the source of her anger that very morning. She couldn't remember the last time she had eaten out in a restaurant. Or eaten out at all. Her mother wasn't a fan of takeaways; she didn't like people coming to the house, even just to drop off food. Summer did the shopping, paid the bills, sorted things that needed to be resolved in the outside world. It was nice to be served for once, not wondering what to make or what to buy. The novelty of just sitting and ordering a meal from the menu was bliss.

Noel was sitting across the table, menu in hand, but she could feel him looking at her. She tried to concentrate hard on her own menu, but she finally risked a peek. He was looking at his menu, studying it hard intently by the looks of things. Paranoid woman, she thought to herself, till she saw him looking again. He flicked his eyes away as soon as she clocked him, and she was suddenly glad that the menu was there, to hide the blush that she could feel spreading over her face. She felt like a frickin' tomato.

'What do you fancy ordering?'

He shrugged, putting the leather-bound folder down on the table. 'Your choice. What's good?'

They were sitting in a little restaurant, off the harbour. It was one of the best seafood places Bridlington had to offer, but they did a mean pizza too, which is what Summer came for. Her father loved it here, and the three of them used to walk from their house to the beach, have a paddle and a nice walk along the shore, and then head to their favourite table together. They had the best times here, back then. Now here she was, right back at their table, sitting across the candlelit table from her new work rival. It had been a bit of a day, to say the least.

'The seafood is gorgeous, but I normally have the pizza. The meat lovers special is pretty awesome.'

Noel nodded, signalling to the waiter. 'Sounds good, to share?'

Summer nodded. 'Might as well. Wine?'

'Fine with me. Rosé, white? I'm not a fan of the red.'

'Either's fine with me, they do a nice Pinot.'

Noel nodded, and the waiter came and took their order. He was polite to the waiter, didn't talk down to him or order for her and she found herself relaxing. In fact, for a non date, it was kind of a good one. Just because it was the first one she had had in years didn't count, of course.

The waiter smiled and collecting their menus, swept off to the kitchen to place their order.

'So, want to talk about your day yet?'

The cloud descended as a vision of her mother's house popped into her head. It loomed dark and dingy in her mind. 'Nope, not really. Just one of those things, you know. I'm sorry about being so rude, I just felt... surprised by your shop. Jean, my friend, told me I was being a little insensitive perhaps.'

Noel nodded, first to her, then the waiter, who presented them with the wine. He waved away the taste test and seemed to wait till the server had filled their glasses and moved on. 'I understand. I normally do advertise the shop first, get a bit of buzz going, but it was a bit last minute this time. I only just saw the shop advert so I decided to jump on it.'

He looked out of the window from the table they were sitting at. The view was right down the harbour, showing the twinkling lights from the boats nestled together on the water. 'It's nice here too, seems a lovely place to live.'

Live? Eh?

'Till January, sure,' she stated. 'The time will fly by.'

Noel didn't answer, just kept looking out of the window, a non-committal hmm sound coming from him.

'So,' she pushed, as always wanting an answer. 'When do you think you'll leave in January? Right after New Year's, or before?'

Noel looked back at her, his eyes focusing on hers. 'I'm not sure yet, to be honest. I have no plans this time, I'm just going to go with the flow, see what happens.'

Go with the flow. Four words that sprang dread into Summer's heart. In her life, she had things organised, compact. Everything ran smoothly. The same, day in and day out. Till the day she got her adventure. Someday.

'Oh, so,' she took a glug of the wine to steady herself, 'maybe the end of January, then?'

Noel cleared his throat. 'Well, no, actually I was considering staying longer.'

Another glug. Thank God for the wine. 'Longer?' she echoed, looking at him incredulously. This was it. This was precisely why her instincts had told her to avoid Noel. It was happening again: having her emotions dangled in front of her at the whim of someone else. 'Why?'

Noel shrugged. 'Why not? I love Bridlington, my landlady says she's happy for me to extend my stay at the B&B and the lease is open ended at the shop. I figured I could sell the Christmas stock off, and then see what happens. I—'

Summer suddenly had an image of Noel, years from now, selling his wares from the front of his shop, Zimmer frame whooshing around whilst she watched in horror from the comfort of her mobility scooter. It was enough to get her to her feet in a scrambled mess of panic and her rubber like limbs flailing for contact with the ground.

'No!' Summer shouted out loud. Half the diners turned their heads, their waiter looking over in concern. 'No, I don't think so.' She caught sight of the diners all staring at her, and she hunched back down in her chair.

Noel looked at her as though she had grown two heads in front of his very eyes and started breathing fire from her nostrils. 'Excuse me?'

'No, I don't want you to stay next door! It's one thing you being here till Christmas, but after, what's the point in that? No one wants Santa on their doorstep come January, Noel. Didn't your mother ever tell you it was rude to outstay your welcome?'

Noel sighed, a huffy, short sigh. 'Summer,' he threw his napkin down at the table. 'I don't really understand what you have against me, but I think we should call it a night.'

He went to stand, to motion for the waiter, and she felt her face flush. She'd made a scene. Damn it. Her and her temper. She was already feeling a little stupid, but she just couldn't help herself.

'I'm sorry,' she said, her voice hard. 'I just don't think that us working next to each other is going to work out. We don't need your type of shops around here; it's just not a good fit. Nothing good will come from you being here, Noel.'

Noel didn't answer her; he was already pulling notes out of his wallet. 'I have to agree with you on that one. This was a huge mistake, obviously. As if we could even have a civilised conversation with each other; you've been at me all day. I just wanted to be nice, to get on.' The waiter was coming over, a concerned, fake smile plastered all over his face. Probably wondering why the nice couple having a date were suddenly sizing each other up over the steak knives. A stabbing over the starters didn't really do much for business. She could feel her anger, already simmering, boil over and hiss at him.

'Get on? Why would I need to get on with you anyway? It's not like we're going to be friends, is it? And I thought that you would be moving on, away from my shop. Now you tell me I have to put up with your tat for longer? Why would I be happy about that?'

'For God's sake!' The tableware jingled on the table as Noel's fists pounded down on the table. 'What the hell is your deal? I get you're in a mood, but you're being kind of a huge bitch!' He bit his lip at the words, fixing her with an intense stare that made his brown eyes look all the larger against his now rather red face.

Summer went to leave, and he grabbed her arm. 'Summer, please—'

'Oh, I would take that hand off me if I were you.' She glared down at his hand, wishing she had laser beam abilities in her retinas so that she could singe the arm hairs off his muscled arm. Or shear the whole limb off in one clean sweep and beat him to death with it. 'You don't want to get any bitch on you; it stains.'

She headed to the door, puffing out her chest and jutting out her chin to try to hide the shame and upset she felt. *How the hell did we end up fighting, again? That guy makes me so angry!* She heard him call her name, but she didn't trust herself to turn around without bursting into tears or flipping him off. She was out the doors and in the back of a waiting taxi before she could process the day's events properly, and that's when the tears finally came. That restaurant, and the happier times she had there, seemed to have eluded her once more. Just once, she wanted her past to leave her alone. She just wanted to get through the day, and the next. That was about all she could handle for now.

4

BEFORE

'Summer, time to get up! Breakfast!' Her mother's cheerful tones roused her from sleep, and she threw back the covers, grinning.

'Coming!' She threw on her school uniform and headed to the bathroom. Passing her parents' room, she saw her dad lying in bed.

'Hey Dad, you getting up?'

Ronnie Hastings was a big man, a meatball of Italian-sized proportions. He loved to get up and 'hit the day square in the face', as he would say. Normally by now, he would already be up, slapping his wife's bottom playfully as she made the breakfast and he made the coffee and moaned about the news headlines. He was a wheeler dealer and spent his time like Del Boy, minus the sheepskin coat. He was always on the phone, selling this and that, buying things and sorting out deliveries. Their garage at the side of the house was always full of random items, from ceiling fans to water heaters. He would always look through the papers, spotting the next heatwave, the newest trend, and then before you knew it, people were buying things from him in droves, heading up to the house on weekends and leaving happy. Even if they didn't see anything they liked, just being around Ronnie was infectious, like laughter. It was odd that he wasn't up.

'Dad?' she asked again, knocking on the door frame. 'Come on, you're taking me to school, remember?'

He lifted his head up from the pillow. 'I'm coming, honey. Ask Mum to put the coffee on, yeah? I need to make a call.'

Summer nodded, heading down the stairs. As she ran her hand along the banister, the smell of polish hit her, released from the cherry red wood of the staircase. Her mother had been polishing again. The woman was a machine, working all day in an office and still looking after them all so well. Just like now. Summer walked into the kitchen and was soon smelling the pull of a healthy grilled breakfast, and a sweeter smell.

'Mum, what are you doing?' She flumped down into the breakfast stool, her mother immediately pushing a glass of orange juice towards her.

'Morning baby, drink up; you need that vitamin C. I'm just making some buns for the office; it's Vicky's birthday.'

Summer smiled. Angie was such a mother hen, even at the office. She never forgot a birthday, an anniversary. The woman had her own gift and card cupboard in the house. She was a walking Clintons.

'Nice, what's up with Dad?'

Her mother shrugged, turning to the grill and laying out sausage, bacon and grilled mushrooms onto two plates and ladling beans from the pan. 'I think he's coming down with something; he wasn't really himself last night either. He's not sleeping well.'

Summer frowned. 'Maybe he's ill. I'll take him a drink.'

Summer made her dad a coffee from the freshly brewed pot and headed up the stairs. She headed to her parents room and noticed that the bed was empty. She heard a noise in the bathroom, like humming. Relief flooded through her at the sound. That was more like her dad. Always singing, and humming, acting the joker.

'So, what do you want me to do? I can't leave right now. I just can't leave Summer, not with her exams.'

Her dad's raised voice stopped her in her tracks, causing the coffee to slosh over the rim of the cup and scald her fingers. *Leave?* It didn't sound like he was just skipping taking her to school. She listened at the door a little more, feeling terrible for eavesdropping but unable to stop herself at the same time.

'I know babe, I know. Just give me time.'

Summer's heart dropped into her school tights. *Babe?* The only time her dad ever called anyone anything like that was when he was talking to her mother. The tone of voice alone was freaking her out. She heard a shuffle at the other side of the door, and putting the coffee down on the dresser, she bolted.

She waited till she was halfway down the stairs before she shouted up, 'Dad, your coffee is on the dresser!' She hoped it sounded cheery. To her ears, it sounded shaky, shocked. Which was exactly how she felt. Why was her dad talking like that? To who? Whoever it was, they sounded familiar to each other.

Heading back into the kitchen, watching her mother tap her watch good naturedly about her cooling breakfast, her heart clenched.

Her dad was his normal self on the car ride to school, but as he drove off, she knew that this morning, she had felt something shift in her life, and she wasn't sure if that was the end of it, or the start of something else altogether. Hugging him goodbye, she shook off the bad feeling and got ready to start the day. The sun was shining. When the sun was high in the sky, nothing much went wrong.

5

The brochure pinged off the back wall, sliding to the floor with its discarded companions.

'For God's sake, where the hell is it?' Summer wrenched open the middle drawer of the filing cabinet and yanked out another pile of travel material. More booklets soon followed the rest of them, slamming into the wall as she hurled them behind her in disgust. The phone rang and she sighed deeply. She had only been in work an hour and already, her mother had called her four times to berate her for not being home the night before. Which just added insult to injury, since the night was such a colossal nightmare. She would have been better sitting at home, talking to the wall. Maybe if she had done that, she wouldn't be attacking the masonry today. She had promised Mr Everett some information on the Maldives, and now she couldn't find it.

'Good morning, Summer Loving?'

'What time are you coming home tonight?'

Summer sagged as she heard her mother's breathy tones down the phone. 'Mum, you just called. I'll be home by seven. I'm going to the supermarket straight after work, and then I'm coming home to make tea.'

A tut came down the line. 'I can cook tea, I already told you that. I just need some mince.'

'For the spaghetti bolognaise, I know, and I told you, I'll cook, to make up for last night.'

Another huff. 'Well, you do owe me an apology. I woke up and you weren't there.'

'Yes Mum, I know this already, and I said sorry.' Summer sat down at her desk, pulling open the filing cabinet in her bottom drawer and locating the Maldives brochure. She punched the air as her mother gave her yet another blow by blow of the evening before. She let her finish, run herself out of steam. It was better this way. If she argued with her, it would just continue, and after the sleepless night she had spent battering the pillow and pretending it was Noel's face, she needed tonight to be easy.

She hadn't seen him yet, thank God. When she had arrived at work at 8 a.m., driven out of the house by restlessness and the fear of her mother's impending ear bashing, she had walked along the beach as usual, stopping to sit on the sand and contemplate the mess that her life was in. Organised boredom. She had been feeling it more and more lately, the pressing, crushing feeling in her chest when she thought of returning home. The house was just so stifling now, and she couldn't remember a time when she felt happy. With the jackass next door, peddling his glittery optimism, she just couldn't take it any more.

'Mum,' she barked suddenly, cutting her startled mother off full flow. 'I'm at work, okay, and I have a ton of stuff to sort out. Listen, if you want to cook tonight, that's fine, but you'll have to do your own shopping. I don't have time.'

The line went quiet. 'What?' her mother croaked. 'What do you mean?'

Summer sighed, sagging down into her chair till she nearly folded in on herself altogether. 'I can't do this any more, Mum. I love you, but it has to stop. We can't go on like this, okay? I know it was hard when Dad—'

'Summer! I don't want to hear it. Don't, please.' Her mother's pleading, broken voice stopped her from going further, but she felt different this time, hearing her mother sob softly down the line. She felt like a tiny chunk of the slab laying on her chest had chipped off, and she could breathe a little better.

'Okay Mum, I won't, but I mean it about the shopping. There's housekeeping money in the tin.' She quickly cut the call off, before her mother could stop crying long enough to protest. There, she had done it. Finally. It was up to her mother now.

'Well my girl, I am so proud of you this morning.'

Summer looked at the doorway to see Jean standing there, black gypsy skirt swaying around her legs with the sea breeze. A waft of sugar and perfume filled the travel agency, making her smile.

'Oh yeah, what for?'

Jean crossed the room, putting the large plastic cake container she was carrying on one of the sides in the kitchen and flicking the kettle on. Summer followed her, one ear out for the phone.

'For finally standing up to your mother.' Jean's eyes crinkled in the corners as she smiled kindly at her employer, and the daughter she had never had. 'How long is it since she left the house?'

She ignored Summer's shocked expression as she made them both a cup of tea. 'People talk, my dear. No-one has seen her around for a long time, and you haven't exactly been using your passport, have you? Does she see anyone?'

Summer opened her mouth to speak, to tell the usual cover story – that she was working from home nowadays, happy but busy – but the words stuck in her throat. 'It's been over a year since she left the house at all. She won't even go in the garden any more. I can't even do a full day at work without her ringing me. I've just had enough.'

A loud banging started up, heard through the wall connecting to the shop next door. Both women turned their heads towards the noise and Jean saw Summer's fists clench.

'So, you told her to do the shopping, which is a start. I'm proud of you.'

The banging continued and Summer flinched. 'She won't do it. I mean, I haven't told her like that before, but she won't do it. She won't even walk to the end of the garden path to get the post. Going to the local minimarket is like asking her to go to the moon. I have to try though, right?'

Jean nodded. *Bang bang bang.* 'Yes, you do have to. I can help if you like. I could go and visit her, maybe even take her a brochure for the courses I do? Might help to get her out of the house, back into work.'

Summer didn't think her mother would let Jean past the front step, but she smiled at her anyway. 'She wouldn't answer the door. I wish she would. Honestly, we could do with the money. The bills aren't massive, but we still struggle, and we need a lot doing, too. The garden for one thing; it's terrible.'

Jean's cogs were turning, but she said nothing. Summer could see her processing the information, and she found herself feeling glad that she had been there, to hear that call. Maybe things could get better. She felt as though another slab chunk had dislodged from her chest.

Bang bang bang. The noise from next door rattled in her brain, pushing the tiny bit of peace she had found right out of her head.

'Anyway,' Jean passed her a cup of steaming hot tea, 'I just came from class, and my tutor gave me a good mark on my cake, so I'm chuffed to bobbins. Plus, we can have a slice now, with our cuppas.'

She lifted the lid off the container, the banging seemingly not even ruffling her usual cheery mood. Summer looked at her cake and burst into laughter.

'Oh my God Jean, what on earth was the assignment?'

Jean grinned. 'It was to make a cake for a special occasion. Granted, not everyone has this happen in their lives, but the usual cakes were just a bit boring.'

The cake was a large, circular affair, white fondant icing covering the sponges, with a red dotted line cutting through the centre. One side was a woman's top half, with the word 'before' written on it, the other side similar, with 'after' written on it. In piped icing at the top, in pink, were the words, 'Congrats on the new boobs!' Suffice to say, the second woman looked a lot perkier in her bikini top than the first one.

Summer gasped. 'Jean, you didn't!'

Jean giggled, cutting a large slice out and putting it onto a plate. 'I did. The tutor loved it! "Very original," she said! I'm going to pitch it to the local bakery when I finish the course, see if they want to buy the design. You should have seen Mrs Ackerman's face, though; I swear, the woman nearly fainted. It's not like they're real nipples, for God's sake!' She passed the plate to Summer, still giggling to herself.

Summer was about to take a bite when the hammering began again, and that's when she got mad.

'Seriously?' She went over to her desk, putting the cake plate down on it and running to the wall that separated the two shops. She put her ear to the wallpaper, head pressed against it, hands at either side of her. 'What does he think he's doing?'

Jean cut herself a piece of boob cake and went to sit down at the other desk. 'I expect he's just settling in, hon; he probably needs some more shelving or something. I don't think he'll be long. We don't have any customers at the minute. It's fine.'

Summer glared at her, making Jean shiver despite the somewhat sunny day. 'It is not fine! I don't come to work to listen to that crap! Who the hell does he think he is, seriously? He pretends to be all nice and gentlemanly, but the minute you ask when he's leaving, or what his plans are, he's running out the restaurant like a mad man!'

'Restaurant?' Jean echoed. 'What restaurant?' She made a sharp inhaling sound. 'You went for a meal! With him next door? When? Tell me everything!'

The banging continued, and Summer jammed her ear back against the wall. 'Oh, there's nothing to tell. We didn't eat anything. It was over before the wine was even poured, really. The man is a flake, waltzing into places willy nilly. I wish he would just *bugger off*!' She yelled the last two words and banged hard a few times on the wall. Jean sat back in her chair, enjoying the moist sponge. Summer was listening intently, but the banging had stopped. The door opened and Summer, facing the opposite way, motioned to Jean with a waggling hand outstretched.

'Jean, can you deal with that?'

'Er...' Jean's voice sounded strange, so Summer turned to look at who it was. Noel stood there, wearing paint-splattered jean shorts and a band T-shirt. 'I think it's for you, love. I'll start cleaning out the back.'

'I'm guessing you have a problem with the noise, right?' he asked, looking at her with his big, brown eyes and an expression that made it difficult to decipher what mood he was in. Cautious maybe, if she had to label it. *Good*, she thought. *Make him squirm. The stupid git might just do one before Santa fills his sack at this rate.*

'Damn right I do. What the hell are you doing? I have a business to run, you know!'

'I'm just finishing off the shop display, that's all. I would have told you, but given our history, I decided to just leave you be. I see now that this was wrong too. Why don't you tell me the rules for being neighbours? Then I won't keep annoying you.'

Summer saw his jaw clench, as he looked at her. His eyes fell onto the piece of cake on the plate, where a solitary boob, complete with nipple, jutted out proudly from the icing.

'Birthday?' he asked, his voice a little softer. To his credit, he didn't raise an eyebrow at the nip. 'Sorry, I didn't realise. I can stop for the day if you like, but I will need another couple of days to get the shop straight. I will be doing it when the shops shut for the most part, so it won't be too bad.'

'It's not my birthday, but I would like you to stop. I close at five; you can bang away to your heart's content after that.' He winced but said nothing. 'If it's only a few shelves, it won't take long anyway, will it?'

'It's a bit more complicated than that, but it's fine, whatever.'

He turned to leave the shop, but Summer noticed that he froze, looking out of her window.

What now? She followed his gaze out of the window and saw two women passing. Attractive women, obviously dressed for the beach. She felt a flicker of something as she glanced at his back, but she pushed it away.

'Do you know that girl?' He asked, turning back around and flicking his head so discreetly, she almost missed it.

'Err, no, I don't – and this is a travel agency, not lonely hearts.'

Noel looked at her confused. 'Eh? She's a *school girl*, Summer. Do you know her or not?'

Summer huffed loudly and walked to the window. On the bench at the other side of the street, she saw the girl from the other day, sitting alone. She was reading a book but kept looking over at the shops.

'Oh, her.' She pulled an apologetic face at him and shrugged.

'Sorry. I don't know her, but I have seen her before. She must be local.'

'Hmm,' he agreed. 'I've seen her every day since I've been here. You think she'd be at school.'

Summer thought of her summers since Dad left, with Mum working all the time to make ends meet, then not being at work at all but spending days under the covers, crying. Of going to school and feeling like an alien.

'Maybe she's just looking for a bit of peace, to be by herself. I'm sure she's fine, and I'm busy.' To help punctuate her point, the phone started to ring, and by the time she had sat back down at her desk to answer it, she looked up to find that he had gone, and the bench was now empty.

'Mrs Peel, lovely to hear from you! Ready for that next trip, are we?'

* * *

The phone rang and Angie snatched up the cordless handset from the arm of the chair. She didn't even wait for it to ring off before she answered it frantically.

'Summer?' she barked, breathily.

'Er, good morning, madam. I'm calling about your recent accident.'

Accident?

'Er, I think you have the wrong number. Goo—'

'Well madam, according to our records, you were in a recent accident regarding medical attention. We are just calling to help you sort out a claim. Can you tell me about your injuries?'

Injuries, she thought. *I can tell you about injuries. Broken heart, for one. Shattered life, for another. Not recognising the person in the mirror, does that count? I nearly battered the hall mirror to death the other day, cos I thought some kind of nutty grandma intruder had scaled the wall. It was me. I'm not even old.*

'Er, I don't think—'

The man prattled on, and she could hear the clicking of keys and chatter of other operators in the background. Everyone had to make a living, but this?

'If you could just confirm to me the location and date of the incident, then we can proceed to the particulars.'

'I haven't been in a bloody accident!' She could feel a ball forming in the pit of her stomach, anger resonating through her veins, like someone had flipped a switch inside her. 'I don't go anywhere, do anything, see anyone! You are the first person I have spoken to other than my daughter for months! Now do me a favour and piss off!' Angie clicked the off button before the man had chance to finish his stutter. She missed the days of clunky phones on the wall, phone boxes. The satisfaction of slamming down the phone on someone was lost to the newer generations. Pressing a button just didn't cut it. A soft click, a tiny beep, it had no pleasure in it. To feel the same effect, you had to throw the bloody thing at the wall, or wave yourself about, spouting expletives to no-one while you gestured with as many fingers as you felt was warranted, aimed at said phone. No wonder people had more rage these days. The outlets were diminishing, the old ways of telling someone to do one with the slam of the phone in their ear, lost forever. Flip phones had even gone out of fashion, so you couldn't even do it on the move now either. She looked at the black plastic in her hands and put it down on the sofa next to her. She couldn't throw it. She needed to be able to get in touch with Summer. It's not like she could nip out and buy another either. Summer would have to, and that would just add to her resentment.

Something had changed in her daughter and she didn't like it.

Now she was demanding she went out to buy food too. She knew what it meant, so why was she doing it, after all this time?

Angie stood and crossed the open-plan living room to the dining area. The table was never used really; half of it was covered in brochures, ready to be made into packs for Summer to send out to her regulars. They ate on the other half. It was a huge, six-seater table, so they only needed a small corner of it. Two table mats, two coasters. Looking past the table, she looked at the thick, red, velvet curtains that covered the patio doors. She always kept them closed, didn't like to be overlooked. She preferred the dark, the quiet, though she knew Summer hated it. Her room was the only one with light in it, her window always open, the curtains always pulled.

She was the same growing up: a real sun chaser. She loved to meet the day with a smile, bounding into their bedroom and chattering away in the early mornings. *Not so much any more, come to think of it. I guess that's my fault.*

The garden lay beyond those curtains, and that was another reason for them staying closed. She just couldn't bear to look. She preferred the memory she had, the one where the flowers were blooming, and the sun was kissing the petals and the leaves, making them stand proudly in their beds.

Summer wasn't going to phone back, she realised after a while. Something *had* changed, and Angie felt all the more vulnerable for it. She headed to the hall table, where her address book sat collecting dust, and looked up a number.

'Hello, it's Mrs Hastings here,' she said, trying to sound normal and not vomit down the phone. 'Yes, that's me. No, not dead, thank you, I'm quite well. Yes, still at the same address. Yes, definitely me. No, no cliffs. Listen, I need to place an order, could you possibly help me?'

6

'How did your nipple cake go down?' A voice called to Jean as she walked up her drive. She could see Benny in the window, giving her his best *what fecking time do you call this?* feline glare. She looked across at Jim's house to see him standing with a piece of timber in his hand, saw plugged in on the drive.

'Good thanks, I won best cake for originality. It caused a bit of fuss though, to be honest. I might tone it down a bit next time.'

Jim chuckled, setting down the piece of wood and sticking the pencil he was holding behind his ear. He had a good head of hair, silvery grey at the edges. It made him look very sexy. Especially with the low-slung jeans and ripped T-shirt. Jean felt herself blush, and she adjusted the cake tin in her hands. He saw this movement and came forward.

'Sorry, I never offered to take that from you. I could carry it if you like?' He held his hands out but then caught sight of the fine layer of sawdust sprinkled into his arm hair. 'Or maybe not, sorry. I forget I'm a bit grubby. The builders are done for the day so I just thought I'd make a start on the bits I can do. I need to have it all done in a week.'

'The children coming then?'

A look of worry crossed his face momentarily. 'Hopefully yeah, it just depends on a few things. I am really hoping so, after all this.'

Jean had to bite her tongue again to stop her from speaking out, asking what was going on. It wasn't her business, but it didn't sound like things were as cut and dried as she first believed.

'Well,' she motioned to the cake tin, 'I should get this indoors and get washed up. You got dinner plans?'

Jim motioned to the house. 'Nope, Pot Noodle and a shower, probably.'

Jean laughed. 'Well, I have wine and I was planning to make something light, a chicken salad maybe. I have enough, so if you fancy some food, you're more than welcome.'

'Are you sure? You fed me the other night.'

'Of course I am,' Jean smiled, ignoring the death stare Benny was giving her through the blinds. 'About seven?'

Jim grinned. 'Sounds good. I'll bring the wine; I have loads.'

Jean smiled back at him. 'Well, bring something that goes with salad and rude cake.'

* * *

Summer walked up the driveway to her house with a slight spring in her step. She was swinging a bag of meat from her arm, and never had she been so glad to be doing so. She had nearly burst into tears when their old butcher had walked into the travel agency that afternoon. She hadn't been out, sure, but her mother had actually picked up the phone and spoken to someone. She had ordered the meat for tea to be delivered to her daughter. It was bloody genius, and a bit of a cheat, but it had given Summer a huge boost for the rest of the day. She hadn't even scowled or flipped Noel off when she locked up at the same time as him that evening. She had managed a smile. A thin one, a begrudging flash of teeth, but still. It was there. He had smiled back too, and hadn't ignored her, which she was surprised at, given how she had been making his life difficult.

The girl on the bench had been there again. Sitting reading *Wuthering Heights*. Summer recognised the cover, one that she had read as a child many times. She'd nipped out for more milk, leaving a *Back in 5* sign on the door. The girl flinched as though she had been watching, so Summer passed her and popped to the shop.

'Hi,' she said, approaching the bench on her way back, reusable shopping bag hanging off her arm. 'No school today?'

The girl shrugged, hunching her shoulders and burying herself deeper into her book.

'I just needed some milk. Need that coffee. Busy, busy, busy.' No response, but she could see that the girl was watching her from the corner of her eye. 'You ever feel like that?'

The girl turned the page, her finger following the words as she read along.

'Good book, that. I read it myself as a child.'

'I know.' The little voice squeaked out. 'Er... I mean... everyone reads it. School makes most people.' She flashed a side look at her again and Summer looked across at the shops.

'Well, good book anyway. I hope you enjoy it.' She pulled a pre-packed sandwich and a can of soft drink out of her shopping bag, placing them on the bench. 'I like to snack while I read.' She had gone back to the shop, and the next time she looked back, the girl, and the food, was gone.

Later that night, she put the key in the lock of her house front door and stilled. There was noise coming from the inside. Music. Diana frigging Ross, with all the gorgeous, glorious Supremes warbling along behind her. *It might just be the TV*, she thought to herself. She stepped into the hallway and felt like crying all over again. There were lights on in the living room and the music was definitely not an advert. She went to the kitchen to put the meat in the fridge, and there she was.

'Hi love, how was work?' Her mother was stood next to the cooker, chopping mushrooms. 'I made a start on tea.'

'Good. Busy,' she replied, taking out a bottle of rosé wine from her other bag and putting it in the wine holder in the fridge. 'I got the meat, thanks.' She felt like she was talking to a bloody unicorn: an elusive, magical creature. She was terrified to overreact, or react at all, in case she scared off the mirage. The pangs she was feeling for her old mother were so strong, they were punching her in the gut, but she kept her poker face.

'I love this song,' she said nonchalantly, though her inner monologue was screaming, *Oh my God, she's got music on and living room lights and she's smiling!* 'I got some wine to go with tea. Shall I set the table?'

Angie nibbled at her lip, slicing through an onion's outer skin now and peeling the layers back. 'Actually, I was thinking that we could clear the table off if you have room at the office for the brochures. It looks a bit messy.'

Summer could feel her jaw drop, and she looked away. 'Er... sure... I need to make them up anyway to be honest, get them sent out before the end of the year. I'll get to work on them after dinner, take them to the post office tomorrow, okay?'

Her mum gave a slight nod of her head, and Summer resisted the urge to hug her. This was sooo going to work. What was it the books on parenting said? Tough love? Who knew it worked the other way round when the offspring tried it? She mentally shook herself.

Play it cool.

'I'll get a bath then, before tea. Will you have some wine with me?'

The onions sizzled as they hit the warm pan, but Angie said nothing. The music played on, so Summer headed up the stairs, pulling out her phone as she went. She opened Messenger and sent a quick message. It beeped back pretty much immediately, and she tapped out a thanks in reply. Tomorrow would be interesting.

She walked into the bathroom, starting the bath running and pouring in some of her favourite bubble bath. When she moved the bottle, the thin layer of dust that had accumulated on the top hit the air, and the motes danced in the last remnants of sunshine from the window. She finished pouring in the lavender scented liquid and put the bottle back on the sill. All of the bottles had dust on them. She hadn't noticed before. Either that or she had just stopped noticing. As the water ran, she sat on the side of the bath, looking around the room as though seeing it for the first time. The wallpaper was out of date, peeling in the corners. It was clean, sure, but dusty, unloved. She knew that the house was a little in need of being updated, but not like this.

'I'm just going through my life like this,' she murmured to no-one but the dusty bottles. 'A little overlooked, unloved. A quiet little guest in my own life, terrified of making a mark. Petrified of kicking up the dust.'

Checking the bath, Summer turned and picked up her phone from the side of the sink. Tapping out another message, she eyed the line of toiletries. One was still in its box, a pretty pink container of her mum's favourite perfume. Still in the cellophane, a Christmas present from Dad. The last Christmas they were all together. She picked it up, turning it over and over in her hands. She'd kept it all this time. Another reminder, another little ghost to rattle its chains around their home. She pushed it into the back of the medicine cabinet and started to undress. They didn't just need help; they needed an exorcist.

* * *

Noel was in a really cheery mood. He was due to open the shop that weekend, the decorating was nearly finished, and all his stock had arrived. His mother, however, was still fretting.

'Darling, I know it's nice there, I've seen many beaches, but that's not all of life, is it?'

Noel tapped the screen to change the camera angle back to him, sighing. His mother brightened when she saw his face again, but the slight scowl was still there.

'I am working, Mum. I just like the beach on a morning. The shop's going well.'

His mother nodded, waving a hand at him dismissively. 'Yes, yes, I know, Santa shops are all well and good, but what about next year? Gap years are enriching experiences, Noel, but gap decades go tend to go on a bit. We miss you here. Isn't it time you came home, started your life?'

Noel sat down on the sand, looking at the concerned face of the woman who gave him life. These little conversations were happening more and more, and he was finding it harder to fob her off. Finding it harder to think of reasons why, truth be told. All of his uni friends were off doing their chosen careers by now, with families, mortgages, the odd beer belly. He remembered how they all used to joke about getting older, being responsible. Becoming their parents, even. Truth was, when he looked through his social media feed, they seemed happy. Pictures of house keys symbolising dream home purchases, funny memes about leaving work early on Friday, the odd gurgling, dribbling baby. Noel's Instagram was like a world map, and he loved it. What he realised was missing though, was people. Sunsets and big waves were all well and good, but did they chat to you at the end of a long work day?

'Mum,' he said, smiling at her frowning features as she folded clothes with her hands that were ever moving. 'What would you have me do at home, if I came back to live?'

His mother rolled her eyes. 'You always ask me that, and you already know the answer. Live, my lad, get a job, go back to uni, get drunk and knock me up a grandbaby, start an anti-Trump movement on my front lawn, anything!'

Noel laughed, a loud belly laugh that rang out loud on the quiet beach. He shook his head at his mother and spotted Summer walking up the beach, her flip flops in her hand. This morning, she was wearing a floaty dress that flapped around her figure in the breeze as she walked around the sand. He couldn't take his eyes off her, and his mother as always, saw something in his face.

'Noel, what is it? Turn the camera around please, show me what you're looking at.'

Summer hadn't seen him, and she looked like she was talking to someone. Which was odd, since she was alone, and her hands were by her sides. Noel wondered momentarily whether she had one of those wireless headsets that poncy businessmen and bike couriers used, but he didn't think her to be the type.

'Noel, turn the camera around!'

His mother was now leaning to one side, as though she could see around the corner of his phone at what he was looking at. He half expected her to try to pull it round with her hand or step out of the screen like a talc-scented version of *The Ring*.

He huffed and, seeing that Summer was getting closer, he flicked the screen around quickly, focusing on the beach area she had just left. 'There, see? Nothing, I just thought I saw something on the beach.'

'Pan to the right now, show me the whole beach.' Her voice was flat, un-amused. *She's not buying it, dude.* He slowly moved the phone to show the rest of the beach till a shriek came through the phone.

'Ooh! That her, is it? The travel agent?'

Noel rolled his eyes and pretended to throttle himself with his free hand. That was the thing about being a so called 'mummy's boy' – when you actually liked your mother, spent time talking to them, sharing your life, being a good son. It came around and pinched you on the bottom when they remembered every little detail of your conversations and used them to find the little bits that you didn't say.

'Well, is it?'

Noel flicked the camera back again and was greeted with his mother's nostrils.

'Mum! Sit back a bit! I can see brain!'

His mother chuckled as she sat back in her kitchen chair. She was at the table, as always, her little office at home. She had a proper office upstairs but she always preferred to sit in the kitchen to work. He knew without needing to ask that her dog Penelope would be laid asleep at her feet, the cats Tolstoy and Shakespeare would be through the open patio doors, sleeping in the shade of the large oak tree at the bottom of the garden. He could practically smell the flowers from the garden, and for once, he got a pang of home.

'It is, isn't it? I know it is, my little tinker. You never said she was beautiful.'

Noel blushed and covered his fingers around the speakers a little. Summer was getting closer now, looking out at the shoreline wistfully. He wondered what she was thinking about, who she had been talking to in her head. She always seemed so stressed.

'I didn't notice. Besides, she actually despises me. She hates Christmas too, can you believe that?'

His mother wrinkled her nose a little before recovering. 'Well, not everyone has the best times at Christmas, do they? Maybe she has a reason to hate it?'

Noel opened his mouth to object but stopped. His mother raised her eyebrows at him, symbolising *I told you so*, and then picked up the latest romance novel next to her. 'I'm going to sit in the garden now to read my book, get the muse flowing a little. Go and talk to the girl, see what happens. And please, come visit your poor old mother. If you don't do it soon, I shall be in a box and then you'll be cross!'

Noel rolled his eyes again. His mother never even looked up from her book as she said, 'Don't roll your eyes Noel. Love you, poppet,' and clicked the call off.

He held the phone between his hands as he sat on the warm sand and watched Summer get ever closer. Perhaps he could say hello, at least.

* * *

'Just book the flight, Summer. Just go to the office, make a drink, book the flight, and get on with your day. Just do it, she'll be fine.' Summer thought of her mother, sat indoors at home, all alone for a whole week. 'She ordered the meat; she phoned the butcher herself. Fair enough, she didn't see anyone, but still, she spoke to a person. She could order pizza if she gets stuck for food, and the post could wait till I get back perhaps. Or I could get it diverted to the office. I can get a temp in for a week, or close even.'

She slowed down, looking at the sea. There were smaller boats coming into the harbour, and in the distance, she could see larger ones, transporting people to far flung places most probably, or maybe just Scarborough. She thought of the beaches in Bali, how blue the sea would be, how soft the white sand would feel between her toes. She longed to just do it, get on a plane, do what she had always wanted to do, instead of living like a teetotal bar manager. Serving drinks to everyone, watching them enjoy them, have the experiences of living in the moment, but never drinking a drop of it herself.

She was sick of lying to people about places, boning up on little bars and clubs to go to in different countries, staying up to date on local customs without ever practising them herself. In truth, the only product she sold with genuine experience and first-hand knowledge was the boat trips around Bridlington, and the day trips to local places. She and Jean had been on most of them on their days off, scoping them out, keeping good relations with the local traders and business people. She was bloody good at her job, but just once, she wanted to be a part of it for real. She didn't want to be a tourist in her own life any more; she wanted to finally be a traveller of the world. It was times like this when she really couldn't help but resent her father for not being there, but that wasn't good for anyone.

'Hi,' a familiar, deep voice said behind her. She felt her shoulders go up to her ears in response, and she gave herself a second to reply.

'Hello.'

'Morning walk?'

'Yep, every day. Clears my head. You?'

'If there's a beach, I'm there.'

She nodded, a little, sad smile crossing her features before she could stop herself.

'What's wrong?' he asked, touching her shoulder with an open hand. 'I'm a good listener. I have the time.' He motioned to the sand, and she took a seat, putting her bag and shoes down in front of her and lifting her knees up to her chin, wrapping her floaty dress around herself. He sat down next to her, kicking his flip flops off and running his toes through the sand. They both noticed each other doing it and stopped.

'So?'

'I lied the other day when I said I'd been to the place you mentioned.'

He didn't flinch, just kept looking at her with his big, brown eyes. His curly hair kept being brushed into his face by the wind, and he pushed it back with his hand.

'The truth is, I want to go on holiday. There's a good deal on Goa at the moment, and I want to see the elephants. I've wanted to go for a while, and it's just a little frustrating.'

Noel nodded. 'Can't get cover for the shop? Why don't you get agency cover, or just close the shop for a week, work remotely? You can get wi-fi there, and most phones do what you need them to. It's a once in a lifetime trip; I say go for it.'

He's pretty much just summed up my thoughts. Not that easy though, is it?

'Yeah, I could, but things are pretty tight at the moment, and there's family stuff too, you know.' She cleared her throat and gathering her things, stood up. 'Anyway, I'd better go open up.'

She started to walk away but he appeared at her side, flip flops in his hand. 'I'd better come and open up too. I'll walk with you.'

She didn't argue; she couldn't stop him from walking her way, after all. They walked up the beach, towards the shops in companionable silence. Not awkward, which was weird.

'It's worth thinking about, definitely, if you can swing it,' Noel said, before slowing down. She noticed he wasn't by her side any more, and she found herself stopping.

'Noel?'

He was there at the waffle stall, ordering. He grinned and beckoned her over. 'You want one? My treat?'

'Er, no thanks. I had juice and toast for breakfast, I'm not keen on sugar-loaded cream fests before, like, at least 4 p.m.'

He batted her away, paying the stall lady, Ruby, with his sweet smile and a fiver. As he turned to show her his strawberry and cream filled waffle, she saw Ruby fan herself with his bank note. She shook her head and Ruby laughed. The women around here, what was it with them?

He jogged over to her, a boyish smile plastered across his face. 'You're missing out; this is the breakfast of champions, I tell you. Perfect way to start the day.'

She giggled despite herself, and they walked up towards the shops. Noel was making all kinds of happy noises, taking bites out of his food.

'You are totally gross, you know that?' She was laughing as she said it, and he growled and pulled a funny face at her. He had a cream moustache, and it made him look utterly adorable. She opened her mouth to tell him so, but then the shops came into view.

'What. The. Hell. Is. That!' She jabbed her finger towards Forever Festive, turning to face Noel.

Outside the shop, right in the middle of the shop window, on the street, was a giant, inflatable Santa. The thing was huge, garish and manically smiling at her. What made it was the slogan hanging from the shop window. It was in festive writing, and it declared *Christmas is coming*. Summer shuddered visibly. The thing would have been less scary if instead of a blow-up Santa, there had been *Game of Throne's* Ned Stark's head on a spike. That would have been easier to handle if truth be told.

'It's... er... Santa. You know, for my shop display?'

Summer looked back in disbelief, blinking a few times as though the hideous apparition would disappear, back to the buggering place it came from. She took a step or two nearer to him and gave him her best *I'm talking to stupid* look.

'I know it's Santa, but your shop is called Forever Festive, and we really need to just keep our shops separate, and classy. This,' another finger jabbed towards the inflatable, 'is not classy! You're going to scare away all my customers with this crap!'

Noel was still eating his waffle, looking at her as though he was expecting her to keep talking.

'Have you nothing to say for yourself?' She dropped her bag on the floor and folded her arms, her foot tapping as though she were a teacher speaking to an errant child in her class. Noel went to take another bite, holding up a 'one minute' finger, and Summer's lips pursed. Pushing her palm up towards his head, she smushed the waffle right into his face, hard. 'You want to eat your waffle, well go ahead!' She flicked the cream from her hand onto his shirt, and grabbing her bag, strode across to Summer Loving. It was then she saw Jean in the window, arms crossed and fixing her with a decidedly cross glare. *Busted.*

Something caught her attention in the reflection in the window and she balked a little. Noel was standing there wiping the cream from his eyes, bits of waffle stuck to his face. Along the beach wall, a large seagull was watching him, and saw its chance. It flew off the wall, aiming straight for Noel. Summer turned around to try to warn him, but it was too late. The seagull went into a full dive and started to peck at Noel as he flapped his arms around wildly.

'Ahh, gerroff!' He ran around in a circle, his arms flailing around. Spinning around, he got one of the flip flops he had in his hand and fired it like a torpedo at the bird. 'Take that, you thieving bastard!'

The seagull, its beak full of waffle and its feathers streaked with whipped cream and strawberry sauce, deftly swerved the blow and made a *ha-ha-ha* sound.

'Keep laughing, ya big feathery twat!' Noel screamed at the bird, who was already flying off to get his next meal. He turned and looked at Summer, shaking his head and flicking more cream around him.

'This, Summer Hastings, is war!' He bunched his fists together and shook them at her. 'Get ready for Christmas, baby!' He saluted her violently with one finger and tore off to his shop.

'Well, that was rude,' Summer said to herself as she headed back to her shop. He needed telling though, and now it was done. Dealt with. He knew the score.

As soon as Summer walked into the travel agents, Jean was on her.

'Summer, what the hell was that all about? Why did you do that to poor Noel? Why were you even together?'

Summer dropped her bag onto her desk and headed to the sink to clean herself up. She had globules of cream on her dress, and her hands were sticky with sauce. 'He came up to me on the beach; I wasn't *with* him. Have you seen that monstrosity outside?'

'You beat him up!'

'I did not!'

'Summer, you pushed something into his face, and let him get attacked by a bird! You need to go and apologise right now. Oh, and your mother called.'

Summer scrubbed her hands clean and dried them off on the towel she kept on a rack nearby. 'Great, that's all I need this morning. She probably rang me to moan about something I didn't do, I have Mr anti-Grinch out there spreading bloody cheer like bloody Peter Pan, and you're mad at me! Fantastic!'

Jean stood fast, arms folded. 'Hey! Just a minute, my girl. I know you're mad, but still, you did wrong out there! You can't keep fighting with people. Don't you think this is all a bit playground, pulling pig tails and sticking tongues out? You obviously like him, so why not go sort this out?'

Summer flounced over to her desk and banged her bottom down on the chair, hard. 'Like him? Like him! As if! He's a curly-headed twatbag!'

'What!' *Shit.* Noel was standing there, a fresh change of clothes on, a towel around his shoulders. 'I came because I felt bad. We keep doing this fall-out dance, but I don't want to keep arguing. I thought we were getting past this, and now I'm a twatbag?' A droplet of water dripped from the end of his nose, and he wiped at it with the towel. His T-shirt had a Chippendale lookalike Santa on it, with the slogan, *Father Christmas does it in his boots.*

Jean stepped forward, a cold drink from the fridge in her hand. 'Have a drink, Noel. Talk about it. I'll cover the phones.'

Noel looked at Summer, but she was focused on her computer screen, tapping away. 'No thanks love, I think I'll just leave it.' He looked at Summer one last time and was gone.

Jean sat down in one of the customer chairs, flicking the ring pull on the can open. 'Do you know, you go on about your mother, but my girl, you are cut from the same stubborn cloth.'

The phone rang and Summer took it, ignoring Jean as best she could and trying not to bite her own tongue off.

If there was one thing Summer hated, it was being compared to her parents. Her mother, mostly. Did all daughters fear that? It was a rite of passage, she supposed. She looked out of the window as the customer spoke to her, on auto pilot as she typed in what the customer was asking for. Her mother used to love the coastline, live for the beach. She always said that she would like to have pets. Chickens, dogs, cats, but she would wait for retirement. She hated the thought of a living thing being left alone indoors all day. She used to worry that they would be pining all day, sad that they were left, worrying that they would be left alone forever. She didn't like the thought of that: the responsibility for a living thing's happiness being thrust upon her and her failing. She and Dad used to laugh at her, with her, declaring it to be a silly notion, but just like her to think of it. They showed her the ads in the paper, offering kittens and puppies, but she wouldn't be swayed. She had no intention of changing her mind, so they stayed as they were, working, going to school, coming home to their home and living their lives, happy as ever. A notion of retirement and animals in their heads. A vision of Angie in wellington boots, standing in her garden, a loyal dog by her side, a brood of chickens clucking nearby. Angie, grey haired and rosy cheeked, loving her new busy retiree life. Thinking of it now, it seemed like a cruel joke. Her mother was the stray dog, wondering why she was left in the house, all alone. Pining.

The phone call came to a conclusion, and replacing the receiver, she finished making a note on the system and sat back in her chair. She felt the familiar lurch in her stomach when she thought of home. Work was her sanctuary, and now that was gone too. Held hostage by a psychotic elf and his massive hammer. Although, she felt sure that in reality, his hammer was tiny. In proportion to an elf perhaps, but a bit weeny for a grown man. She needed to take back control, and she knew just how to do it.

She ran through her Rolodex, her long nails skimming through the cards till she found the number. Picking up the phone, she dialled. She would make her stamp on this little parade of shops if it killed her doing it. She had no intention of letting Christmas screw up the rest of her Indian summer. She would hold off the festivities as long as she could. The thought of spending another Christmas at home with her mother, still alone, still single, still missing her father, her family, and the future they never got, was suffocating. There was no way she was going to start living through the horrors early, that's for damn sure. Noel and his festive shite would learn its place.

***

Noel woke up in his B&B feeling awful. He hadn't slept well, and he was pretty sure it was more than just the errant springs in his mattress. He kept replaying the last few days in his head, and it felt like he was missing part of the reel. Somewhere, on the cutting room floor of his brain, there had to be some snippet of footage, some big reveal that would explain to him the different sides of the enigma that was Summer Hastings. Jekyll and Hyde looked like Ant and Dec compared to her epic mood swings and finding out her triggers was proving to be quite painful. He still didn't fully trust seagulls, and their screeching outside his window still felt a little like being laughed at all over again. And to think, he had spent weeks once freeing birds and other little creatures from an oil-slicked beach on the other side of the world, and now he was here in the UK, a mere hour or two from home, and he was hiding from the local birdlife. He would never enjoy a waffle in the same way again, and he would never forgive her for it. *She's a joy sucker,* he thought, pulling himself out of bed and heading to the en suite for a shower that would consist of thirty seconds of boiling hot water that stripped the meat off his bones, followed by a ten-minute blast of aqua so chilled, it would make a penguin's scrotum shoot up into his stomach. *She is a glass-half-full girl. A sucker of joy from life. The opposite of me.*

'What is her damage?' he blurted out loud as he pulled off his PJ bottoms and stepped under the shower head. He turned the shower on and scrubbed himself quickly, barely getting everything done before the cold-water jet caught him on the bare butt as he jumped out.

Picking out a warmish jumper and a pair of skinny, black jeans, he threw on a pair of stripy *Harry Potter* socks and his comfiest trainers. The weather had changed overnight, and he was beginning to feel the first vestiges of the impending coastal winter.

He made his bed, still chuntering to himself. 'She's pinched so tight, I'm surprised she can walk. I mean, who on Earth hates Christmas? Does she not watch the John Lewis adverts? The Coca-

Cola Truck? The X-Factor Christmas single!' Picking up his backpack, he shrugged on his black jacket and headed out.

Mrs Simpson, the owner of the establishment, caught him as he was headed out of the front door.

'Noel, don't go without some breakfast; you never have it and it's included in the price.'

Noel opened his mouth to politely decline, but she was on to him. Waving her neon-pink spatula at him, she pointed to the dining area. 'Come on, I have fresh local sausage on the go and bacon...'

Noel's stomach gurgled at the thought of the breakfast that he could now smell wafting through the air. Mrs Simpson, her blonde hair piled on top of her head in a beehive style that somehow worked, her body encased in a frilly, pink apron with teapots adorning it, raised her brows. It felt like a challenge to defy her, rather than a gentle offer. Still, he was hungry. He could be a little late to work. If he skipped his beach walk, he would still make it on time.

Summer popped into his head again. Maybe avoiding her for one morning wouldn't be so bad. He didn't trust himself not to throw her moaning arse into the sea if she had one more pop at him. Although, that would be very therapeutic. Some of the locals might even pay to see it. He could charge a viewing fee, give the proceeds to the council to help keep the beaches clean. Hell, they could probably clean all the beaches for what he would give to see her dunked. She was so annoying, yet here he was, staring dumbly at his landlady, thinking about her.

'Thanks, Mrs Simpson, sounds perfect.'

She beamed at him before heading back to her kitchen. 'Janice, honey, call me Janice. Do you like tomatoes, mushrooms?'

'Yes please, love them. Do you want me to sit anywhere?' He got to the door of the dining area and saw a few guests sitting, eating, chatting and reading the paper. It was homely, as always. Little touches around that made you feel like you were in a family home, rather than just renting a room. The tablecloths were pretty fabric pieces in pastels and floral patterns, little teacups on the tables and cute and quirky little table centrepieces. It was Mrs Simpson's personality down to a pot of tea, and it made Noel smile. He walked across the room, taking a seat at a little two seat table in the window. It looked chilly outside, and he noticed that people walking past were a little more wrapped up than usual. Good job he had plumped for the jumper and jeans combo.

Forty-five minutes later, Mrs Simpson finally stopped shovelling food onto his plate and allowed him to leave. He headed to work, burping from time to time as his stomach struggled to digest the amount of food that had been thrust upon it, and the richness of his brekkie. It was just after nine when he rounded the corner, taking the keys out of his bag ready to start the day. He heard a whooping noise and looked for the source. There, at the doorway of Summer Loving stood a woman, dressed in a skimpy bikini. He did a double take. He felt the chill even in his jacket; how was this woman still smiling? She was stood there, grinning like an idiot, a bottle of something in her hand. Was Summer flogging sun cream or something?

He walked up to his shop, doing his best to appear unrattled. He was sure that this was aimed at him somehow. He could hear whooping and girlish screams and cackles, and it was then he realised that the woman in the doorway wasn't the source of the noise. As he put his key into the shutter lock, he glanced across and realised that the crazy bikini lady was a cardboard cut-out, holding a bottle of tanning solution. *What the hell?* He finished opening up and started putting out his metal baskets of stock, listening intently for noise. He'd only been open for a couple of days, and he was eager to get going.

'What are you doing?'

He swivelled around, realising belatedly that he was filling the baskets willy nilly, whilst practically humping one of them in his efforts to reach over enough to peek through the window. He was very relieved to see it was Jean standing there with an amused look on her face and not his opponent.

'Sorry, I was just...' He looked again at the baskets, which looked ever so slightly worse for wear, tinsel chucked in with baubles, Santa dog toys looking dishevelled as though a few hounds had already had a bit of a taste test. 'I... er...' He tried and failed to think of something clever, nonchalant. Or even anything that made sense and didn't look stalkerish. 'What's going on next door, anyway?'

Jean eyed him, and then looked through the window. 'Promotion day. Summer has asked the local college beauty department to come in. She's offering free spray tans, for the students to practice. Plus, five per cent off any holiday booking for next year.'

Noel twigged. 'This is aimed at me, isn't it?'

Jean's mouth twitched. 'Well, you do look a bit pale.'

Noel made a 'ha-di-ha' sound and started to sort out the baskets. Jean chuckled and he heard her enter the shop. Grabbing one of the squeaky Santas, he grabbed it and pretended to choke it.

'You won't win me, woman!' he said to the cuddly fabric face. Then he had a thought. Running into the shop, he flipped the sign to closed, dumping the toy into the basket.

* * *

Next door, Summer was in her element. The students and their teacher had arrived that morning, full of bubbly energy and brandishing various products and machines. They had installed a huge, pop-up tent in the back, and there had been a steady stream of people coming to get a free spray tan. The college had been over-joyed for the opportunity to give their students practice on the general public, and she had sold two holidays to two people already, new customers as well. To say it was all about hacking the neighbour off, she was already up on the event, even after the refreshments and giving the college some money for their materials. The shop was buzzing and happy, people reading through brochures in the seating area as they waited. It was lovely, and the college girls were professional and friendly, caring and – best of all – quite loud. She just knew he would be able to hear it, and the thought felt like balm on her frayed nerve endings. She tidied away some of the empty mugs and glasses and was just in the back dealing with them when she heard Jean's voice.

'Hello! What brings you here?'

A male voice started speaking, but she couldn't make it out and carried on with her cleaning. Jean knew everyone in Bridlington, so it wasn't unusual that someone who came into the shop had stopped to chat. One of the college girls, a seventeen-year-old called Imogen, came into the back brandishing two cups.

'These are from the customers that just left, sorry. You should see the guy who just walked in; he's lush. I swear, he looks like that bloke off the telly. What's his name, Outlander? Me mam watches it, he's a bit old for me really. Fit as, though.'

Summer thought of the red-haired Scottish hunk from *Outlander. Wouldn't that be a treat,* she thought. She heard an explosion of laughter and whoops in the shop and came out to see what everyone was so excited about. Heading for the tent, she soon saw why. She was aware of Imogen coming up behind her, giggling to herself, and she felt her face freeze in an *I'm fine* expression.

Noel was standing there, in the spray tent. He was just pulling a hair net onto his springy locks, and his feet had little stick-on soles attached to them. His chest was defined, a sprinkling of thick curly hair across his pecs. The women were all flocking around him, chatting away, but Summer couldn't take her eyes off one thing. His pouch. The man was standing there, naked except for a black thong. A thong that showed his butt cheeks off, and a front piece of material that had a nose on it. A flashing, red, tacky nose. Noel, her neighbour, was standing in her shop wearing a singing, flashing Rudolph faced pair of skimpy pants.

'It's Poldark, not Outlander,' she murmured as an afterthought. Imogen jabbed her in the arm excitedly.

'That's it! Summer's right, guys! He looks like the bloke from *Poldark*, not *Outlander*!'

The women all joined in on a chorus of *ahhhh's* and *oh yeah's*, luckily drowning out Summer's groan of anguish. Jean came and stood at the side of her, nudging her elbow with her own.

'Shame you don't get on, love,' she said, out of the corner of her mouth. 'That is a real shame, because he is going to be beating them off with a stick once word gets out.' She tipped her head in the direction of the women, who were all engrossed in him, including the beauty course tutor. 'See?'

Summer headed back to the sink, trying to keep the scowl off her face till she was in private. 'Shout me if any customers come in. Good work, ladies!' She headed out of the room, shutting the door behind her firmly. 'Jackass.'

* * *

Noel was in his element. Oh, it wasn't the booth, or the free tan – that actually looked rather good. Though he did smell a bit biscuity. It was the look on Summer's face. She looked like the end scene of *Terminator 2*, when the bad robot gets thrown into the molten lava. Her face changed from confusion, to recognition, embarrassment, anger and, he liked to think, a little lust. Just a tad. The college girls had found it hilarious, and even the tutor and Jean had laughed after the initial reveal shock had worn off. Now he was getting sprayed down, and she had disappeared into the back. Presumably to lick her wounds. I mean, it was worth it. Totally. Even being a bit orange for the rest of the day, till it developed, and he could shower the rest off at the B&B. The girls were all chatting away, Jean had gone off to clean, and he was happy to just get it over with. Although, the longer it took, and the longer Summer wasn't there, the worse he felt. He had kind of stolen her thunder with the shop promo. He knew that she had aimed the whole thing at him and his shop, but still. He hadn't been raised this way. Things didn't get to him. She did, though. She really did. She got under his skin, worse than the exotic worm that had burrowed into his skin a few years ago and taken up home in his arm, making him itch and wanting to cut it off himself out of sheer panic and revulsion. If he could cut her off, it would be better. Bloody, fast and effective. The thing was, then he calmed down, and he thought about how cute she was. How adorable she was, even when her nose was all scrunched up when she was yelling at him or staring at him like a piece of seagull crap on her slinky sandals. He turned this way and that when asked, lifting an arm, moving a leg, and then he was done.

'Right,' the tutor said, doing her best to maintain whatever professionalism she had before the pouch incident. 'If you can just step forward onto the mat, and we can take off your sticky feet, and check your tan.'

He did as he was asked, looking down at his feet as one of the girls, Tanya, took off the little stick-on soles from his now very tanned feet. He stood forward onto the mat and looked up as he heard the snap of a camera. *They never said they would take photos,* he thought in panic, but when he looked up, there was no camera, just the girls looking at the tutor, who was peering forward at his body. She noticed him looking and blushed.

'Sorry, I'm just checking that there are no drips.'

He nodded, now feeling a little chilly, given that he was standing there in a furry scrap of material and nothing else. She straightened up, smiling.

'Excellent job Tanya, you excelled yourself here! You girls will all be pleased to know that you have passed your first assessments! Well done! Now, if you can head back to the college and send the next three please.'

The girls' *yays* and *yips* turned to grumbles as they nodded along to their teacher, before reluctantly waving goodbye to her and Noel and heading out.

'Thanks so much, Noel,' she glanced at him whilst she passed him his clothes. 'We don't get many males coming to our student sessions, and it's great practice. Men can get tans too; it's the twenty-first century, after all!'

Noel nodded awkwardly. He wouldn't be one of them, after this. He'd made his point. 'No problem, happy to help.'

That night, his landlady gave him a plastic sheet to sleep on, and some fabric that looked like it was once towels, but was now used to clean up spills in the garage, or to wipe the dog's feet on after a muddy walk. She knocked at his door about five seconds after he got home. He spent the night feeling and smelling like a plastic-packed biscuit you get in airports.

Summer didn't appear on the beach the morning after. He took his usual walk before work, this time with a sausage sandwich to go from Mrs Simpson, who then pushed him out of the door before he could ask for brown sauce. Probably in her mad dash to check if there were any orange arse prints on her furniture. He made a mental note to get her some flowers on the way home, to say sorry for the inconvenience. No wonder the stag and hen parties were not allowed at her house; the poor woman would have a coronary.

7

Angie was laid in bed when she heard the gate go. Looking at the clock in panic, she realised it was still the middle of the day, far too early for Summer to be home. She pulled her head slightly out of the duvet, listening intently for any sounds. She could feel the blood pumping in her ears, and... footsteps. Definitely footsteps. She wished she wasn't so intent on keeping the windows shut all the time; she couldn't hear well enough to decide whether it was just her own paranoia she was hearing.

Bang bang bang! The door went. Definitely not paranoia then. Angie darted out of bed and grabbing her dressing down from the back of the door, crept to the top of the stairs.

'Hello?' A man's voice could be heard at the other side of the door. 'Mrs Hastings? I have a delivery here for you.'

'What sort of delivery?' She found the words flying out of her mouth before she could push them back in with hands of fear.

'Er, from the garden centre? I need a signature please, and do you want them putting in the front or the back?'

'I didn't order anything, sorry. You have the wrong house.' *He said my name, though.*

'Er, your daughter placed the order, Mrs Hastings. Do you want me to just leave the order outside? I just need a signature.'

Angie couldn't make much out through the frosted glass of the door. She had a curtain she usually pulled over the front door of an evening, but Summer had obviously opened it when she left. She could only make out a uniform through the door.

'Leave it there,' she managed to squeak out. 'Thank you.'

'Err okay,' the delivery man was obviously a little confused by her behaviour. *So am I, for the record.* Seconds later, a clipboard was half pushed through the letterbox, and she scurried to sign it and push it back through.

'Thanks,' he said cheerily, pushing a pink sheet of paper back through the slot.

She sat on the step, waiting till she heard nothing but the birds singing outside, and then pulled the paper through the slot, unfolding it.

It was from the local garden centre, addressed to her. The invoice was addressed to Summer at the shop. There were pots, and bulbs and bedding plants, everything you would need to make a garden. All of her favourites, she noticed. Was Summer replanting the garden? She wasn't exactly green fingered. Then the penny dropped. The delivery was in her name. Summer wanted *her* to do the garden. What was with her lately? First the meat order, now this?

Angie scrunched up the delivery note and flicked it onto the hall table. She wasn't going to win this one. She went to head back up the stairs, to bed, but instead found herself heading to the dining table.

It was clear. Summer had cleared off all the brochures, and the table had been cleaned and a tablecloth placed over it. One of her old favourites: a blue and white floral one that really brightened the room up. Or used to. Now it looked a little muted in its drab surroundings. She crossed the room and slowly lifted one of the thick, velvet curtains. A cloud of dust flew up and smacked her in the face, making her sneeze. The window was grubby too, and she felt a pang of shame, thinking of how she used to love these windows to gleam, to frame the room with a gorgeous picture of the garden outside.

The reality was far different now. The garden looked awful. The flowerbeds were a mess, the lawn both overgrown and patchy in places, which was an achievement. Her favourite wooden reading chair was on its side, the peeling paint punctuated with flecks of mud and overgrown blackberry bushes. It wasn't like she hadn't missed the garden. Hadn't wanted to sit in it with a paperback, a nice cold glass of wine, the radio on low in the kitchen while her food cooked. She used to love that. She had just packed the feelings and thoughts in a box, right along with the rest of them: a box in her mind. She realised now she had always thought the garden would just stay as it was: perfect. Just waiting for her to come and sit in it, like two old friends greeting each other after an extended absence. Needing no explanations, no apologies. She realised now that she had been dreaming.

'I'm sorry,' she said to the garden, putting her hand up to the dusty glass. 'I'll do better.'

Taking one of the curtains in her hands, she gripped it tight, and with one swift pull, yanked it off the runners.

* * *

Summer managed to avoid Jean for the rest of her time there, making sure that she was on calls as much as possible. Jean, to her credit, didn't linger either. She was suspiciously fast too, racing around doing her work and heading out of the door right on time, bag on her arm.

When she had gone and Summer had finished her call, she decided to close the shop for ten minutes and go and get her lunch. As she left Summer Loving, she noticed that Noel had a sign up in his shop window, saying,

WEEKEND HELP WANTED.

Underneath it said,

GRINCHES NEED NOT APPLY. TRY NEXT DOOR.

Summer huffed. 'The bloody cheek!' She kept walking, not trusting herself to pass close by it and not kick the window through. 'Grinch indeed. The man snorts candy canes.'

The girl was there, sitting on the bench once again, facing the beach. She had pigtails in that looked a little windswept, and her usual thick-rimmed glasses. She was always alone. Always here. Summer tried to think of the people she knew, who she could belong to, but she came up blank. Who was she?

As though she knew she was being watched, the young girl turned and stared at Summer. Her features seemed familiar somehow. They were in a panic now though, and the little girl turned to run, grabbing her backpack. One of the straps got caught in the wooden slats, and as she ran, it yanked her back hard. Propelling her straight into the metal edging of the seat with a loud *clunggg!*

'Sugar!' Summer ran to her side, getting down on her knees. 'Are you okay, love?'

The girl made a 'nnngg' sound and tried to get up but sank back down to the pavement with an equally disturbing noise.

'Sugar!' Summer said again, louder. There was a lump forming the size of a quail's egg on the side of the girl's forehead, and Summer started to fumble around in her bag for her mobile phone.

'Can I help?' Noel stood behind her, pulling off his T-shirt in one smooth movement. He had a fine line of hair running from the button of his jeans to his belly button. Which was, of course, a cute little innie. It looked fuzz-free and Summer licked her lips thinking about what it might taste like if she licked it. *What???!!!*

'Er...' *Oh my God, I can't even believe I just ogled him. It's like finding Santa a turn-on. Getting a wide on for Rudolph. No, no, no. The girl! Concentrate on the girl!*

Noel put his balled-up top under the girl's head, feeling for a pulse. 'She's breathing okay, and pulse is normal. Did you call for an ambulance?'

Summer rummaged again through her bag. 'I think my phone's in the office. You got yours?'

'No. No ambulance.' The girl went to sit up, and they helped her move slowly to sitting up on the bench.

'You need to get checked out; you had a nasty knock. Did she lose consciousness?'

Summer realised he was speaking to her, and she was still halfway between being concerned and *The Full Monty* playing in her head. 'Er... no, she didn't. Are you okay? Where's your mum?'

The girl shook her head slowly, wincing at the movement. 'I don't need the hospital. I'm okay.'

Noel glanced at Summer and nodded his head towards his shop. Summer nodded her head back. 'Come on then, let's get you inside so we can at least get you a drink, check on you properly.'

The girl said nothing, pulling on her backpack strap.

'Okay? Come get a drink with us?'

She didn't argue, so Noel hooked his arm under hers, and slowly pulled her to her feet. Summer threw her own bag on her shoulder and went to take the backpack off the girl's shoulders.

'No!' The girl grabbed for it, half spinning herself out of Noel's arms.

'Careful,' he said softly, picking her up and carrying her instead. She didn't argue, and just laid there, holding the straps tight in her hands. Summer followed them into Forever Festive, trying not to shudder at the godawful shop window display.

Noel turned and pushed the shop door open with his back. Summer followed and couldn't contain her gasp. On the adjoining shop wall, there was a whole Christmas scene laid out. In the middle of the wall, it had been set out to look like a living room. Flock wallpaper and a fake fireplace was set out, fake candles on the fireplace casting a warm glow over the shop.

Noel headed over there and sat the girl in the soft fabric armchair that was placed on one side of the fake fire. There was a full Christmas tree at the other side, complete with decorations and presents. It looked like a whole family, perfect Christmas scene, and it made Summer's heart plummet into her stomach. She could smell cinnamon and something else in her nostrils. The whole shop was a red and green nightmare.

'I should go,' she said, walking backwards to the doorway. Noel stopped her just as she was leaving. He reached for her hand. She grabbed it without thinking, and they both stood there, hand in hand.

'Don't go, please. First of all, being a man in a shop alone with an injured young girl might not be the best idea, you know? People make all kinds of assumptions. Secondly, I have no idea how to help her. She seems to like you.'

'Me? She freaked out when I tried to help her.'

'I see her, watching the shops. It's your shop she's watching.'

Summer looked through the glass at the girl, who was now sitting with her backpack on her knee, speaking to someone on a phone. 'I don't know why. Who's she speaking to?'

'I gave her the shop phone to call her mother to pick her up. Please, at least stay till then.'

Summer looked again at the fireplace scene. 'Was that what you were doing when you were making all that noise?'

Noel looked where she had jabbed her finger, and then back at her with an odd look on his face. 'Meet me for dinner, tonight? Let's start again?'

The girl was finished on the phone now and was looking around the shelves of pretty things that Noel had for sale.

'She's finished. We should go back in.'

Noel rubbed the skin on her hand, pulling her to him a little closer. 'Summer, I don't know what's going on with you, but I like you. Can't we just stop all this fighting?'

Summer turned to look at him, his deep, brown eyes looking at her with such intensity, it made her draw a sharp breath.

'Just come out with me, please.'

She opened her mouth to say yes when her phone rang in her bag. Her mother's ring tone. 'I can't,' she said, turning to leave. 'Sorry. Tell her I said bye.'

She walked away on shaky legs, willing herself not to turn around and look back at him. *He likes me. I've been nothing but mean, but he still likes me. Get a grip!*

She whirled around, and he was still standing there, looking right at her. 'Half seven, outside the shop. Wear something casual.'

His grin was contagious, and she carried it on her own face for the rest of the day.

* * *

Angie growled at the phone as yet again, her feckless daughter didn't answer. She lowered herself to the floor again, opening the letter box as far as she could to look through the hole to the outside. The plants were all still there, just looking at her. She needed them brought in before they attracted attention. Summer had planned it all, of course. I mean, why wouldn't she have? It was ridiculous. They were only plants, after all. The neighbours wouldn't think much, but the last thing she needed was someone commenting, or coming round to ask if she needed help. Summer had obviously spent a fortune, which wasn't the best use of what money she had. Not that Angie had room to comment, of course. She felt the pang of guilt once more about not bringing money into the house. They survived, but she wasn't so stupid that she didn't feel the pressure that their current situation put them both in.

She slapped the wooden door hard in frustration and pulled herself up till she was leaning against the door.

'You can do this, just grab the boxes, and bring them in. Just do it. Come on, come on, come on...' She turned the key in the lock and yanked the door open. She was through it and out in the daylight before she could give her brain the chance to process the terror. With shaking hands and a hammering heart, she grabbed the first box and ran inside. Her feet felt cold and wet, the dewy grass having made an impact on her usually insulated indoors skin. She dropped the box in the hallway and sat down on the stairs. Her whole body was shuddering, her knees knocking together, her teeth chattering from the force of her body's reaction. She went to stand and fell back onto the stairs. Closing her eyes, she concentrated on her breathing, taking huge gulps of air. *Bad idea, bad idea.* She felt like she was about to pass out. It was then that she smelled them. The scent of the flowers by her feet, and the breeze from outside. They hit her nose hard, evoking memories of days outside, in the sunshine, in her garden. An image of baby Summer, playing on a rug on the grass while she read a book. BBQs, days out in the car. She closed her eyes and sat for a long time, letting the memories and the fresh air roll over her, permeate her skin.

After an age of sitting there, she stood up slowly, leaning forward and placing the palms of her hands on her knees to lever herself up. Digging her nails deep into the flesh of her palms, she walked out of the front door again. And again. And again. Her heart pumped wildly the whole time, but taking in deep breaths of air, scented with the outdoors and the aroma of flowers, she moved every box and bag that was outside. When she closed the front door, turning the key in the lock, she burst into tears.

8

Noel wandered back into the shop, light on his feet. What that woman had, he didn't know, but he just couldn't get her out of his head. She was a total pain in the arse, and had real issues, but he couldn't shake the feeling that she was supposed to mean something to him. He'd travelled the world and seen many things, but it was her face he thought of when he woke up now. His mother had picked up on it from a phone screen, and now he was starting to admit it to himself.

'You okay?' the girl asked, sitting in the armchair now, rubbing her head.

'I should be asking you that,' Noel smiled. 'Will you have a cup of sweet tea before you go? Your mum's on her way, is she? I don't even know your name.'

'Avril.' She stood up, pulling her backpack off her shoulder and pulling out a bottle of water. 'I'm okay thanks, I have a drink. Can I er... have a job, though?'

'A job?'

Avril pushed her thick-rimmed glasses further up her nose and pointed at the sign in the window.

'Yeah, a job. I'm bored of school, and I can help out here. I could use the money and you need someone who loves Christmas! I had the best Christmases as a kid.'

'I don't know, Avril. It would mean working together, and I really wanted someone to dress up and hand flyers out. It might be better with someone older. Besides, you need to go to school. It's where you should be, right? You're not expelled or anything?'

She pulled a face. 'No, I just skip sometimes. It's boring, and the teachers don't even care about anything but exams.' She scowled, and Noel got a flash of recognition he couldn't quite place. 'You mean a man. You want someone to dress up and hand flyers out, I assume for minimum wage. You really think many people will want to do that, in autumn, when the other jobs around here are inside, or cooler, and they can pick up girls? I don't think so. In fact, I bet I'm the first one to ask about the job, right?'

He chuckled to himself. 'Right. What about your mum, your parents?'

'They'll be fine. Dad's working away, and Mum's busy with my little brother. He's only two. They'll be fine with it, I promise. Does that mean yes?'

Noel looked her up and down. 'Is that why you were watching the shop, for the job?'

She looked at him, and he knew then there was a reason, something she wasn't saying. 'Yes, that's why. I told you, I love Christmas.'

Noel picked up a sheet of paper from his desk and handed it to her. 'Job application form, just the basics, but I want your mum to sign it, okay? You can do one day a week, starting this Saturday. You need to rest that head of yours for a few days and go back to school too. No school, no job.'

'Yes!' she squealed, shoving the paper into her backpack and throwing her arms around him. 'Thank you, thank you, thank you!'

Noel gave her a quick squeeze back and heard a car outside. 'Okay, okay, I think your ride's here.'

Avril was out the door in two seconds flat. Noel followed her to the door, but it wasn't a normal car that picked her up; it was a local taxi. Avril waved at him, and he waved back.

Her mother sent her a taxi? It seemed like a little bit lapse parenting-wise, leaving her to her own devices all day and not coming to her aid after a fall, but he wasn't one to judge usually. After all, he didn't live a conventional life, did he? His biggest commitment in life, other than phoning his mother, was to his Netflix account. He lived his life one backpack at a time, and that was fine to him. Others would never like how he lived. Something told him though, that Avril wanted or needed something, and it wasn't just a bit of pocket money. Still, he needed the help. Maybe they could help each other, figure out how to live alongside each other till January. He felt a pang in his chest when he thought of Christmas being over, and his next move. Truth was, he was getting quite used to being around here. Drama and all.

* * *

Summer left work bang on five fifteen and she noticed that the shutters for next door were already down. She smirked to herself, thinking of Noel in his bed and breakfast, getting ready for their date. They'd probably end up arguing again, but she had to admit that the prospect of an evening with him did intrigue her somewhat. Jean was going to laugh her head off.

She needed to make amends with her friend, though; she knew that she'd been awful to her the last time they had been together. The poor woman always had her back, and she'd been nasty, mean. Jean didn't deserve that.

Summer pulled the shutters down on her shop, smiling and

chatting to the people who passed her as she locked her beloved shop away. The sun was still high in the sky, only just starting to turn the sky from bright blue to brush strokes of orange, umber and blood red. The air was humid, thick with heat, but the breeze brought welcome relief as it brushed against her skin. She loved nights like these, when you could sit outside till the stars came out and not catch a chill. People often knocked Yorkshire, saw the coastal towns as tacky, 'kiss me quick', binge drinking, but it was far from the truth. They didn't call it God's Country for nothing. There was a beauty here that was well worth seeing. She wandered down to the beach on her way home, kicking off her shoes to feel the sand under her feet once more.

In the early days, when it had been just her and Mum, she had spent hours here. Sitting on the beach, reading a book, crying her salty tears into the cold sand. January meant that their little corner of the world was quieter, people at home sleeping off the excesses of the season, knuckling back down to the world of work and normality.

New Year always meant more possibilities. New beginnings. People quit jobs in January, they put their houses on the market, they left bad relationships. Or good ones, come to that. That January on the beach though, it was just her and her mother. Adrift. Alone. Treated differently than normal by everyone around them. Everyone except Jean, of course. She had always been there, offering support, bringing around food, distracting them both with her chatter.

'Time will heal you, Summer,' she had said often. 'Get on with life, or it will get on without you. You don't want to waste a drop, my girl.'

They had healed, in a way, but all wrong. Like a bone not set properly. Weakened, bent out of shape, a shadow of its former self. Her mother lived like a ghost, hugging the walls of their crumbling house, and she herself sold dreams to other people, but never fulfilled any of her own. Now, as she walked along the beach on the way home, she felt a sense of things changing. Maybe things weren't going to be too bad; the terrible season she was always dreading was coming, but maybe it would be different this year.

She turned the corner to her street and started walking down the path. The gate was closed as normal, and the house looked just the same. Her heart sank a little, but then she saw the grass. On the right-hand side of the front door, there was a patch of flattened, green blades. *The delivery!* She rummaged in her bag for her keys, desperate to get the door open, see what had happened. She hadn't been notified that they had been asked to take the delivery back, and it wasn't like someone had come along and half inched a load of plants, surely?

She had just got her key into the lock when the door opened. Summer, caught off guard, ended up smashing into something hard, banging her head on the hall floor.

'Ow, what the hell!' Summer rolled onto her back and looked straight up into the face of her mother. Dressed in jeans and a green top. 'Mum, what are you doing?'

'Well, I was letting you in; I heard you come up the path. Do you want to tell me why you had a load of plants delivered to the house? The peace lily you bought last year lasted all of two weeks before you killed it off. Don't you think killing off a whole load of them is a bit of a waste of time and money?'

Summer pulled herself up, tossing the scattered contents of her bag back into the zip pocket. 'Well, it's my money to waste, remember? Given that I'm the one working to keep this shack from completely falling apart. Did you tell them to take it back? God knows when I'll get that money refunded. You could have at least stopped them from unloading it all before you...'

As she walked past her mother in a huff, she saw the light in the living room. It looked different from usual. Brighter. She walked into the room and saw what had changed. The thick, horrible, heavy curtains had been taken down, and the light she was seeing was from the garden outside. She wandered over to the window, not trusting her own eyes. She could hear her mother walking behind her. Looking out into the garden, she saw the boxes of plants, all sat in crates bearing the garden centre logo.

'How?'

Her mother came and stood next to her, gazing out through the glass. 'Well, I couldn't just let them sit out there all day. I didn't want people nosing into our business, so I brought them in.'

Summer looked around the dining room, now suspiciously clean and sweet smelling. 'You cleaned too. Where are the curtains?'

Angie shook her head. 'I ran them through the washer, but I think it was only the dust keeping them together. I've put them in the wheelie bin. I thought we could order some more, pick them together.'

Summer could feel herself well up, but she choked it down. 'That's fine, we can look online. Be nice to have things looking fresh.'

Angie nodded. 'We'll need some more compost too, and grass seed. Some of it is very sparse. I was thinking I might get the mower on it tomorrow, if you can get it out of the garage for me?'

The garage wasn't connected to the house. Summer thought about saying no, but she didn't want to push her luck. 'Sure Mum. Listen, I'm out tonight. You okay without me? I can bring some food home?'

Her mother was looking out of the window at the garden. 'No love, I'm fine. We have stuff in. You go out.'

Summer was halfway up the stairs, bag in hand, before she realised that not only had her mother not moaned that she was going out, but she hadn't even asked where she was going. Progress really was happening, and now she was off on a date with a man who annoyed the hell out of her. Go figure.

A short time later, Summer was walking back to Summer Loving, trying not to vomit up the nerves that were fighting against the two slices of toast she had grabbed before getting ready. Her mother had left her alone, and the music had been put on again. It was weird, to say the least, but the house actually had some life in it for once, so it was something she was happy to get used to. Anything but going back to what they were.

She had dressed in her best outfit: a yellow, billowing skirt that showed off her curves, and made her tan look all the better. She had teamed it with her favourite white silky blouse, and her cute red pumps and small leather bag. It had been hanging in her wardrobe for a while. Her someday outfit.

She resisted for once the urge to walk on the beach, not wanting to be sandy for her date, and walked along the front, past the families and holiday makers all out having fun, going on the rides. For once, she actually felt part of it, someone out to meet someone, someone with plans.

Walking around the corner, she saw the shops come into view. She noticed that Noel's *help wanted* sign was gone, and she smiled. He'd probably taken it down because of the grinch barb. She had to give him points for that.

'Hey,' a voice from behind her made her start.

'Hey! Stalk much?'

His face fell and as she looked at him, she wanted to bite her own tongue off. Again. 'Sorry.'

'I know you are, it's fine. These are for you.' He handed her a large bunch of beautifully wrapped sunflowers, tied together with yellow ribbon.

'I saw them and thought of you. They match your outfit too.'

'They're beautiful Noel, thank you. I feel like a bit of a prize bitch now.'

He waggled his eyebrows. 'All part of my dastardly plan. To be nice to you until you use up all of your snark and have no choice but to be nice to people.'

'Me? Being nice to folk? I can't see it.' She gave him a little sarky smile, leaning in and smelling the flowers. 'These are lovely, thank you. So, where are we going?'

'Well, I was thinking we could nip to Italy, and then you could show me some of the sights that Bridlington has to offer.'

'Italy, eh? You brought your jet pack?'

'Ah well, we only have to get to Regent Terrace; apparently it's lovely food. You been?'

Summer shook her head. There she was, feeling like a tourist again in her own life. She hadn't even seen half the sights in her own home town.

Noel grinned. 'Oh great! Another new experience for both of us then.'

'Another?' she asked. 'Do you mean as well as the sights?'

Noel blushed. 'Er yes, of course.'

* * *

Noel held the door to the restaurant open for her and she felt her mouth water as the scent of garlic and herbs reached her. The whole place felt heavenly. It was a dimly lit little place, all set out in dark oak and white linen tablecloths. Candles sat in bowls on each table, flowers around the place making it look romantic and inviting. All thoughts of the nerves and the toast were gone. Summer found herself feeling hungry.

Noel ushered her in, nodding to an approaching server.

'Good evening! Do you have a reservation?'

'Pritchett, table for two? I called earlier.'

She nodded, smiling a mega kilowatt smile at the pair. 'Ah yes, this way please.' She gestured with her hand, and Noel put his hand around Summer's waist, pushing her gently to follow along with him. They walked through to the back, where some cute little tables for two were set out. A single sunflower was laid on one of the place settings.

'I thought you said you hadn't been here before?' she murmured.

She felt his breath on her neck as he whispered close to her ear. 'I might just have called in on the way over, to check it was a nice place. I kinda wanted to make the right impression for once.' He pulled her chair out, and she sank into it.

'Thanks.'

The server passed them a wine list each and a menu. 'I'll give you a minute, unless you want to order drinks now?'

Noel looked at her in question. 'Wine?'

She opened her mouth to say no, ready to trot out her standard response of having to get home, needing a clear head. 'Yes, please.'

The meal was delicious, and soon they found themselves laughing hysterically as Summer recounted the days when Reg, the previous owner of the Forever Festive shop, was working in his little shop next door, and all the shenanigans he used to get involved in.

'You sound really fond of him. I get now why you were so...'

'Hostile?' Summer offered, eyeing him over her glass as she took another sip of her wine. The candlelight was dancing in Noel's eyes, making them look like little pools of chocolate, and she couldn't help but make eyes at him. Just a little.

'I would have said *upset*, tactfully,' he laughed, leaning back in his chair and resting his left forearm on the tablecloth. His sleeve was rolled up, and she could see tanned skin underneath, made all the darker by the stark white of the cotton cloth. 'I get it now: Reg leaving, me coming. It was a lot.'

She went to agree with him but found herself unable to get the lie out. 'Actually, it wasn't just Reg. He's enjoying his free time now, and he feels better without the stress of the shop. It was more about the other thing.'

Noel's eyebrows raised. 'Ah, the other thing. Right.'

Summer took another swig, and not trusting herself, she put the glass down and pushed it away with her fingers. 'Yeah. I know, ridiculous isn't it, from a grown woman.'

Noel looked her in the eye, dead serious. 'Your rampant sexual attraction to the sexy new business tenant is never ridiculous.' He waggled his eyebrows, leaning forward and giving her a look that made her want to blush. 'It is most definitely,' he paused for effect, 'a thing.'

'Dear Lord, you really do love yourself don't you,' she countered, shaking her head but laughing at the same time. 'That was terrible, by the way.'

Noel winced. 'Not my best work; I think I set my own teeth on edge.' He rubbed at his lips with his fingers, as though to scrub something off. 'What thing do you mean?'

The moment was gone now, and Summer found herself not wanting to tell him this part of her. She had kept it hidden for long enough; a bit longer wouldn't hurt. She felt like telling him now would be akin to passing wind in a lift: ruining the mood, and the atmosphere. Not to mention the smouldering look he was throwing her way. Hurling the equivalent of a smelly fart at him wouldn't do much for the ambience, so she kept quiet.

'Ah, nothing. Another time, perhaps.' She looked away, signalling to him that the conversation was over. She felt his eyes rake over her, but when she eventually looked back, she saw that he was looking at her and the last thing she could denote from his face was pity or concern.

'Okay,' he said slowly, leaning forward and placing his hand on the tablecloth, a hair's wisp from hers. She looked at them, imagining how it would feel if he put his hand to hers. 'So, next question then, and this one will need an answer.' He flicked his gaze from her face to their hands and back again. He flicked out one finger, running slowly along her index finger from top to bottom, and back up and over the back of her hand. She wanted to swan dive over the side of the table and jump into his lap. *Holy sexy fingers, Batman.*

'Yeah? Try me,' she retorted, tracing the path he made on her skin with her own finger on his. He smiled, and his eyes darkened.

'Do you want...' he leaned forward, clasping her hand in his and pulling her gently towards him.

'Yes?' she said, her voice hoarse with the zing of lust zapping through her.

He leaned closer still, and she copied the action without even realising, drawn to him.

'Pudding?' He reached for the dessert menu, and the spell was broken.

Bugger.

* * *

They rounded the corner to her house, and Summer released the breath she didn't even realise she had been sucking back into her lungs. The sense of dread flowed through her from the minute they had headed towards home, Noel ever the gent offering to walk her back.

The lights in her house were on, the curtains closed, but in a normal, cosy home for the night way. Like someone was in there, living their life, not skirting around the edges of existence. Her mother had less of a carbon footprint than the ants they got in the kitchen every summer. One ant, even. The house looked different now though, and she had a good feeling. For the first time in a while, she was actually looking forward to going home. Not that much in a rush though, since the night was going so well outside the walls she grew up in, too.

'You okay?' Noel asked, softly. 'You've gone quiet.' She could feel his eyes on her. 'You look a little tense. Your shoulders went up over your head as soon as we turned the corner.'

She turned to look at him, trying and failing to be annoyed that he seemed to know her so well. The light from the lamppost was lighting up his black hair, giving him a halo effect. Things were better, and she couldn't help but think that he had something to do with it somehow.

'I'm good. Where did you come from?' She asked, a murmur of wonder in her voice.

'Leeds,' he quipped, his voice deep and smooth. 'But that's not what you meant. Is it?'

She shook her head, taking a step closer to him, before she could talk herself out of it or ruin the moment with a nasty barbed comment. He looked her up and down, his eyes raking over her body, a sly smile crossing his features.

'I'm here for you, Summer.' He reached out and ran his fingers down her left cheek. She turned into the warmth of him, and he cupped her chin, taking a stride forward and taking her face into his other hand. He looked down at her, his big, brown eyes searching her face, his floppy curls over one eye. She brushed it back off his face, and he dipped his head, brushing his lips against hers. She gasped at the contact, and he pulled back ever so slightly, looking at her in question. She smiled at him, and saw her own happiness mirrored in his face. He kissed her then. Slowly. Deeply. Tenderly. He moved his hands from her face, down the sides of her neck, taking her into his arms, wrapping her in his touch. He felt like a security blanket around her. Solid, strong, his hand rubbing her back and the other came up to nestle in her hair. She leaned into him, wanting as much of her body to be enveloped by his as possible. She felt alive, young. Sexy. The thought thrilled and surprised her, and she wanted more. She matched him kiss for kiss, her own hands wrapping around his waist tight, locking around him in a desperate plea to keep him there.

His tongue teased hers, and she teased him right back. They kissed for a million years, and then finally, agonisingly, they came up for air. He released her, but only enough to look at her. His eyes were unfocused, as black as a shark's up close. His hair was ruffled from her fingers running through it, his breathing ragged. She knew she looked exactly the same. Her lips felt swollen, on fire from his kiss, and she giggled with awkward happiness. Noel's face lit up into a huge smile, and he laughed along with her.

'Well,' he said finally, 'that was amazing.'

Summer nodded. 'I know.'

He kissed her again, short, sweet, building to frantic, and she reached for him too, grabbing his bottom and giving him a squeeze, making him laugh again. She could feel him smile against her lips.

'See me tomorrow?' he asked, between stolen little pecks. 'After work?'

Summer nodded her head, her heart hammering in her chest at the thought.

'Come on, you can do better than that,' he said, pulling her into his arms a little tighter. 'Tell me you want to see me, Summer. In fact, tell me you want to date me.'

She frowned up at him. 'Why?'

Noel looked down at her with such an intensity, she felt her legs just about collapse beneath her and she was grateful he was holding her up. 'Because, Summer Hastings, since the day we met, you have pushed me away, and I have wanted you all the more for it. I need to know that you are in this, that you feel this too. Us Pritchetts have weak hearts.'

She wanted to scream, *Yes, take me now!* but then she thought of the shop, and him leaving. What was the point?

He was looking at her, waiting for an answer, but the words felt trapped in her throat. Held captive by all the worries, and fears. 'Don't overthink this, Sum, just trust me. Do you want to be with me, or not?'

She felt him tremble around her and she knew then, he was just as nervous as her. Yet he was here, telling her what she had been waiting for all along. Someone to step up and declare himself for her. Someone to want her and be prepared to fight for it. Not just someone either. Him. The man who had swept into her life like a tornado, and blown the dust off her life, shaken things up. This was it, it was time to take a risk.

'Yes, I do.' She took his face into her hands, his slight stubble rough against her fingers, and lifted herself up onto her tip toes, kissing him with everything she had, telling him she was all in. He kissed her right back, and they held each other tight, both not quite believing the turn the night had taken. Neither wanting the moment to end.

He gave her a final, blistering kiss and pulled away reluctantly. 'Good night, Summer,' he said softly. 'Sweet dreams.'

She walked to her front gate backwards, both wanting to prolong the moment till the last. She finally got to the door and turned the key in the lock, looking back at him before she went inside.

'Night, sexy' he said, a silly grin on his face. She grinned back, waiting till the door was closed between them before she started squealing like a teenager. Running to the front room window, she peeked through the thick curtains. Noel was dancing in the street, high kicking his heels as he walked away.

'Idiot,' she said, laughing at him. He was so damn cute. She watched him till he was out of sight, and then she reluctantly went upstairs to bed. Her mother's door was closed, and there was silence within, meaning she had no doubt turned in for the night. She was secretly glad; it meant no nagging, no guilt eyes her way, no awkward questions.

After her shower, she lay in bed, thinking of her date, the kissing, his tender words to her. She was smitten, hook, line and sinker. If she could bottle the feelings she had swirling around in her, she could live on them forever and never feel empty again.

Her phone buzzed on the nightstand, and she lunged for it. Noel had left a text message for her.

Best night ever. Wear something a bit dark and casual for tomorrow. Rock out time. Noel xxx

Under his text, there was a YouTube link. She clicked on it, turning the volume down quickly as a band started to play. The footage was roughly shot, from a spectator in the crowd. The band were all dressed in black, guyliner in full force as they played and crooned about a girl who never noticed them. On the drum, the band name said *The Dirty Lemons* and a lemon with a bandana sporting a V sign and sticking its tongue out completed the look.

What on earth was she in for? She hadn't been to a rock concert in, well, ever. She was about to text him with an excuse, a palm tree emergency perhaps, but then she thought back to his words. *Do you want to be with me?* She wanted to, badly, and everything that went with it. What would she have been doing instead? Pretending not to be upset with her mother? Doing the laundry? No, she would be with the man she liked, and fancied rotten, seeing a band. This had

come from nowhere, and it wouldn't, couldn't last, but so what? For
once, she wanted something enough to take the leap, accept the risk
and reach for it.

I'm in, she typed back with a kiss emoji. It pinged back within
seconds.

Looking forward to kissing your face off, N xxx

She held the phone to her chest, her head half buried in the
pillow while she suppressed another squeal. *God, yes*, she thought
to herself. *I'm looking forward to that too*. She sent a row of kisses in
reply, and finally drifted off to sleep.

* * *

The train pulled into Leeds train station and Summer could see the
crowd of pasty-looking, suited people peering through the windows
with disinterest, knowing that they would still have to stand on the
platform while the train was readied for the next journey. Noel
nudged her with his elbow, reaching out his hand to help her out of
her seat.

'Come on, we can go for a drink first before the concert. I know
a little place. Let's get off this train quick.' He jerked his head to
the people waiting outside. '*Shaun of the Dead* auditions are
starting.'

'Not a fan of the average worker bee, are you?' she asked as he
pulled her to her feet and guided her onto the platform. 'Not
everyone can be an elf, Noel. Not everyone sprinkles unicorn glitter
wherever they go.'

He snorted. 'I'm not that bad.' He smiled at a man who was half
reading the paper, half listening to their conversation, and was
rewarded with a sour look, making Noel blanch. 'I just have an aver-

sion to idiots.' He looked directly at the man as he spoke. 'Have a good evening, sir.'

He led her away from the platform and, taking the ticket from her hand, he waved them in front of the barrier screen, taking her hand in his and leading her past the busy, tired working commuters and the early evening drinking crowd.

'People have to work, Noel; there's nothing wrong with that. Life is routine, no matter how hard you tried to rebel against it.'

Noel squeezed her hand tight and pulled her into him as a drunk lad ambled past, almost taking her eye out with a skateboard he had wrapped in his backpack straps.

'Steady, geezer,' he admonished the man, steadying him and sending him in a new direction like a little wind-up toy. 'Safe journey home.'

They headed out of the train station and into the night, heading for the crossings with the other people all heading out, heading home, heading somewhere. It was pitch black already, the night chilly, and Summer was glad she had gone for the black jeans and puffy jacket now, with a thin knit cream sparkly jumper to break up the dark look. She'd bought some little pixie boots for the occasion, and she was now thanking her lucky stars that she'd not gone for heels. They were just heading into a bar called Banyans when a woman came tottering out, shouting something about Greek Street cocktails and making it look as though she was straddling an imaginary camel, with over cautious steps on the uncovered cobbled area of the street.

The pair headed to the bar, which was packed with office drinkers and early revellers. Noel wrapped his arm around her, pulling them together tighter and leading them both to the bar.

'What would you like?' he asked, close to her ear. 'Wine, lager?'

'Wine, please.'

She looked around the bar area. It was a nice place, all

reclaimed wood surfaces and brass lighting fixtures, giving it a rustic, cowboy-type look. It suited Noel, funnily enough.

Noel ordered their drinks and they headed to a booth in the corner that a rather subdued pair of men in suits had just vacated. Summer sat and snuggled deeper into the circular seating, shuffling along the leather seat as lady like as she could. Noel matched her shuffle for shuffle, their legs constantly touching each other. He put her wine down on the table and raised his pint of beer.

'To us, and to your first mosh pit,' he made a Gene Simmonds Kiss face and she snorted with laughter. 'Ooo, piggy!' This made her laugh even more.

'Give up,' she said, slapping him on the arm. Noel hugged his pint protectively.

'Hey, watch me beer!' He took a huge drink, half finishing it. 'Ah, I missed that. A good old Yorkshire pint. They don't taste the same anywhere else but in Leeds.'

Summer rolled her eyes. 'Of course not.'

He clinked his glass against hers. 'Here's to a fun night!'

The Dirty Lemons, it turned out, weren't half bad. After their drink turned into three, Noel had walked her through the back streets and down into a nothing-looking doorway, and there they were. As soon as the double metal doors were opened, she could hear the music, feel the bouncing energy of the crowd. It was a showcase night, bands from all over trying to make their way in the world, get spotted by that agent, get that deal. The Dirty Lemons were headlining and were tipped to be the next best thing. According to the man at the bar, anyway. Noel bought them both a drink, and got chatting away to the barman, Summer tucked into him as usual.

'So, the mighty Noel has finally succumbed, eh?' The barman, a thick-set man with a huge hipster beard laughed, dodging the pretend punch that Noel threw his way. 'What's next? Franchises of your shop? A puppy?'

'Shurrup,' Noel jabbed him in the arm, making a *ha ha* face in triumph. 'As I was saying, Chaz, this is Summer. Chaz here owns the place, so he's got no room to talk in sticking it to the man.'

'Hey,' Chaz said, holding out his hand and shaking Summer's, 'this is mine, lock, stock and barrel, dude. Jen and the kids do their own thing; we've got it good. Nothing wrong with making a life, bro.'

Summer would have liked to have heard what his answer was, but a commotion on stage signalled the next act, and the moment passed. They found another quiet little corner, and sat drinking steadily, laughing and chatting about nothing. Favourite books, worst fear, Noel mocking her lack of musical knowledge.

'I like pop, what can I say? I don't really buy music; I just listen on the radio. I have tastes, I… I suppose at mine, music isn't really part of life. It used to be, Mum loved it, but something is a little disconnected now.' She grinned at him, not wanting to bring the mood down again. 'Besides, some of the newer stuff really is just white noise.'

'Speaking of which,' Noel looked behind her, his face sparking with recognition. 'They're on! Grab your drink!'

Summer did as she was asked, barely managing to keep the liquid in the glass as he pulled her to the front. The crowd was already bouncing, but one nod to one of the security staff, and a little spot was opened up near the front. Summer looked to Noel in surprise.

'I used to work here a while back, help Chaz out. I followed these guys for a while, the whole showcase night thing was something I brought in, so they let me get a decent view.' He shrugged, reaching for her free hand. 'You okay here?'

She curled her fingers around him. Everything was so easy with him, so selfless. He made her feel like a prize jerk just by being near her sometimes. Which wasn't his intention, of course. He just made everything seem effortless. Possible. Achievable. The man was a walking, talking, Instagram meme.

He looked Insta-delicious tonight too. He was wearing dark-blue skinny jeans, trainers, and a fitted T-shirt and jacket. His hair was on point as always, springing around his head, and the few beers he'd had had made his eyes look even more sparkly than normal, and his hands less nervous around her. He was standing off to one side slightly, behind her now, his arms wrapped around hers as they moved to the music together. Summer had never felt so alive, so... so normal. For once, instead of reading about the girl in the bar, or watching her story on the screen, she was here. She was her. The girl in the bar, being hugged by a boy who likes her, while they drink, laugh, and listen to a band. It was scary and exhilarating, and Summer was just as scared to embrace it as she was to lose it. More, even. If she got to like this new life, this new version of her world, what would be left when it was over?

Noel ran his tongue softly along the edge of her ear, making her shiver. 'I'm so glad you're here,' he whispered to her huskily, barely heard over the music and the roar of the crowd.

'So am I,' she said earnestly. 'I'm glad to be here too.'

9

Jean hadn't seen Jim since the night they had shared dinner together, and she hadn't seen him coming to or from the house recently. His car had left the next morning and hadn't returned. A building firm had turned up later that day, and they had been hammering and sawing away ever since. When she woke up this morning however, it was oddly quiet. Benny the cat was overjoyed, judging from the fact that he had woken her this morning with his customary sitting on her chest and purring session. When the builders were here, he had sulked, choosing instead to lie on the back of the couch, turning his body away from her when she spoke to him, and showing her his bum hole at every opportunity. The cat's equivalent of flipping someone the bird. This morning however, all seemed forgiven and she had woken up to his fishy breath, his nose millimetres from hers and his whiskers tickling her cheeks.

'Oh, happy today are we Benny?'

He stuck his tongue out and give her one quick sandpapery lick on the end of her nose. She wrinkled it at him, and his eyes bulged with the tracking of the movement. She listened a little and was rewarded by nothing but the low hum of the central heating clicking on. October, regular as clockwork. She always wanted to turn the thermostat down and hang on to the summer, but when she reached her hands out from under the duvet to pet Benny, it did seem rather chilly.

'I wonder where our new neighbour went,' she said to her cat, to herself. It had hurt a little that they had been spending time together, and now he had seemingly scarpered. Was something wrong? Maybe something had gone wrong with the children? Was he going to sell the house? Maybe he had already left, and the builders were just getting the house saleable. Or maybe he had been kidnapped by Martians whilst out buying milk in his car. Or he was a spy, and the whole doting granddad thing was a cover. Jean had considered everything from espionage to Elsie from her cake class trying to throw her off her baking game by throwing a hot silver fox into her path as a distraction.

Benny jumped down off the bed, heading out of the door to the stairs, giving her his best pitiful look and *feed-me-now* miaow. The cat was a creature of habit, that was for sure. Ten minutes past breakfast time and you would think he was being tortured. Garfield was less high maintenance, but she did love him dearly. He squawked again, and she sighed theatrically, tossing back the eiderdown.

'Yes, yes, I'm coming. I have class today anyway. Breakfast time.'

Summer woke up to the smell of bacon and sat bolt upright in bed. 'Oh Christ, it's happening. Oh God, oh God!' She jumped out of bed, slamming to the floor face first when her leg, caught in the mess of covers, yanked her short in her stride. She crushed her boobs on the carpet as she hit the shag pile.

'Ow, ow, ow, ow! Broken boobs! Broken boobs!' She rolled onto her back, cradling her battered bosom in her arms. The door flew open and bonked her on the top of her head.

'Ow!'

'Summer? What are you doing?' Her mother looked down at her and ran to her side. 'Oh God, are you okay? Shall I ring an ambulance? Oh no, I can't do that, I—' Her mother went deathly pale, and Summer groaned, knowing that she was picturing having to make the 999 call, having to let paramedics, strangers, into their home to scoop her up off the floor.

'Calm down, I fell out of bed. Aside from a slightly dislocated areola, I'll live.'

Her mother grimaced. 'Oh God, a dislocated...' Realisation set in, and she giggled. 'Summer! You silly girl. What were you doing?' Summer remembered her urgency and sprang to her feet, running to the long mirror on her wall and looking at her eyes up close. 'I could smell bacon, that's a sign of a tumour. I read it online.' She swirled around to face her mother, who was now sitting on her bed.

'Do my eyes look weird to you?'

'I'm making bacon for breakfast, that's why you can smell it. And it's burnt toast you are supposed to smell, not bacon. I can make toast too when you come down. I thought we could sit and have breakfast together before you went to work.'

Summer pulled her outfit out of the wardrobe, where she had laid it all on a hanger the day before. 'You made breakfast, that's great! I thought we didn't have any bacon?'

'The butcher dropped it off this morning. I ordered a fruit and veg box too, from the grocers. They're coming later.'

Summer felt like reacting, but she knew she shouldn't, so she tried to focus on her clothes instead, hoping that her voice wouldn't come out all high pitched and give her away. 'Oh cool, I'll just get a quick shower, and I'll be right down. Thanks, Mum.'

Angie left the room, and a minute later, she could hear the downstairs television click on, the morning news being read out. It sounded and smelled so normal, so domestic. Summer took a deep sniff and stood for a moment on the landing, drinking the atmosphere in. Her mother was getting better; the tough love was working. She couldn't believe it.

'Mum,' she called down the stairs, wanting to get it over quickly. 'I'm going out again tonight, is that okay?'

There was a pause, and then her mother's voice came back. 'That's fine dear, I'll be all right here, I have plenty to do.'

Summer didn't ask what that was. As long as it wasn't sleeping, or sitting and staring into space, that was fine with her. Those days were long gone, and she had no intention of letting them come back. The house was waking up, and it was glorious.

She didn't see her mother try to hold her nerve as she climbed down the stairs. Angie made sure she was smiling and happy when her daughter came down to breakfast. Just like she wanted.

* * *

Noel burst into laughter when Avril walked into the shop precisely on time. He had to quickly swallow his coffee before he shot it out of his nostrils.

'What on earth are you wearing?' he asked, wiping his mouth on a piece of festive napkin. Avril looked down at herself, a confused look on her face.

'Er... my uniform! First day, remember?!' She grinned, and the movement pushed her glasses further up her nose. He found the action familiar somehow, a sense of déjà vu passing over him. She put her backpack on the hook by the door, taking off her pink duffel coat and hanging it next to it. The little gold bell on her hat tinkled with the movement.

'Well that's gonna get annoying real fast,' he murmured. Avril shot him a mucky look and he pulled an apologetic face. 'Sorry. You know that we don't actually have a uniform though, right?' He pointed at his own clothing: a pair of ripped, blue, denim jeans and a T-shirt sporting a picture of Homer in a Santa outfit, saying *D'oh d'oh d'oh.*

'Er, yeah, I got that,' she retorted, giving him a look that made him feel like a dad dancing. Badly. Even for a dad dancing. 'This is way better, trust me. I am going to spread the festive cheer today!'

She did a twirl, and Noel realised that the bell on the tip of her hat wasn't the worst part of the costume. She was dressed from head to foot in red and green, a full-on elf costume, complete with curled shoes (with bells on) and candy-striped socks, with tiny bells all around the top hemmed edges. She looked like a Tim Burton Christmas nightmare. Noel loved Christmas, so he knew that this was bad if *he* was balking at the sight. He thought of Summer and his stomach clenched. Whether it was the thought of her clapping eyes on Avril the elf or the thought of getting to kiss her remained to be seen.

'You look... er... nice.' A voice from the doorway flipped his stomach again, and he had his answer. Summer was standing there, looking gorgeous in a yellow sunflower-patterned summer dress and yellow flats. She looked gorgeous. Apart from the slightly horrified look on her face as she took in Avril, the ridiculously happy munchkin. The two stood side by side, facing each other; they looked as different as night and day. Summer and Christmas. Their expressions, however, were comically similar.

'Hi!' he said, far too enthusiastically. 'Hi,' he tried again, going to lean on the flip-up counter but falling to the floor as he missed it entirely. Avril laughed her head off as he scrabbled to his feet.

'What a smooth move,' she guffawed. 'Good one.' She turned to Summer rather shyly, jingling her bells as she moved.

'Summer, you look very er... summery! Do you like my outfit? Noel doesn't.'

Noel cringed at her forthright imagery. 'I never said that, exactly. You do look nice, Summer. You both do, in your own ways.'

Avril grunted. 'Whatevs, this little number is going to have the customers flocking to buy your baubles, trust me.' She smiled at Summer, and tinkled off into the back, presumably to er... tinkle.

'You have your hands full there,' Summer said kindly, walking further towards him. He moved closer to her, suddenly nervous. Should he just run up and grab her, or maybe go for a handshake? A high five, perhaps? She thankfully answered his question for him, as she slipped her hand into his.

'So, I wanted to ask you something,' she said softly, biting her lip. He followed the movement with his eyes.

'Yes,' he said, leaning in to kiss her. She kissed him back, half laughing.

'I haven't asked you yet!'

He kissed her again, wrapping his arm around her. 'I don't care. What do you want, a kidney? Yours. My babies? Any time.' *Whoops*, he thought. *Dial it back, Mr Mop!*

She laughed again, thankfully. 'No, nothing like that. I actually wanted to know if you would help me do my garden. It's a bit of a project I need to get started, and I could use a hand.'

'Sunday?' He asked, and she nodded.

'We are both closed then. So, if you're free, I'll treat you to lunch after somewhere, to thank you.'

'You don't have to do that, but yes, that'll be nice.'

She smiled, but this one didn't quite meet her eyes. 'It's a bit tricky though, because my mother is... well, I live with my mother, and she is a little shy of visitors. I wouldn't be able to invite you in.' She blushed furiously, and his heart went out to her. It was obviously a lot for her to deal with, and he was so glad that she wanted his help.

'That's no problem. I can come with a big flask of tea, and I have outdoor plumbing anyway.' He waggled his eyebrows. 'It's good for the plants too.'

She burst into laughter and hugged him tight to her. 'Thank you,' she whispered into his ear. 'Thanks for understanding.'

He squeezed her back, till the sound of approaching bells broke them apart.

'I'll get off to work; these holidays in the sun don't sell themselves!' She gave him a swift peck on the lips and headed out the door. 'Bye Avril, have a happy elf day!'

Avril beamed. 'Same to you, Summer!'

Summer closed the door and they both watched her cross the front of the shop window to her own.

'She is so cool!' Avril trilled. 'Isn't she cool, Noel?'

Noel nodded dumbly. 'She sure is.'

'And pretty, and clever. I really like her.' She twirled around to face him. 'I knew I would. Are you her boyfriend now then?'

Noel went to flick the kettle on. 'Er, I don't know about that; we haven't exactly talked about it. Glad you like her, though. Did you know her before or something?' Her comment had struck him as odd.

'No,' she said, her eyes and hands now focusing on the box of Elves on the Shelves that had just arrived. 'But you can kinda tell you are going to like a person, or not, can't you? I think we'll be best buds soon.'

Noel looked at the sweet little whirlwind in front of him and wondered again just how these two females had been plonked into his life. 'Yes, I know what you mean. Right, quick cuppa, then we'll get you out there with some flyers, eh? I have a feeling these elves will be flying off our shelves soon, eh?' He laughed at his own joke, but Avril just looked down her nose at him, her glasses perched at the end like an octogenarian librarian.

'Wow, Noel. That was really lame. You should write your own cracker jokes.' She picked up one of the elves, clipping him to her costume like a mascot. 'I'll flog these outside. Let's see who can sell more.'

The kettle clicked off.

'Deal,' Noel said, filling his Mrs Claus tea pot with hot water. '£3.99 each.'

'Prepare to be beaten,' she said in a deep, menacing voice. Then in her sweeter voice, she simpered at him. 'Got any chocolate biscuits?'

* * *

Summer ended her call and finished off her booking for the customer, updating his client file before returning it to her cabinet of regulars.

She had been putting it off all morning, but this was it. She was going to see to her mother and plan the weekend. She just hoped that it wouldn't set her back. She had been doing so well. Summer could see both the glint of freedom and a life for herself, and a slice of guilt for feeling that way at all. She had to get her mother out of this rut, for her own good, but she knew that really her reasons were not entirely selfless. Especially now she had Noel in her life. She thought back to his baby comment and couldn't stop her stomach from flipping. She had suddenly had the image of the pair of them driving to her mother's house for dinner, a fat cheeked, little, Poldark-haired baby in tow, the pair of them blissfully singing along to the radio as they drove. She really had to lay off the rom coms. All this idea for happy ever after and babies and hot blokes and normal mothers, it just wasn't for people like her. The sooner she just clung to what she could and expected no more, the better. Bastard daydream.

She picked up the phone handset crossly, dialling her home number. Her mother answered on the first ring.

'Hello?'

'Hi Mum, it's me. Listen...' It clicked. She had answered on the first ring. The first time of calling. 'Has someone just rang?'

'No?' Her mother said, sounding confused. 'I was just cleaning and was near the phone. What's wrong?'

'What's wrong is you answered on the first ring. The very first ring.'

Silence down the line.

'I mean, I didn't ring twice and ring back.'

Silence again.

'Mum?'

'Yes, I heard you love. I... I didn't realise actually. Fancy that.'

They both sat in silence for a few moments on the line, digesting how momentous an occasion it was that Angie had just picked up the phone, naturally, because it rang, as millions of people did every day without thinking.

'So, love,' her mother eventually broke the silence, 'what did you want?'

Emboldened by this occurrence, she smiled down the line, her nerves all but gone. 'I have some help, this weekend, for the garden. I have asked someone to come round tomorrow, just to the garden, not the house, a friend. I just wanted to check you were okay with that, really.'

'A friend? Well, okay then. I'm sure that will be okay.'

'Really?' Summer stuttered. 'I'll take him out for lunch after, to say thanks, and he won't come into the house.'

'Oh, a male friend is it?' Angie asked in a funny way and Summer realised that her mother was teasing her.

'Er, yes, Noel, he works in the shop next door. Actually, he runs it.'

'Ahh, I see,' Angie replied. 'Good looking, is he?'

Summer felt her face bloom like a tomato. 'Well, er yes, he's okay.'

Her mother laughed. Actually laughed, and Summer felt the urge to cry, swallowing hard.

'I bet,' she said, giggling again. 'Okay Summer, I'll see you later. Oh, and listen, don't get any tea tonight. We'll order in.'

Summer smiled. 'Okay Mum, see you soon.' She put the phone down and promptly burst into a spate of hot, salty, happy tears. Her mother was coming back, and it felt like she had died and come back to life all over again. She thought again of the fat-cheeked, mop-haired baby, and suddenly, it didn't seem so *Mary Poppins* after all.

* * *

Meanwhile, next door, the Elf Wars were in full swing. Tinklebell, as Noel had dubbed Avril, had been outside all day, chatting to punters, doing little elf dances and selling the little cuddly elves faster than Noel could have a hope of keeping up with. She was really getting people into the shop with her sheer enthusiasm, and things were building up nicely with customers, all telling Noel how lovely his shop was, and how good his shop assistant was outside. At one point, Avril had even produced a skateboard from her back-pack and started doing tricks outside! Someone came with an empty paper coffee cup, and people were throwing change into it like she was a street performer. Noel worried about the police at one point, as a pair of local officers came up and seemed to take an interest, but then a couple of minutes later, by the time Noel had served his customer and dashed outside to explain that she wasn't some mad illegal busker, she saw one of the officers whizz past on the board, whilst the other was buying four elves for his grandkids. It was then that Noel not only threw in the towel of the competition, but he also rang his supplier to order two more boxes of the elves. They were nearly wiped out, and the day wasn't even over.

Noel used the quiet times in the shop to answer his emails, and he noticed one from a charity that he often worked for, asking him for his availability in the new year. They were looking to set up another village project, this time a school for children affected by the recent natural disasters that had ravaged the country. Normally, he would jump at the chance to be gone for three months, possibly longer, but now things seemed so different. Thinking of leaving Summer for that long left a bitter taste in his mouth, a clench in the pit of his stomach. Could he put down roots here? He couldn't live in a B&B forever, that was for sure, and he thought of his mother's plea for him to visit home, start his life. The thing was, he always thought he was living his life, but now he had something tangible, something new, and he didn't want to cut that short. The truth was, he wanted to spend all his time with Summer. And then there was Avril. What about her? He had been toying with the idea of offering more long-term work in the holidays, but how would that even work? Was she a project for him? For that matter, was Summer? She hadn't given him the easiest of starts in Bridlington, but he knew in his heart that her issues were the reasons for her aloofness. The putty that kept her walls up and strong. He could see through the cracks in those walls now though and he wanted to keep knocking them down. Eugh. He was doing his own head in now with his metaphors. He googled local gardening suppliers, writing the address and opening hours down for one in case they needed to get some supplies beforehand. He would need a pair of wellies too; his had been left on his last job for one of the workers to wear. He never came home with more than a backpack of basics, and he shipped over what he could afford. This time though, would he want to take more with him? Would Summer consider going with him? How would that even work?

He sighed, looking out of the window at Avril, who was now apparently performing some sort of musical number for a couple of clapping pensioners. He could see one of them reaching into her shopper for her purse and knew that they were another willing customer for her manic little elves. He had balked at the idea of the little guys himself at first, even being as festively forward as he was. It seemed a little eerie somehow, and also a lot like hard work. Surely parents were busy enough without having to dream up scenarios for the little buggers to get themselves involved in night after night? Still, his Facebook feed was always full of them every December, his friends who were married off and sprogged up posting them daily for posterity. He wondered if he would ever be that dad. Or any dad at all, really. Summer did hate Christmas...

He blushed, suddenly aware that he was yet again painting a Hallmark moment with the shop girl next door, and they hadn't even known each other five minutes. Still, it didn't feel too much like pie in the sky. Scary thought, but that was the truth. She seemed to be in there, buried in his head, whether he wanted to fight against it or not.

Avril bounded in, tinkling up to the counter with a fist full of notes. 'I sold loads today!' Her cheeks were pink from the fresh air and the exertions of the day, and he couldn't help but smile broadly at her.

'I know, I have had to order more in! You did great,' he took the notes from her proffered hand, pulling a twenty off the roll and handing it back to her. 'Bonus for you, well done.'

She shook her head, but Noel side eyed her and pushed his hand closer. 'Take it, you earned it.'

'I know,' she said, giggling. 'I made £34.72 in tips too, from that cup. I am so gonna buy myself a bike this year!'

'Not asking Santa for one then?'

Avril's face darkened a little, and Noel felt like kicking himself for prying.

'Nah, my parents are a bit skint at the moment. I thought getting a job, I could help them a bit and get myself a bike. We can ride them to school, and I don't fancy walking in winter.'

Noel said nothing, knowing a little about parents and children struggling and helping each other. Worldwide, it was very different, but often, First World Problems were still that. Problems. Food banks were full of hardworking people with families and mortgages, after all.

'I think that's lovely Avril, and if you have another day like today, there's another bonus in it for you.'

Avril stuck her chin up. 'You don't have to do that; we don't need charity.'

Noel held his hands up in surrender. 'Hey, not charity, you whupped my ass on the bet, and the mark up on the bulk buy elves is pretty good. The bonus is nothing on what I make.'

She looked at him for a minute, adjusting her hat as seriously as a black and white movie star would a trilby. 'Deal. You were rubbish. I don't know how you would have managed without me.' She tipped the banknote and the contents of the cup into a bum bag she produced from under her costume, zipping it up with a flourish. The noise of the coins only added to her body percussion skills. 'It's time for home, so I'm off. Same time next week?'

Noel nodded. 'Yep, and listen, I still really need to see your parents at some point, just to check they are okay with you working here.'

Avril, on her way out of the shop, froze momentarily and then kept walking, grabbing her stuff from the hooks. 'Yeah, I'll get Dad to text you! Bye!'

'Bye,' Noel echoed, watching her run off down the street. That girl reminded her of someone at times, but he just couldn't quite place it. Maybe it was himself.

* * *

Jean was decidedly tired, and a little bit ticked off when she arrived for work at the travel agents. Summer was staring at her computer screen, looking surprised when she saw her standing there.

'Jean, it's almost five. What's the matter?'

'I know I'm late, I am sorry. I'll get on; you can leave me to lock up if you need to get off.' She walked straight through the agency, heading to the back to dump her gear and grab her cleaning supplies. Summer followed behind her.

'No, I didn't mean it like that, I just thought you might be ill. You look tired.'

Jean looked at her, all dressed in yellow. 'Well, you look like a canary, and I haven't commented, have I? Can I just get on? I have the arcade to do after this.'

Summer raised her eyebrows, returning to her desk. Jean felt awful, but she just didn't want to talk about it. She felt a bit foolish and last night it had occurred to her just why her neighbour disappearing had affected her quite so much. She didn't want to verbalise it and Summer would no doubt have an opinion. She just wanted to be left alone, so she could do her jobs and get home, back behind locked doors, with Benny and her knitting. At least she knew where she stood there. When Benny didn't want to speak to her, he would bugger off upstairs, or give her evil looks from his arm chair. This was new territory with a human man, and Jean didn't bloody like it one bit.

'Tea?' Summer asked. 'I'm making one for myself.'

'No thanks,' Jean said, 'and please, wash your cup out if you're not finished by the time I leave. The mugs stain when left in the sink.'

Summer said nothing, and Jean didn't give her another glance. She just wanted to get home and jolly well ignore the world from her sofa. Men. She must have been mad. Cats were much less complicated. She scrubbed harder at a non-existent stain on the toilet wall. Relationships were messy, and who needed that anyway? She would just go back to normal, and none of this would matter. She was fine before, and would be again, goddamn it. She had her house, her courses, and her cat. She had friends, and when she wasn't shouting at them, she loved them. Sometimes, the devil you knew was better.

Sometime later, she heard Summer go and finished up her work. She had been lurking in the back, truth be told, and the whole place stunk to high heaven of her organic cleaning products, but she just couldn't face her just yet. Shrugging her jacket on, she picked up her bag and headed for the door. The keys were on Summer's desk, along with a piece of paper, folded in half.

She grimaced and taking the keys, opened the note.

Jean
I don't know what's wrong, but you know where I am. I have a lot to tell you!
Ring me, please?
Summer xx

She felt a fresh pang of guilt as she read Summer's kind words. She had been rude, and Summer was a bit misguided at times, but her heart was in the right place. She decided she would call her tomorrow once she had had a bit more time to lick her wounds.

* * *

Summer walked into her house feeling a little distracted. She hadn't been able to speak to Jean, leaving her a note instead, but she couldn't help but worry. What was wrong with her? She had been so happy, even happier than normal lately, but this was a side that she hadn't seen before. A snippy side. Angry, even. All this from a woman who lived life on her terms, and never failed to embrace a silver lining. Something had happened, she knew it.

She headed straight to her bedroom, looking at herself in the mirror. Did she look like a canary? Was that what people thought? She opened her wardrobe, having a look inside. It was true, looking at it in light of the comments, that her wardrobe was a bit on the bright side, but how was that a bad thing? The magazines were always full of bright clothes for summer, and she wasn't an undertaker, after all. She sold rest, sunshine and beaches for a living; she had to look the part. She tried to remember what she wore last winter but couldn't recall. Other than her pastel cardigans and long, yellow coat, she never much altered her wardrobe. Maybe Jean had a point. She thought of Noel, who wore dark jeans, sexy, black T-shirts. He wore the hideous bright (and sometimes flashing, dear God) yuletide stuff too, but his wardrobe was a mix, it had to be said. Maybe this rut her mother was in had affected her more than she thought. Maybe it was time to mix things up in her own life, too.

She was just heading for the bathroom to get showered but she stopped in her mother's doorway. Angie was sitting on the floor, cross legged in front of the wooden blanket box she kept there. It had been buried under a mountain of clothes in recent years, but now instead, there were black bags all over, stuffed with various garments.

'Having a clear out?' she asked, gently.

Her mother looked up at her, and she could see that she had been crying.

'Hi love, I just thought I would make a start. I was getting a little bit sick of looking at the same things.'

The thought of her wardrobe popped into her head, and she nodded. 'I get it. Do you want some help?' Summer stepped into the room and took a seat on the tatty carpet next to her mother. 'I could get the charity shop to come and collect the stuff.'

Angie nodded. 'They're coming on Friday. I rang them; I found a charity bag in the post box this morning.'

Summer put her arm around her mother, rubbing the top of her shoulder. 'I'm proud of you, Mum, I really am. I know I have been a bit hard on you lately, but I know how hard you're trying.'

'You were outright brutal,' she snipped back. 'I thought you were going to drag me outside and change the locks, make me live on the front lawn in a tent.'

'Would you do that? Cos, you know, I can buy a tent. We could dig a hole in the garden for a toilet too.'

Angie swatted at her. 'Hey! I know I've been a little bit... scruffy lately, but I do want to try. Just... bear with me. I'm still struggling with some things.'

She looked at the blanket box again, brushing off a layer of dust from the wood. 'I can't even open it. This thing has been buried under stuff for years, and I just can't open the lid.'

Summer squeezed her tighter. 'One day, eh? We knew that this wasn't going to be easy, but at least we're trying, right? We have the garden to sort too.'

Angie shook her head. 'I have to get on with this, I really need to just... stop being... me.'

She knelt forward onto her knees and pulled the lid up, hard. Dust motes hit the air, and they both coughed. When the air settled, they looked into the box. Photo upon photo were stacked into boxes, and Angie reached for one, sitting back on her bottom on the carpet.

'I remember this one. We were teaching you how to ride the bike on the street out front.' She smiled through watery tears. 'You were terrified, but your dad...' Her smile dimmed, and she swallowed hard. 'He was so calm, so sure that you would just learn. And you did it. You rode your bike all summer long. You had such a tan from the sun. He was really proud.'

Summer took the photo from her, looking at the smiling faces, captured forever. 'Do you think things would have been good, better if we hadn't lost him?' She asked her mother, thinking of how things would be, how much brighter life might have been, like it was before.

Angie shook her head, shutting the blanket box and standing up. 'I don't know honey, but I know that you were right. This thing we've been doing, it's not a life. We need to stand on our own two feet for once.'

Summer stood, tucking the photo into her back pocket and her mother brushed a strand of hair back from her face.

'Well, you already do that. You did that too much, truth be told. It's time for your old mum to step up now.'

Summer grinned. 'Well, you're not that old, not yet.'

Angie's lip twitched. 'Still bloody cheeky I see. Shall we go make some dinner?'

Summer nodded. 'Sounds good.'

10

Sunday, and Summer was up before the birds had a chance to clear their throats, scrubbing the front steps of the house. They hadn't been cleaned for a while, and the debris of winters past was still evident, making the front of the house look uninviting, like an unused, scary house that was always portrayed at Halloween as being the worst end of town. Usually inhabited by a strange wizened old woman, who lurked indoors and scared the neighbourhood kids. Well, the element of truth in the tale was starting to slough off, just like the ingrained dirt on the stone steps of their porch.

She thought back to the early days, after it had happened, that Christmas. She had come down the stairs, woken by the cold air chilling her arms as they lay on top of the covers, her Christmas nightie short sleeved and leaving her arms bare. The front door was wide open, a smashed bauble on the welcome mat. Her mother was laid on her back at the bottom of the garden, looking straight up at the sky. Her blood had chilled, and she had called out her mother's name. Angie just raised her head, flopping back down onto the snow she had been using as a pillow.

'Go back to bed, Summer. It's okay.' Summer saw it then, poking out of the wheelie bin at the bottom of the drive. The Christmas tree, still dressed. Her mother had dragged it out of the house and binned it. Christmas was over.

She shook the image out of her head and scrubbed harder. The closer it got to Noel coming to the house, the more she worried about it. What would he think of their house, her mother not wanting to come out, or let him in? The state of the garden was bad enough. She couldn't believe she had even asked him to help. This new life thing was hard enough, and she felt like she had just pressed the fast forward button on everything, and now it was all going to implode, right in her face. She had kept her worlds segregated for a long time, and now she was pushing them together, hoping they would gel, stick somehow, form a new shape. A new shape with new things as part of it, Noel, and her new life. A holiday, to start with. She wanted things to change, to evolve. She just wasn't sure that she could pull it all together and keep it together.

She finished scrubbing and looked at the time. Noel would be here in an hour, and she was a little bit grubby and scruffy looking. Time to get showered and changed. They would be digging around all day but there were no rules against being a little dressed up for the occasion. Time for her new outfit.

Noel headed up the drive to Summer's house, taking in the house in the daylight for the first time. It was a nice street, with her house being right in the centre of the cul-de-sac. The closer he got, the more he could see the differences between the other houses and hers. It looked a little unloved: no flowers outside, no real signs of life. The paint was peeling just a little from the window frames, the front door a muted, washed-out colour. Some of the gutters had seen better days too, grass tufts sticking out of the plastic of one, a bird nesting in the corner of another. The house looked like it was trying to blend into the background, to disappear, and it seemed totally at odds with Summer, who was always so bright, so engaged. Once again, he wanted to know about her family, what secrets she kept beyond the walls, but more than that, he wanted to help her. To wrap her up in his arms and protect her. She probably would have something to say about that, but still, it didn't stop the feelings stirring up inside him. He wanted to help, and here he was.

He walked up to the house and stood on the porch, which gave off a smell of cleaning products, floral scented, and was neat and tidy. He knocked on the door gently, smoothing his unruly hair down. It sprang back into place as soon as his hands left it.

The door opened and Summer was standing there, looking at him with a nervous smile on her face. 'Hi,' she said, so softly he barely heard it.

'Hi. These are for you.' He passed her the bunch of flowers he had bought from the local florists on his way there. 'I know it's not a date, but still.'

She took them from him and wrapped her other hand around his arm, pulling him into a hug. 'I love them,' she whispered into his ear, making him shiver a little. She closed the door behind them both, putting her hand into his and leading him off the porch and down the side of the house.

'I thought we could have a walk to the coffee shop, if you like, before we start, once we've had a look and seen what's what.' She squeezed his hand tight, and when they rounded the corner, away from the windows, she pushed him against the wall and kissed him. Surprised, he gave a little yelp and they ended up knocking teeth rather than locking lips, Noel smacking his head on the brick wall behind them.

'Ouch!'

'Ow!'

Noel rubbed the back of his head, rubbing at his mouth with the other hand to see if she had drawn blood. Both hands came back thankfully clean.

'Oh God,' she said, grabbing his head in her hands and moving it quickly from side to side, checking for injuries with an anxious expression. 'I'm so sorry. I was just trying to be spontaneous!' Noel started to laugh hysterically, and she looked at him with concern. 'Oh God, are you concussed? You're concussed, aren't you! It's all my fault!' She started to rummage in her pocket, and Noel grabbed her hands.

'No,' he soothed, between chuckles. 'I'm fine, you just surprised me, that's all. Don't worry.' She kept rummaging in her pockets. 'What are you doing?'

'I'm getting my phone to ring an ambulance!' He reached for her hands again and held them by her sides. It was only then that he noticed she was wearing indigo blue jeans, green wellies and a navy-blue, knitted jumper. She looked cute as hell, but different than usual.

'Your outfit's nice, different.'

She looked embarrassed, her face turning a deeper shade of pink than the flush of the failed kiss. 'Thanks. I'm trying something new.'

He pulled her arms around him with his own, and she sagged into him. 'I like it, not that I didn't like what else you wear. Now, what about that kiss?'

She leaned in and pressed her lips to his. His whole body sprang to life, remembering how good this felt. He kissed her back, deepening the kiss, and they held each other tight.

'Now,' he said, pulling back slightly, still brushing his lips against hers ever so gently. 'That was worth the injuries.' She jabbed him in the stomach, and he winced, laughing. 'Hey, still hurt here! You need my help today, remember?' He made a muscle man movement, pulling a macho face. 'These guns need looking after.' She tickled him where his T-shirt rode up under his jacket, and he tittered like a schoolgirl.

'Oh yeah,' she retorted, raising a brow. 'All man right there.'

He grabbed her and turned them both till she was against the wall. Pushing his body close to her, he put his mouth close to hers, teasingly close, whispering. 'You have no idea, baby.'

The laughter on her face turned to lust, and she swallowed. *Man, she's beautiful.* He kissed her again, and eventually, when they finally pulled apart, they headed round the back of the house, arm in arm, her head resting on his shoulder.

The garden itself was much like the outside of the house, only more worse for wear, with the whole area looking overgrown and unloved. There was a set of patio doors leading into the house, and they lead out onto what was a patio area, now full of weeds and the first leaves that were starting to fall from the trees. Some of the fencing was down, pushed back up from the ground in places by the weeds and ivy crawling around the weather-worn wood.

Noel looked at the garden, and saw that once, it was loved, well kept. You could see the bones of the framework of the space, could see that once, someone had really cared about this little corner of England. It made him sad as he looked around him. He saw it often, decay and destruction, things very much loved left to die and return to the earth. Worldwide, it was still as sad, still felt such a waste. He could feel the tension in Summer's body permeating through her hand to him, and he stroked his thumb along the back of her hand.

'So, we can start by snipping this lot back, and then we can fix the fence.' He had noticed a garden bin at the bottom of the front garden, but he didn't think that this was going to cut it somehow. 'I think we should order a skip. I'll ring one tomorrow. Do you have any gardening tools?'

Summer came and stood next to him, pointing to where a small, dilapidated shed sat behind a large oak tree along the far corner of the garden. It looked as though the foliage around it was pretty much the only thing holding it together. It reminded him of his own mother's garden, though the differences in state were huge.

'There are some in there, but I'm not sure how decent they'll be.'

Noel nodded. 'Good enough, let's have a look, then we can go get coffee and make a plan. Do you have a budget for this?'

She looked at him sheepishly. 'I have bulbs and planters in the house, compost and stuff, but not much else. I need to do this on the cheap, with winter coming.'

'Cool,' he brought her hand to his mouth and dropped a kiss onto her skin. 'Cheap is my middle name, baby!' He pulled her with him through the undergrowth, to the shed door, and they got to work, weaving their way to the shed.

* * *

Angie watched from the upstairs window as Summer weaved her way through the garden, laughing and chatting away to the man beside her. She looked so happy, so... Summer. Angie felt a wave of nostalgia ripple over her as she thought of how much she used to laugh. She filled the whole house with her laughter, her sheer volume of just being awake. It kept hitting her, harder and harder as she thought of the things that her girl used to be, before her parents snuffed out her sparkle between them.

She had dressed well today in one of her old outfits that she loved to wear for the office. She always felt good wearing it, powerful even. It was her confidence suit, as she called it, a light-weight trouser suit with a lovely cream blouse. It still fit her, if a little on the large side now. She hadn't realised just how much weight she had lost. Wearing nightgowns all the time had obviously helped her with her own deception and denial. She glanced across into the cheval mirror, newly cleaned and free of clothes and sheets. She looked good, better than she had that morning. *Presentable*, as her mother would say.

'Well, Mother,' she said to the mirror, 'you wouldn't be too pleased with me these days. It's time to change that.' She headed down the stairs, towards the sounds of people chatting in the garden, and taking a deep breath, she slid open the patio doors.

'Hello, you two, would you like a drink?' She kept hold of the patio door to keep herself steady, and then risked a glance at the pair. Summer looked shocked, and Angie felt a little thrill at surprising her daughter. It was worth the wave of nausea she felt, if she ignored the voice in her head telling her to shut the door and run and hide. The man next to Summer was smiling at her, and she gave him one back. Or at least, tried to. She felt like her face was going to melt off, and the smell of the outdoors was still something that hit her in the face every time, hard, a slap of reality around her chops.

'Hello,' the man said, not moving from where he was stood. 'We were actually about to go to the coffee shop, could we bring you something back instead?'

'Yeah Mum,' Summer said, 'Noel and I, we were going to get some snacks too, sandwiches?' She nodded encouragingly at her, and Angie found herself nodding back.

'Perfect, thanks, that's fine with me.'

Noel grinned. 'Nice to meet you, Mrs Hastings.'

Angie flinched, but recovered well. 'Please, call me Angie.'

'Angie, no problem. Thanks for having me.'

The fact that he was stood in her rather shabby garden, about to do a full day of unpaid labour, and thanking her made Angie smile at him again, a real one this time that lit up her face. 'Oh no, Noel, thank you. I really appreciate you being here.'

She withdrew back into the dining area, closing the patio doors shut behind her, and headed to the kitchen as fast as her wobbly legs could carry her. She could hear them now talking, laughing, working together. She knew she should feel happy, but she just felt sick. How could she protect her daughter, if she insisted on going out into the world and doing things? It was easier when she was younger, and she was a lot more 'whole' back in those days. She didn't see the world as she did now. Summer still didn't see it, and now there was this 'friend', here in their lives and kicking up the dust and the ghosts and Angie wanted to grab her daughter and run into the house with her. She wanted to climb into their blanket fort in the master bedroom and just be there with Summer and nothing would change. Summer wanted her to do better, and she was trying. Trying with all her heart, but some things are just broken. Summer would never get that, so all was lost. It was just a matter of time, but Angie knew she needed to prepare. The day was coming soon when Summer would leave and Angie couldn't help hoping that she wouldn't even be here to see it.

She walked straight up the stairs, and headed for her bedroom, slamming the door after her.

* * *

'Wow,' Summer said, once her mother was safely inside. 'I can't quite believe that happened.'

'So that doesn't happen often?' Noel hadn't asked many questions, none at all really, and Summer found herself wanting to share things with him. To share part of herself.

'My mum never goes out. I can't remember the last time she left the house. She used to go out all the time, and work, and laugh. After Dad... she kept it together for a while, but people were always coming around, asking if they could help, bringing food and stuff.

She just kinda lost her confidence, her shine, and that was that. She started ringing in sick to work, then she just stopped altogether. Everything. This garden used to be amazing, her baby. It's all part of a plan, all this, to get her out again. I sort of threatened to leave and told her she had to change. She's trying to.'

Noel said nothing, just reached for her hand. 'Well, I thought she did great. Shall we head out?'

Summer fell into step and they headed back around the side of the house. They both hesitated a little at their make out spot. Noel waggled his eyebrows at her.

'Our little hot spot. After lunch, I shall be having you up against that wall again.' He blushed slightly as the words registered. 'Or... something less sleazy and more romantic.'

'I know, not your best work.'

'Hey, I tried!' He pulled her tight against his side. 'Maybe I can do better tomorrow night? Your choice what we do, but I was thinking we maybe have a night at mine?' He held his hands up. 'Nothing sinister, I promise. My landlady does a mean shepherd's pie. I thought we could maybe have some food, watch a movie?'

Summer thought of the idea of spending the evening away from home, and her heart beat a little faster. 'Sounds perfect.'

Noel dropped a kiss onto her lips and together, they walked towards the cafe as slowly as they could, along the sea front.

11

Noel's back was close to breaking, but he carried on. Summer was busy planting bulbs and taking little potted shrubs and placing them in the flower beds that they had spent the best part of the day raking over. Once the grass was cut, and the weeds taken care of, it had seemed like a slightly easier task than they had first thought. Summer was on one, knowing the best places to plant certain bulbs, and chatting away about how they would look lovely in the summer. A summer that he wouldn't be here for. He couldn't seem to shake off the feelings of sadness he had as they worked. In August, would she be sitting in this garden, enjoying their hard work, thinking with fondness of their time together? Would she still be in this place, lonely, looking after her mother, sitting and reading alone? Reading about other people and their lives, their loves, their travels? He couldn't picture it in his mind, and he knew that was because he didn't want it to happen. He couldn't imagine her being alone again. He looked across the garden at her as he dragged and carried the debris out of the area to pile up at the front of the house, ready for the men to come. Jean again had come to the rescue, saying that her neighbour had contacts in the rubbish removal game, so they were coming the day after to remove it all from the front garden. No mush, no fuss. Angie wouldn't be disturbed, and it saved them hiring a skip and dealing with the whole delivery/removal drama. This was better for everyone.

'Noel, you listening to me?' He heard Summer speak and realised that he hadn't been the best guest.

'Sorry, I was miles away. You okay?'

She beamed at him, standing up and rubbing her soil marked hands together. She had a little smudge of dirt on her nose, and she looked freaking adorable.

'I'm great, I can't believe we got so much done!' She slowly started to turn around in a little circle, raising her hands in the air, out at her sides like the Angel of the North. 'It's so nice to be out here now!'

The light was starting to fade, and the day had been so long, yet Noel still felt cheated. It wasn't enough. He could quite happily stay in this garden forever. He almost wished that he'd asked her to come to the B&B tonight instead of tomorrow but at least he had that to look forward to. He looked towards the house as Summer stood twirling and looking in awe at the garden, which was beginning to take shape well. Another few days in it and they'd have it looking beautiful again. The house needed work too, but he wasn't going to be the one to bring that up. Angie hadn't appeared again, and Summer had taken her lunch but come back out somewhat downcast, so he was guessing that his presence there wasn't welcomed to the same degree by both Hastings women.

'So,' he checked, 'still on for tomorrow night at mine?'

She stopped twirling and looked right at him. He could see the blush creep across her face. 'Yes, I'll be there,' she said softly. 'Do I need anything?'

Just that face. Those lips. The boobs too, obvs. I am a man.

'No,' he dismissed her with a shake of his head. 'Just your lovely self. Mrs Simpson will have everything else covered, and I'll get some wine. A couple of bottles should do it.' He winked at her, and was rewarded with one of her best smiles.

'Okay,' she agreed. 'Thanks for having me.'

He said nothing, because he didn't trust himself not to blurt out a daft joke or declare his love for her eternal.

'No worries,' was what he actually said. *Smooth Noel, smooth.*

* * *

'Noel love, I haven't heard from you in days! Are you okay?'

Noel was sitting behind the counter, talking to his mother on the laptop. A slow start to the week, Mondays. Always the same. People sloughing off their onesies and tracksuit bottoms to head back to work and school, squinting at the light. October was upon them and he missed his little buddy. Avril had gone back to school, but still wanted to work Saturdays, which was fine with him. He had been googling the latest films to see what they would buy to watch that evening. His movie knowledge was a little sparse, given his travelling. He normally packed a Kindle and a few paperbacks. Easier to watch on the go, more relaxing. It wasn't really Netflix and chill territory where he had been staying. The last movie he watched was some obscure French film he had happened to see with a nurse he was working with overseas. That had been a fun night, but somehow, he didn't think he should share that with Summer. With her trusting him now a bit more each day, the last thing he wanted her believing was that he was a bed hopper as well as a nomadic traveller. It wasn't true, anyway.

'I'm good Mum, sorry – busy weekend. The shop's going well though. I've even hired a Saturday girl.'

'The girl on the beach?' His mother came close to the screen, tea cup in hand as she sat on her floral couch, iPad propped up on the coffee table.

Noel rolled his eyes. She never missed a bloody trick. 'No Mum, a local school girl, Avril. The girl on the beach works next door, remember? At the travel agents?' She knew full well. She'd probably hired a PI to check her out.

The shop bell went, and Noel flushed as Summer walked in, takeaway coffees and a couple of paper bags in hand. She came over to him. Now or never.

'Mum, Summer is here actually, do you want to meet her?'

His mother's face exploded into a picture of excitement. She jumped forward and sloshed her tea down her front. 'Ow, bugger that's hot!'

Summer put her goodies on the counter and went to stand next to Noel. He noticed that she looked different again, a long, dark trench coat covering black slacks and brown knee boots. She looked very autumnal.

'You look nice,' he said, putting his arm around her. 'Mum, this is Summer, my... girlfriend.'

'Hello Summer! I am so very pleased to meet you!' She dabbed at her top with a wad of tissue. 'I am sorry, I spilt my tea. So, when are you two coming to see us? We have our annual bonfire coming up at the Woodman; why don't you both come and stay over for that?' She looked at the pair of them expectantly, and Noel looked across at Summer.

'You don't have to,' he said quietly, out of the side of his mouth.

'I heard that Noel Patrick Pritchett, and yes you bloody well do have to! Your family hasn't seen you for ages. I'm getting tired of hugging your photo.'

Summer smiled at him. 'Yes, Noel Patrick, you should go and see your mother.' She turned to the screen. 'We would love to come, Mrs Pritchett. Can I bring anything?'

Sheila clutched the tissue to her chest tight, grinning like a loon. Noel cringed. 'Nothing dear, just yourself, and my daft son. See you on the fifth then, yes?'

'Looking forward to it.'

Noel turned the screen a little, giving her his best *you're dead later* glare and his mother just looked at him triumphantly, a butter-wouldn't-melt expression on her face.

'Right Mum, I'd better go.' He gritted his teeth a little. 'I will talk to you later, though.' His mum took a sip of her tea, sitting back amongst her plumped cushions. She looked as though she was drinking the blood of her fallen adversaries whilst sitting on a throne of crushed bones and skulls. *Mothers*, he thought to himself, *can't live with them, can't push them off a seaside cliff*.

'Ooh, twice in one day,' she quipped. 'I shall look forward to it, my sweet. Bye, Summer!' She waved wildly at them both, and Noel cut the call.

'Hey! You didn't say goodbye!' Summer tapped him on the arm, moving round the counter and looking into one of the paper bags. 'Bacon, no sausage right? I wasn't sure if you liked sauce, so I got these.' She reached inside her coat pocket and pulled out little sachets of red and brown sauce, holding them up. 'I warn you though, your decision will impact on my opinion of you.' She waved the two choices in front of him, and he pretended to really consider the answer.

'Well, if I was having bacon and sausage, as you are,' she looked surprised and pulled out her sandwich, which was indeed bacon and sausage, 'Then my decision would have to be brown sauce.' She nodded approvingly, taking one of the packets and pouring it on her own breakfast. 'However, as my delightful lady knows, sausage and bacon sandwiches are the Devil, so the only choice for me would be the rather sexy bacon and tomato sauce combo.'

He poured it onto his sandwich and took a deliberately huge bite, growling. 'Mm!'

'You are such a cave man,' she giggled. 'I got you a pumpkin spiced latte too, if that's not too girly for you.'

He groaned loudly in pleasure, rolling his eyes and taking another huge bite of his sandwich. Some red sauce dripped out and landed on to his T-shirt. This one said *Habitat for Homes* on it and had a logo of a house with hands wrapped around it, in shades of blue.

'Gross!' She took a napkin out of her other pocket and rubbed it off gently, putting her other hand on his chest to steady herself. 'You need a bib.'

He swallowed the rest of his mouthful and leaned in to her, pressing his lips against her forehead.

'I hope your lips aren't covered in sauce,' she said softly, wrapping her arms around his chest. 'I don't want to scare my clients off.'

He ran his stubble along her cheek, making her shiver. 'I am sauce free, now kiss me.'

She lifted her head to his and smooched him. She tasted of spice, and coffee, and the scent of her perfume filled his senses.

'You always take care of everyone, don't you?'

She rolled her eyes at him, flicking the hair away from her face. 'I do not, I just don't want you to lower the tone any further around here. A tat shop just opened up near here, the house prices are plummeting. It's obscene, really. The local folk are already sharpening their pitchforks and garden hoes.'

'Really?' Noel looked around in mock horror, clutching her close to him. 'Well, don't worry, I'll protect you. No one will hurt you on my watch.' He thought back to how she was when they first met. How guarded, and alone. He didn't want anything or anyone to do that to her again.

'Cos I'm your girlfriend?' She asked, head to one side. Just hearing her say that was music to his ears, though he wasn't sure how to make it happen for real. How he could keep things like this.

'You caught that, huh?' He tried to gauge her reaction, whether she was freaked out, but she gave nothing away. She looked calm, her tone borderline teasing. The fact was that when his mother had been there on the screen, and Summer there suddenly at his side, it had just slipped out, but wasn't that what they were anyway? 'You okay with that?'

Summer took the lid off her coffee and licked a little at the foam. Noel suddenly wished he was a cream topped beverage. She didn't answer for so long, Noel started to worry that he had completely freaked her out. 'I'm okay with it. I'm looking forward to seeing your family, actually. I don't quite know how I will spin it at home, but I'll worry about that later. I have to get to work, but what shall I bring for tonight?' She was trying again, ever the accommodator. Ever trying to fit in with everyone, making herself smaller to fit.

Noel almost said pack an overnight bag but stopped himself just in time. He shook his head, trying to dislodge the image of the coffee foam from his mind. 'Nothing, just you. I'll pick you up at about six, okay? From yours?'

Summer nodded, flicking the head of a stuffed reindeer on her way past, coffee in hand. 'Watch out for flying pitchforks,' she blew him a kiss and was gone, leaving him standing there with a sappy expression on his face.

October, and they already had plans for November. He couldn't help but feel the excitement of planning things, even if his mother had railroaded him into it with her own special brand of smothering agenda. Maybe Christmas might be very different this year. He already knew that December wasn't the problem, though; it was what happened after that concerned him.

* * *

Summer walked into her shop and, putting down her coffee, headed to the back room. Sitting down on the floor, she took out her phone and called Jean. The phone rang out, and she decided not to leave a message. She put the phone down and scrolled through her numbers, looking for someone else to call. Someone else to tell her news to. She ran through name after name and realised that she didn't have a good friend among them. She knew lots of people, sure, but there wasn't one person in this whole address book that she could just call up and talk about her feelings with. She felt the pain of the loss of them, these friends she had once and let slip away, watched walk out her life without recognising what was happening. She had made her world so small, so tiny and inverted in on itself. The truth was, Jean and her mother were it. That was the sum total of her relationships now, and they were dysfunctional at best. She didn't even know how to rectify it. How do adults form friendships? Should she join a class, or the gym? Start talking to random people on the street? It wasn't the school playground, she couldn't just break the ice with a lollipop and a sticker set.

She slammed the phone down onto her desk and opened up her emails. She might as well get back to work. She thought of going to see Noel that night, and her mood improved somewhat. She resolutely pushed the thought of January out of her mind. She'd deal with him leaving when she had to. After all, she was used to people leaving. She could pick up the pieces one more time, as long as the memories were worth the pain.

Before either of them really had a chance to prepare, the time for closing was soon up and the date was upon them. Summer waved off the Burtons, who were journeying to Australia to see their daughter and her family, as they did every year. They left with their money exchanged and their hearts light. Summer could see it in their walk as they headed towards the beach, arm in arm. Mr Burton had linked arms with his wife through the bag, to protect the money.

'Safety first,' he'd said, grasping his wife's hand. 'We can't go over all mugged and without money to spoil the grandkids, eh?' Mrs Burton had rolled her eyes, clearly loving her husband's wit and charm, and he'd looked back just as adoringly at her. On any other day, Summer might have felt a little jealous, but today was not that day. Today, she was closing up her successful business, and her boyfriend would be coming from his successful business. They'd link arms along the beach, all the way to his place, where dinner would be waiting. Sounded normal. Mundane, even. Millions of people did this every day, living their lives. Today, Summer would once again be one of them. She turned off the lights to the shop, and stepped out of the shadows.

Noel was just locking his door, and he bounded over to her. He had a thick, reusable shopping bag in one muscular arm, and it clinked when he moved. The wine. He wasn't kidding about the two bottles then.

'Hey,' he said, enthusiastically running rings around her like a happy spaniel. 'Good day?'

They talked about the sales they'd gotten, and the customers they had had in the shop. It turned out the Burtons had shopped in Forever Festive too, stocking up on stocking fillers for the children, who seemed to be missing out on the festive tat that England's finest had to offer. Neither of them mentioned Angie, or the house, or the garden. Noel knew that the removal men had been and collected all the rubbish; he had been in the shop himself bringing Summer a coffee at the time when her mother had called to scream at her for men being in the garden. Summer had taken the verbal bashing, letting her mother rant on and on, and Noel had stood there, drinking his coffee and pretending that he didn't want to take the phone and slam it down on the table, cutting her off. He knew Angie couldn't help it, he got that, but why did Summer have to be the blasting board all the time? Any outsider could see that this situation needed to change. He just didn't feel like he could be the one to do it when he was already leaving anyway. How could he upheave her life and then just go? It felt like a cruel act in the making, and he wanted no part of it. He'd just have to make the most of their time together and ignore the voice in his head telling him to stay.

They were nearing the B&B now and the pair walked into the foyer, glad to be indoors and out of the slight chill that was nipping the air around them outside. The Indian summer would soon be a distant memory once autumn turned to winter.

'Hello, my loves!' Mrs Simpson flew into the reception area, spraying Febreze on the curtains on the way past and shuffling them inside. 'Take off your jackets, make yourselves comfy! It's been a bit nippy tonight, I've even shut my upstairs windows!' She put the bottle into an umbrella stand near the door and came and stood in front of Summer.

'My, Noel, you didn't tell me she was this pretty! Although of course, I knew of you, from your shop, but me, well! I don't tend to go on holiday; I'm too busy looking after everyone else!'

Summer laughed, an easy, relaxed motion as she took off her jacket and allowed Mrs Simpson to take it from her. 'I know the feeling, Mrs Simpson. Thanks for having me!'

Mrs Simpson wafted the air in front of her, like a quick karate chop. 'Oh, don't be silly; I'm always glad to meet the nearest and dearest of my guests. Noel here is not a bit of bother: house trained, polite. Always happy, aren't you Noel?' She reached up and patted him on the head, and Summer pressed her lips together firmly to stop herself from laughing. 'Dinner won't be long. You guys go through to the dining room; the table's all set!' She scurried off with their coats and Noel's wine bag, and they were left feeling rather shell shocked in the hallway.

'I swear,' Summer smirked, 'if she brings you a meaty treat, or scratches your belly, I'm gone.'

Noel pulled a face and Summer exploded into fits of giggles. 'All right, all right,' he groaned. 'She took my wine too! Shall we go through?'

Summer nodded, still laughing, and followed him into the dining area, a charming space clearly decorated by Mrs Simpson. She thought of her mother, sitting alone at home again, and pushed the feelings of guilt and worry away. She had her phone; if her mother wanted her, she would call. Noel ushered her towards one of the tables that had been laid out with candles and a bowl of floating roses in the centre. The whole room screamed romantic evening, and Noel was both a little embarrassed and grateful to Mrs Simpson for making the night so cheesy and gooey. Just how he felt at the moment, not that he would ever tell Summer that. She went to pull her chair out but Noel sidestepped her and got there first, settling her in before taking his seat himself.

Mrs Simpson came bustling in with one of the bottles of wine in an ice bucket and two glasses, and she left them on the table, backing out of the room and half curtseying as she swept back into the kitchen. Noel poured them both a glass, and they sit there in the empty room, feeling a bit like goldfish in a doctor's waiting room tank.

'So, I bet you've stayed in some amazing places,' she stated, looking around at her current surroundings and observing him with a little teasing smile on her face.

'Not as weird and wonderful as some I can think of,' he turned his head, tilting it towards the picture above the roaring fireplace. It was a donkey wearing a bright-pink flat cap and winking into the camera. She followed his eyes and hers widen in shock.

'Oh God, I think my dad had that photo up at ours a while ago; they were in fashion a while back!'

Noel sniggered. 'Well, I've seen worse in houses. I lived for a whole week in a hut made of animal dung and sticks, so a donkey print would have broken up the decor.'

Summer's eyes sparkled. 'So cool though, dung aside. I wish I could have been there; I would have loved to see something like that.'

'You'd have loved it, it's a whole other way of life, but so rewarding. They don't care about the things we bother with here: how many Twitter followers they have...'

'Paying the gas bill?' she offered. 'I bet it's a different world altogether.'

'It is; their problems are far different to ours. Each corner of the Earth has its own stories, and I've been lucky to see a lot of them. Still, one day, eh? I'm sure I can drag you off at some point.'

Summer took a gulp of her wine and said nothing. Her eyes had dulled now, her stance closed off once more. She looked like the first day they'd met, over the Christmas tree. She was coiled up again, trapped in that house not fulfilling her dreams or able to help her mother. He'd said too much.

'So,' he said, brighter, faster, better. 'You ready for some dinner? Mrs Simpson has been cooking all day.'

Summer spoke back, ate well, talked to Mrs Simpson and the other guests who wandered in and out in search of food, a pint of beer, a read of their book by the fire. She was there, with him, in body at least, but Noel knew that her mind was elsewhere. He had popped their balloon, and the air was escaping, deflating their earlier good mood. The bubble couldn't last forever, and they already had a slow leak. In three months, the air was going to run out, and Noel already felt breathless at the thought.

12

NOVEMBER

Summer heard a beeping outside the house and ran to her bedroom window. Noel was leaning against a hire car, a jeep-type vehicle. She could see some bags on the back seat, and her stomach flipped over. She was really doing it; she was really spending the weekend at someone else's house, away from her mother, and Bridlington, and work. She felt as though she was going on a huge expedition, like Scott or Christopher Columbus, minus the dangerous terrain and high chance of death. It was only Leeds, but still. It was a different postcode. That was a start to her travel plans; she would take that. She waved to him out of the window and he blew her a kiss back. Damn, he was sexy. She wanted to vault out of the window and run to him, but she managed to hold herself back, pulling her big plastic case down the stairs behind her. She had treated herself to a new one, along with a few other bits. She had had a good week at work, so she felt like her splurge was justified. The truth was, a few people had come in after being next door, saying they fancied planning a Christmas break, or booking a short trip for a present. She hadn't told Noel, of course. Not a chance would she admit that his shop had boosted business instead of tanking it.

Bump, bump, bump. The case bobbed along, down the stairs behind her, and she just reached the door when her mother stood in front of it. The only hurdle to her weekend.

Things hadn't been good. They were bad even by previous standards, but Summer was determined to squash down the guilt and the worry and just go. Even jailors got the odd day off, right? Angie hadn't been right since Summer had plucked up the courage to tell her about today. She hadn't wanted to spring it on her, but the closer the weekend got, the snippier and more agitated her mother had been. Last night had been the worst. Her mother had cried most of the night, locking her bedroom door and leaving Summer to talk futilely to the mute painted wood.

'Summer, do you really have to go?'

Looking at her mother, her clothing crumpled from being slept in, Summer's heart broke. Angie looked so tired and beaten down by life. How had she come to this? How had *they* come to this?

'It's just for the weekend,' she started, her voice soft, gentle. She put her case down at the foot of the stairs and went to take her mother's hand. Angie pulled it away, folding her arms and backing up to the door, blocking it further. 'Mum, please.'

'You're not leaving, I won't have it!' Angie was panicked, jerking movements rolling through her body. She started scratching her neck with her fingernails, and when her hand came away, Summer could see the red marks she had left from the pressure. 'Go back upstairs, he'll leave.'

'Mum, please!' Summer reached for the latch, but her mother covered it with her arm.

'No, please, don't go! Go another time, maybe I can come then, when I'm better.'

Summer shook her head. They'd been here before. School plays, the first day of college. The day they opened the shop. Every time they had this, but nothing quite like. She didn't recognise her own mother. 'Mother, you won't get better till you try to help yourself more and get some professional help. I need to get a life of my own. I can't keep living like this. You need to do this; we both do.'

Her mother shuddered at her words, and held her breath in, shaking her head. 'I don't need someone listening to my pathetic life, Summer. I won't do that; you know I won't. I can't actually believe that you're going to walk out on me for the whole weekend, without a care for your poor mother.'

Summer gripped her case handle tighter. Through the grubby net of the window next to the door, she could see Noel there, looking at the house, leaning against the car, waiting. He hadn't even made a move to the house. He was just there for her, as always. It was looking at him that made up her mind for her. She had to do this and hang the consequences. She felt suffocated, and he was clean, fresh air. She took a deep breath and tried again to reach for her mother. Her hand was slapped away, a hard, sharp tap. She tried again but lowered her hand when her mother's eyes flashed.

'I'm not doing this without a care, Mother, and you know it. I know you have had it tough, God knows I know it's true, but you need to get on with your own damn life! Seriously, I can't believe that we're still here, after the garden? Can you not see what we've been trying to do here? Can you not see any of this?'

Angie looked at her, baffled. 'No, what?'

'Mum, I want you to stop living this nothing existence, so I can leave!' She pulled the handle of her case closer behind her, grabbing her jacket from the hook. 'I want to leave, to have a life!' She went to open the door, and her mother grabbed her arms, her fingers digging into her daughter's flesh.

'Leave? To go where?'

'*Anywhere!*' she screamed. 'Get off me!'

Angie held her fast, her lips pulled back over her teeth as she gritted her jaw. 'This is still my house, my rules. I forbid you to go!'

Summer, crying now, grabbed her mother by the hip, and pushed her hard to the right with her hand, quickly reaching for the door latch and wrenching open the door. 'Noel!' she shouted, pushing her case out of the house. 'Can you get this?'

Noel was there in an instant, taking her case in one hand and grabbing her hand in the other. 'You okay?'

She didn't answer, wiping at her eyes. 'Please, take it to the car, Noel.' She turned back to her mother, who was now standing in the doorway. She wanted to reason with her. Leaving like this wasn't the plan. She couldn't leave while they were both so upset, so mad at each other. It was then she heard the slap. Heard rather than felt, and she spun her head from side to side, looking for what caused the loud crack. Noel flinched at the side of her, and she looked at him for answers.

'Don't ever do that again,' she heard him growl in her mother's direction. 'Summer, you got everything?' His voice was softer when addressing her. It washed over her, oddly soothing in its timbre.

Summer put a hand to her now smarting face and looked at her mother in disbelief.

'You hit me. Why would you hit me?'

Her mother stood in the doorway, arms folded, face like thunder. 'You know why, my girl. Now get back inside this house, right now.'

Summer went to take a step forward, out of habit, on auto pilot and then she felt Noel's fingers wrap around hers. His touch was warm, hot even. 'Let's go, okay? Mum's expecting us.'

She looked back at Noel, who smiled at her, his eyes blazing with something she hadn't seen before. His jaw flexed, and he headed down the path to the car, her case and coat in his hand. She felt like she was being ripped in half yet again, and she didn't welcome the sensation. An image of her father flashed up into her head.

'You go, and you can stay gone. Don't expect to come back under my roof.' Her mother was sneering at her, her face sweaty. She was shaking, her hand vibrating on the door frame. She didn't mean it, not really. Summer could hear Jean's voice in her head, telling her friend her mother was still there, under the bravado. Looking at her now, Summer didn't care.

'That's fine. I mean, it's not like I paid for anything, is it? You'll probably be a lot better off without me. No problem.' The sting of her cheek intensified as a single tear ran down her face, and she rubbed at it crossly. 'Have a nice life, Mum.'

She turned to leave and her mother reached out for her. She could see Noel's face darken and him go to open the car door and get out. She shook her head at him, and he stood there, not moving, one hand on the open door. She shrugged her mother off and kept walking. Her mother was screaming now, shouting horrible things, words she had never heard from her before, and wished she could ignore now. She started to run to the car and Noel came to meet her. Wrapping her in his strong arms, he walked her around the car, opening the door for her and slotting her into her seat. He closed her door and just like that, she was in a bubble. She couldn't hear her mother, and soft rock was playing low on the car CD player. The heat was on, and she started to cry, feeling oddly comforted. Noel got in fast, and saying nothing, he put her seatbelt on for her, clicking his into place before pulling away from the street. Summer went to look at her house, and he said softly, 'Don't look baby, don't look.'

Something in his voice made her cry even harder, and he sat

saying nothing, taking her hand into his as he drove the car straight out of Bridlington. Within minutes, she was fast asleep.

* * *

Noel pressed a couple of buttons on the car phone, and the phone started to ring out, Noel turning the speakers down. He needn't have worried; she was out cold. He looked across at her. Even in sleep, she looked exhausted, sad. The palm print across her cheek was a vivid red, and Noel couldn't help but feel angry again at Angie. What type of mother slapped her own child? He had wanted to pick her up right then and there, throw her into the car and take her away.

Jean answered the phone, and Noel gave her a potted history of their morning. 'I'm really sorry to bother you with this Jean, but I just wondered—'

'If I would check on her?'

'Yeah,' Noel winced. 'If you can't, it's okay.'

'It's fine, I'll go round in the morning. I'll give her today to cool off.'

'Yeah, probably best. Summer's phone hasn't stopped ringing in the boot. I ended up pulling over and putting it on silent, but you have my number if you need us. Summer stocked up for her, so she'll be good for food till we get back.'

'I won't need you,' Jean said, firmly. 'You look after our girl, honey. Have a good time.'

Noel looked across at Summer, who was now wrapped in Noel's winter coat, sleeping soundly. She might have a bruise tomorrow, he thought to himself unhappily.

'We will. She's safe with me.'

* * *

Jean put the phone down and padded back into the lounge. Benny looked at her from his spot on the windowsill.

'That was Noel,' she said to him, sitting back down in her easy chair and flicking her feet out of her slippers. 'They've gotten off for the weekend. The poor lass bloody deserves it too.'

She looked around her room, thinking about what her upcoming weekend would entail. Aside from visiting the seemingly delightful Angie, it would be more of the same. Reading, baking, cleaning, the odd romantic movie or sporting game show. Having a weekend off used to be really appealing to her, but now it just reminded her of how lonely she was.

Benny hissed out of the window, and Jean saw a car swinging into view. Jim was home. Benny stood and arched his back, jumping down from the windowsill and looking at her with a fixed gaze before heading to the front door. The little bugger sure picked his toilet times. 'I'm coming, Little Lord Fauntleroy.' She pushed her feet back into her slippers and walked to the front door. Opening it up, Benny skulked off to do his business, and Jean stood in her dressing gown, enjoying the scent of the season outside. The smell of smoke hung in the air already, as though in anticipation for the night's festivities. Benny, as ever, couldn't give two hoots, and was busy heading to his normal spot in the middle of the green to tend to his bladder. She couldn't just leave him out; pranksters had been known to pick on black cats at this time of year. Halloween had a lot to answer for, and the fireworks and over excited idiots would be out in full force later.

'Come on Benny, hurry up!'

'Hi,' a voice said to the side of her, and she turned in surprise.

'Jesus Christ, you frightened me to death!'

A little giggle came from the darkness, and Jim walked out, a sleeping toddler in his arms, and a girl and boy at his sides.

'Is this the cake lady, Grandad?' The girl dressed in a pony onesie asked, looking up at Jim. He smiled at her bashfully.

'Er, yes, this is my friend, Mrs—'

'Miss, and call me Jean,' she stepped down off the step, moving closer and bending down to chat to them. 'Hello, you two. Your granddad has been really excited for you to come.'

They both beamed and she straightened up, taking a closer look at the little sleeping boy in Jim's arms. His arms were both wrapped around Jim's neck, his dark eyelashes sweeping over his adorable little face.

'Well, you have some lovely grandchildren, Jim.'

Jim beamed proudly. 'Thank you so much. We just got home. It's been a bit of a long drive.'

Jean raised her hands in apology. 'Oh gosh, I'm so sorry! I just came out to let Benny out, I'll let you get on. Benny!' She half screamed, half whispered her cat's name and was rewarded with a bored miaow in response. Benny was sitting at the front door as if to say, *Here, idiot!*

'Actually Jean, if you aren't busy, I was kind of hoping...' He looked embarrassed, and as he jigged the child in his arms, she realised he looked exhausted too.

'Do you want some help?' she asked, kindly. 'I just have to put Benny away for the night, then I can come over and help if you like. He hates the fireworks, but he'll be fine indoors.' She looked down at the children. 'Have you had something to eat? I have some lovely ham if you fancy a sandwich.' She bent closer and tapped the side of her nose. 'I might even have some cake.'

The two children gasped. 'Yeah, cake!'

She looked at Jim and he mouthed *thank you* at her. She winked at him and turned to her house. 'See you in a minute.'

Jim started to walk to his house, the two children following closely behind. 'Just let yourself in, okay? I'm going to get the little guy down for a nap and run a bath for these two. They've not really slept.'

* * *

A few hours later, all three children were snuggled up in their new bedrooms, too tired to even express any delight or curiosity at looking around their surroundings. Jean was just cleaning the work surfaces in the kitchen when Jim came down, an empty cup in each hand.

'Wow, you made them lunch, tea, a bedtime drink and it knocked them straight out. Did you put something in it?'

Jean folded the tea towel over the oven door handle and started to laugh. 'Just a shot of whisky, couple of pills crushed up, the usual. They're lovely kids, they really are. Are they home for good now?'

Jim beckoned to the breakfast island, where some stools sat, and tapped on one. 'You sit, you've done enough.' Jean did as he asked, and he reached into the fridge and pulled out a bottle of white wine. 'Wine?'

'Please,' she said, glad that she was here and that she had been able to help. The children were lovely, and she could see Jim in the two older children. He poured wine into two glasses, and bringing the bottle too, he motioned to the kitchen door. 'Let's go sit in the lounge; it's comfier there.'

The two walked through the house, and Jean looked around her properly for the first time. It was a lovely home, nice touches everywhere: photos of the children on the walls, a toy box in the corner of the living room. A doll house sat on a coffee table under the far window. It looked as though the children had always lived here. She felt her heart swell once more for this man, followed by a pang at his ignorance of her lately. Maybe she had come on too strong?

Maybe it was all in her head. They'd never actually discussed their friendship, had they?

Jim put the wine onto the coffee table, all on coasters, and they sat down on the soft grey couch.

The heating whirred in the background, punctuated by the odd firework noise.

'Thanks for today,' he said, eventually.

Jean took a long sip of her wine and Jim did the same, both of them settling back into the seat. 'It's no trouble at all. I'm happy to help. They're great kids, Jim.'

He smiled then, a real smile that lit up his tired features. 'They are. I had to leave here in a hurry. My daughter, she... er... she died. She has been sick for a while, not looking after herself, hanging around with the wrong sort. She became an addict, and the poor kids got taken into care.'

Jean took another glug of her wine, grateful to have something to hold to stop her from throwing herself into his arms, comforting him.

'I lived in an apartment at the time. I travel a lot for work, or used to, so I never needed much. I said I would step in, have the kids with me. She has no other family, and bugger knows who the fathers are. I'm not sure Carla even knew. I had to get them out of care, so I bought the house. I wanted Carla to go to rehab, but she kept skipping the appointments, and the judge was going to give her one more chance, but then she disappeared. That's when I went to get the kids, to tell the judge the house was nearly there, and I had taken early retirement from work. I can still work from home, if I need to, but round them. I was there a day, and then I got a call.'

His voice broke, and he lifted a shaky hand to his lips, draining half the glass of wine. 'She'd run out of rehab, and not even tried to see her kids. She didn't ring anyone, bother trying to contact anyone for help. I guess she was too far gone.'

He drained his glass and refilled it, filling hers without asking. 'They found her sometime later. She'd taken some drugs, and this time, she didn't wake up.'

Jean reached for his hand and held it tight. They both sat in silence, wine in hand, the other engaged in comfort.

'I had a husband once.' Jim looked at her teary eyed, and she stroked her thumb along the back of his hand. 'Oh, no one knows around here. He died young, silly accident. He was drunk, of course. We'd been married two years, though it felt like an age. He wasn't a nice person when he was on the sauce. I can't even say I grieved for him, really. Nothing to grieve for. The man I married was a big fake. The drink killed him long before the accident did. I think I was all cried out by the time the police knocked at my door.'

She took a deep pull on her wine. 'I buried him, collected the insurance, sold our house, and moved here. All on my tod. I wanted nothing to do with being his widow for the rest of my days. I was going to start living again, fall in love maybe, fill the house with kids.' She gestured with her hand around her. 'Just like this, in fact. You've done a wonderful job, Jim; the kids will love it here. It's a nice place to raise a family.'

'I have no idea what I'm doing. I can't even believe that they let me take them really, but I guess it was me or having to try to rehome them. The social worker was saying that splitting them up might be easier, but I just couldn't do it.'

'It's a brave and wonderful thing that you did. You will do fine. You have to, you know that. You did this whole house for them, and it's incredible.'

Jim started to cry then, softly at first, then wracking sobs.

Tears dripped into his glass, and he set it onto the coffee table.

'I failed her,' he said between cries. He sounded like a wounded animal, and Jean put her glass down and pulled him to her. He fell into her lap and she cradled him, stroking his back soothingly.

'What the hell am I supposed to do for those kids? What am I supposed to say to them? I'm just gonna screw them up too. I wasn't there really; her mum was... difficult.'

Jean said nothing. She knew what it was like to live with someone like that. She always thanked her lucky stars that she didn't have a child with her husband. That would have made everything far worse.

'I tried to be there, but with work, and them moving away... I could have done more. Her mum died a few years back, and it went downhill from there.'

She sat and let him cry it out, purge himself of all his guilt, and shame, and loss. He was helpless, in that moment, and she had never felt as close to someone.

They sat and talked into the early hours, one bottle turning into two, sharing their lives with each other, while the ghosts of the departed swirled around them.

* * *

Jim was woken up by a prod in the face. He opened one eye gingerly and was greeted by the face of his daughter. It shocked him, and he sat up with a start. The little girl was still dressed in her nightgown and was holding one of the teddies that he had put in her room. She really was the double of her mother at that age.

'Granddad, is this for me?' She held up the plush brown bear and his heart soared. He pulled her onto his knee and sat back with her in his arms. He looked around the room, but Jean was nowhere to be seen. The wine glasses had been cleared away, the coffee table cleaned.

'Come here sweetheart.' He touched the bear's nose and made a *boop* sound, making Isobel laugh. 'This is Bradley Bear. I got him for you so you would feel like you had a buddy. I know that things are sad at the moment, but I want you to know that this is your home now: you and Kyle and Alex. You are going to live with Granddad now if that's okay.'

Isobel looked at him with her baby blue eyes and nodded slowly. 'The boys are asleep; shall I make them breakfast?' She was looking around her, as though sussing out the place, bear in her arms tight, and he realised. She had been taking care of her brothers when her mother couldn't or didn't. His heart broke all over again, and he put her down, standing up.

'I tell you what: from now on, it's my job to take care of you guys, okay?'

Isobel smiled slowly, nodding and hugging Bradley closer.

'It's your job to be a kid, and enjoy school, and take care of Bradley Bear. I'll handle the rest, all right?'

He reached for her hand and she took it, her little fingers wrapping around two of his. He cleared his throat, swallowing to push away that feeling of despair.

The door went then, and the pair just looked at each other in shock.

Jean walked into the hallway, coat on, laden down with bags. She started to head to the kitchen and then caught them both staring at her from the doorway. 'Oh, sorry, I was just bringing you some shopping.'

Isobel stepped forward. 'Coco Pops, are they for us? Alex loves them.' She pointed at the bags, where the monkey's face could be seen poking out.

'Is that right? Well, I like them too, but to be honest, blueberry pancakes are my favourite, so I got some stuff to make those too. Would you like some?'

Isobel was already halfway to the kitchen. 'Yes please! Can I help?'

Jean winked at Jim. 'Of course you can, honey. That okay, Jim?'

Jim didn't say anything. The lump in his throat had closed off his windpipe. Jean dropped her bags and went over to him, giving him a hug.

'I'm here to help,' she whispered. 'Now, go see to those boys. Let us girls get some food going.' Jim walked up the stairs, suddenly ever so grateful for neighbours and the British need for a cup of tea.

13

'Summer?'

She stirred at the sound of her name being called and opened her eyes.

'Noel?' He smiled at her, sitting across from her in the car. She looked out of the window and saw that they were parked on the drive of a large house. 'Are we here already?'

'Yep, I let you sleep. Figured you needed it.' He touched her cheek gently with his fingertips, and Summer felt a zing of electricity, followed by a throb of pain. 'Are you okay?'

She moved her head away from him, looking out of the window again. 'I'm fine. Shall we go in?'

'I'll get the bags. You go say hello to my mum.'

There was a loud tap on the window, making Summer jump. Noel's mother's face was pressed up against the window, and she had a sparkly jumper on, with flashing fireworks emblazoned on it.

'Hello!' She mouthed through the window. 'I'm so glad you're here!' Her face dropped a little. 'What happened to your face?'

Summer turned to Noel, a look of horror on her face. Noel shrugged apologetically. 'Mothers, eh?'

Summer wished for a sinkhole. Just a small one, just big enough to swallow her up and help her to disappear from her tragic life. How the hell was she going to act normal and whole enough to get through the weekend?

Noel took the bags into the house whilst Sheila proceeded to drag Summer out of the car, cover her in Noel's coat and shepherd her into the house. By the time Noel had taken their bags upstairs, Summer was settled on the couch with a thick patchwork blanket around her and a cup of tea in her hands. Sheila gave him a look and turned her head to the kitchen. He followed her in.

'What happened? Is she okay? She looks like she's in shock!' She peeked around the kitchen door at her guest, who was staring into space, the cup still in her clasped hands. She closed the door slowly, with a quiet click, before rounding on her son. 'Answer me!' she said, as crossly as she could whilst whispering.

Noel held his hands up in surrender. 'Okay, okay, I yield! She's okay, I got her here, she slept in the car. She'll be fine, just a bad morning.'

'And her slapped face?' She punctuated her question with a tapping of the foot and hands on hips stance.

Noel flinched. 'Well, it wasn't me!'

Sheila slapped his arm, then yanked him in for a hug, winding him in the process. 'I know it wasn't you,' she said to his chest. 'I never thought that, but did you get whoever did it?'

Noel put his arms around his mother, kissing the top of her head. He could smell her typical mum smell: a mix of cookies, Parkin cake and her coconut shampoo. The woman always smelled fresh, and of whatever seasonal baked goods she was cooking up at the time. He looked around the kitchen, and noticed she had made about a hundred cookies, all decorated with fireworks and sparkler icing. A couple of pumpkin pies were cooling behind them. His mother never stopped. In fact, since his dad died, she had even stepped it up. Keeping herself busy, she would say.

'It's not that easy; it's not some arsehole ex I can punch out or something. It's her mother, but it's complicated.'

His mum squeezed him tighter. 'Well, she has us now. We'll look after her. Have you eaten?'

'No, not yet.'

Sheila headed to the fridge. 'Right, well, lunch then. The guests aren't coming till later, so you have time to get washed up. I put some towels in your room.'

'Did you put some in the guest room?'

'For Uncle Russell? Yes love, I did.'

Noel, one hand on the door handle, froze. 'Mum, I thought Summer was going to be in there? Where is she going to sleep? Nana and Granddad are in the other bedroom. Did you get some kind of Narnia extension I wasn't aware of?'

The look on her face told him everything he needed to know. 'Mum, you can't be serious.' He looked at the kitchen door in a panic. 'Muuum!'

Sheila was already slicing tomatoes and making sandwiches. 'Don't "Mum" me Noel; I'm a hip woman. I'm down with the kids. You don't have to be married to share a room nowadays, and besides, we are pretty full up.'

'Uncle Russell lives five minutes away! I could take him home. Hell, he could walk from here, even half cut and hopping on one leg!'

His mother started humming to herself and clicked her kitchen radio on. Noel tutted and she waggled her finger at him.

'Don't tut at me, boy. Just get on with it. Don't be such a fuddy duddy! You like the girl, sharing a room for a night won't kill you. She looks like she would be glad of the company.'

Noel bit his lip, thinking of the pick-up debacle that morning.

He wanted to be there for her. He wanted to help, but even this wasn't an easy fix for him. He could dig ditches for wells, build school buildings, help to drive food and medicine where it needed to be, but this was beyond him.

'Mum, how did you cope when dad passed?'

Sheila paused in her lunch-making frenzy and turned to face him. 'I didn't, at first. I didn't want to, really. I wanted to curl into a ball and never unfurl again. But I had people, responsibilities. You were a teenager, so you had your own life to live, so I just helped my family, volunteered more, baked more. I dragged myself out of the house every day. I dog walked half the neighbourhood hounds in that first six months and babysat for most of the children around here. I just got busy living Noel, that's all. I wasn't about to waste what life I had left. Your dad would have hated that, and I don't want any earache when we finally meet again.'

He thought of Angie, and how she was. She had done the opposite; instead of reaching out, she had dug in for the winter.

'I wish you had known Summer's mother, you could have helped.'

'I doubt that,' a flat voice came from behind him. 'I tried everything and look what I got for my trouble.' Summer was standing in the kitchen doorway, the empty mug in her hand. She pointed to her cheek, where the palm print of her mother's hand was just starting to fade. She crossed the room and put the mug into the hot, soapy water in the sink. 'Besides, my father isn't even dead. If it's okay, I'm going to get ready for later?'

Sheila nodded encouragingly. 'Yes love, of course. Noel, you go and show her where everything is.'

Summer smiled thinly at them both and headed out of the room. Noel followed her and heard the radio volume go up and his mum chatting to the dog, who was scowling at the two cats that were mocking from the windowsills outside. His mother, ever the diplomatic host. He followed Summer up the stairs, taking care to stand a little back, not overcrowd her. They reached the top of the stairs, and she stopped.

'Where?'

He pointed to one of the doors, belatedly realising that his mother had still got his name plate on the door. His name in zoo animals, written across the door. She never had let him get rid of them. No wonder he had never brought girlfriends to stay over.

Summer walked over to the door and touched the little, brightly coloured animals. 'Cute. Where are you sleeping?'

'Ah, well, my mother—'

'I heard. I'm teasing.' She turned to face him. 'I heard everything, actually. Why did you think my dad was dead?'

Noel opened his mouth to tell her, but he couldn't think of any reason why. Had she ever actually said it? 'I... I think I just assumed, with your mother and everything.'

Summer laughed, but it came out all wrong, angry. 'I sometimes think that if he had died, it would have been a hell of a lot easier, but then I hate myself for thinking that. It would have been better for Mum though, I think. At least that way, he wouldn't have left on his own accord. He would have left because he died, not because he didn't want us any more.'

She pushed the door to the bedroom open and moved forward a little bit, allowing Noel to enter the room and close the door behind them both. She leaned back into him, and he wrapped his arms around her. 'Do you think I'm damaged?'

His heart broke a little, hearing her words, seeing her like this. She seemed beaten down, and he detested whatever and whoever could make a woman like her feel beaten down by life.

'The day we met it wasn't the first time I had seen you. The truth is, I saw you a few nights before, walking along the beach.' She started to stroke his arms with her fingers, and he struggled a little to keep focus. 'It was nearly night time, and the sun was just setting on the horizon. I was sitting on the beach, eating a waffle.'

'Of course,' she laughed.

'Yep, food for every mood.' He kissed her hair. 'I was eating my waffle, and I saw you walking along the shore. There was a dog there, with its owner, and the dog was jumping in and out of the water. You started playing along with it, hitching up your dress, and running in and out of the waves, laughing your head off.'

Summer remembered that day. She never thought that someone could have been watching. She remembered later that night too, when her mother had told her off for coming home late, for being wet. She had screamed and wailed about her getting sick and leaving her mother all alone.

'I thought you were so beautiful, so carefree. I looked for you for the rest of the week, but I never saw you again, till the morning with the Christmas tree.'

He turned her to face him, and she pulled a face. 'Sorry, I was a bit of a bitch that day.'

'Yes, you were, but I know you now. I get it.'

'Hey!' She pushed him, and he stumbled backwards. 'You should say, of course you're not, dearest girlfriend.'

He moved closer to her, moving her towards the double bed at the other side of the room. 'I'm sorry, dearest girlfriend, of course you are nothing but sweetness and light. I was the one in the wrong.' The back of her legs touched the bed, and their bodies touched.

'That's right.'

'And furthermore, I am declaring now that you will always be beautiful, and I will always be wrong.'

She laughed, and Noel was glad to hear that it was happier now, carefree.

'You are learning. Excellent, Mr Pritchett.' She put her hands around the back of his head, running her fingers though his hair and pulling him in. 'Now, kiss me. We don't have long before the guests arrive.'

Noel kissed her, and they sank down onto the bed together. The sheets smelled of fabric softener. 'Your mum is a bit of a domestic goddess, eh?'

Noel laughed, a low rumble in his chest as she laid side by side with him. 'She likes to meddle and keep busy. You don't mind sharing a room with me tonight?'

She shook her head slowly. 'I don't know, I've never done it before.'

She looked at him, and he clicked. With her life being as sheltered as she was, where would she have found the time and freedom to date?

'Never?' he asked softly. 'Anything?'

She blushed, one cheek going redder than the other, a remnant of her mother's handiwork. 'Not really had the time to pursue an actual life, let alone a love life. I have had a few first dates, second ones even, but then they want to see where I live, ask about my life, go on sodding mini breaks. I can't do any of that.'

'Till now,' he countered, undoing the top button of her blouse, looking at her in question.

'Until now,' she agreed, moving her hands up under his sweater. 'Now is good.' She started to lift his sweater up, over his head, and Noel's expression turned to surprise.

'What are you doing?'

She looked to the door in panic, as though his mother was standing there with a Polaroid camera. 'Sorry, is it your mum?'

Noel shook his head, as best he could with his sweater bunched up around his neck. 'No, she won't come in, but... are you sure you want to?'

Summer's expression turned to relief and she lifted his sweater up over his head. 'I'm sure if you are. I want this to be with you.'

Noel looked at her, laid there next to him, her hair fanned out against his bed sheets, and he stood up. Walking over to the door, he clicked the lock closed. She watched his movements, and he slowly took his jeans off, throwing them to the side before walking back over to her and lying next to her.

'I really do like you Summer, you know that?' He took her in his arms and rolled them both until she was beneath him. 'I'm here.'

She reached up and ran her hands along the contours of his chest, moving down slowly to his stomach and the waistband of his pants. He had a thick patch of hair on his chest, curly yet soft, matching the hair on his head.

'You have Poldark chest hair,' she giggled. and Noel froze.

'What?'

She ran her fingers through it, gently touching her fingertips to his skin. 'Nothing, an inside joke.' She moved her hands to her blouse, and started to undo the buttons, one at a time. He lay over her, his arms at either side of her head, watching her. She should have felt nervous, sick, but she didn't feel any of that. She had thought about this moment so often over the years: how it would happen, and with who. Now it was here, it was better than she had ever hoped for. She lifted herself up a little, taking her blouse off, and he started to kiss her, touch her.

'Tell me if you want to stop, okay? There's no rush for this; we can wait.'

She kissed him back, pulling him to her. 'I'm ready, Noel. I don't want to stop.'

He looked at her again, taking her in with his eyes, and she laid there, looking right back at him. He smiled down at her and kissed her again.

* * *

A few hours later, Summer woke up naked in Noel's bed. The covers had been wrapped around her, and there was a note on the pillow next to her.

Best fireworks ever. Gone to help Mum with the rabble. Come down when you are ready.
    Love, Noel xx

Love. He had written it, right there on the note. She clasped it to her chest, feeling her heart beat that little bit faster. She was here, in a city she had never been to before, with a man she had just made love to, in his childhood home. Her mother was miles away, doing God knows what, and for once, she was okay about that. She was okay about having a life for this one weekend. If this weekend was all she would ever get, she would cherish the memories.

Her bags were sat at the bottom of the bed, and she tucked the note inside one of the side pockets. Her fingers bumped against something in there, and she pulled out her phone. She knew instantly why it was in there, and on silent. Noel had obviously wanted to protect her from her mother's rantings. She had voice-mail messages and missed phone calls. It looked like she had been calling for hours. She felt a flash of panic, but she stopped herself from calling. Calling her mother would never end well, not now. She would deal with it all when she got back home, when she had to. Calling her voicemail, she quickly deleted all the unread messages and tapped out a text to Jean, telling her that they had arrived safe, and that her mother hadn't taken it well. She left out any details, not wanting to put them into words before she had even processed them herself. She had a party to get to, with her boyfriend and his family, and just for one night, she was going to be normal. Even if it killed her.

* * *

'You comfy?' Noel asked, passing her a steaming hot mug of coffee. 'I'll warn you now, Mum will have Irish'd that up, knowing her.' Summer took it from him carefully, not wanting her gloves to drop it through their lack of woollen grip. She took a sniff.

'Wow, yep! Definitely a bit of Irish luck in there,' she blew the contents and took a hesitant sip. The heat from the coffee hit her first, together with the slow lick of caffeine, and then the alcohol snuck up on her, warming her through. They were all sitting in a semi-circle on and around the patio, while at the bottom of the rather large garden, two men were sizing up various fireworks and talking about wind 'disturbance' and 'ideal conditions'. They were all snuggled under blankets, various patio and dining chairs scattered around like little rafts on an open sea. Little islands of blanket forts and people laughing and joking with each other. There must be thirty people there but it felt so chilled and relaxed, Summer found that her usual social anxiety radar wasn't even flickering. Not for the first time, she wondered at how the other half lived. While she sat in her room, studying for exams, headphones on, reading late at night by torch under the quilt, devouring teen stories of love and adventure, just how much she had missed out on? Was Noel doing the same, all teenage spots and hormones? Looking around here at the neat flower beds, the gnomes discreetly sitting in the rockery, and the fairy lights strung all around the fences and trees, she doubted it.

'You okay?' Noel asked, once again sensing that her mind was elsewhere. 'No regrets?'

'No, no regrets.' She thought of their time together earlier, how he had made her feel so cherished, so protected. Safe. He really saw her. 'I'm just enjoying the night.' She smiled at him, and he pulled his camping chair up closer to hers, touching the handles of each together as though they were kissing.

'Good, I'm glad.' He nodded at the men, who were now very efficiently sorting through the boxes and packing the fireworks away in order. 'Those two get worse every year. Dad used to be right up there with them, arguing and trying to take over. The first year, him, Dave and Rajesh set fire to the back fence and ruined my mum's potting shed.' He looked at her dramatically. 'The fire service came and told them off, and then she told *them* off for walking through the house in muddy boots. I swear, it was hilarious.' He looked back at Dave and Rajesh, a faraway look crossing his features. 'You have to enjoy your time here, Sum. Things happen, good and bad, but it's all life.'

She took a sip of her strong coffee and thought about the day she had had. 'I'm beginning to get that idea,' she said softly, and he winked at her.

'Good. You warm enough?'

She nodded, pulling him in closer by the arm. 'I am, but I can still huddle up, if you need the heat.'

Noel put his arm around her, and she dropped her head onto his shoulder. 'Girl, I bring my own heat. You need to stick with me.'

She grinned and tucked in closer. She wasn't going to argue with any of that.

14

Jean headed up to the cul-de-sac where Summer had lived her whole life, and gasped when she turned the corner. It looked right out of place against the other, neater houses and she was suddenly very angry with herself that she hadn't been to the house years earlier.

She remembered when they had moved in: Angie all excited about her new house, her dream home. It was huge, plenty of room for her family, her husband and her daughter, and their lives together. Jean was the cleaner in the office building that Angie managed and the two had become good friends. She was a woman you couldn't help but like. She was always happy, cheerful, on the go. She used to pore over interior design magazines in her lunch hour, picking out what she wanted for her home, her garden. She was a woman who could turn the sourest, most cantankerous customers into little pots of walking sunshine just by chatting to them. The woman had been Mary frikkin' Poppins on acid, and then it had ended. He had left, and that was it. The beginning of the end of Mary Poppins.

Jean had been inside this house many times, before. Angie was one for parties, and she invited everyone from the CEO to the office cleaner and treated them just the same. The house always looked welcoming, full of life, but the house she saw in front of her today wasn't nearly the same. She jiggled the cake tin in her hands, adjusting her handbag and opening the front gate. The front path seemed to take forever as she walked to the front door.

She knocked, and when there was no answer, she knocked again. She tried to look through the front windows, but the curtains and drapes were all shut tight. She thought about going around the back, but she knew it wouldn't do any good. Everything would be locked up tight there too. She sure as hell wouldn't just be out or sitting in the garden. She took a seat on the front porch, setting the cake tin to one side, and pulling out a flask of hot tea from the large handbag she had brought.

'I'm here Angie, and I am not leaving, okay? I'm here for the long haul, so you need to open this door and get your arse out here.' She looked behind her back at the door, and thought she saw movement. She took her mobile out and rang a contact.

'Hey love, I'm here. Yes, she's in. Yep, same address. Okay, see you soon.' She plopped the phone back into her bag and took a long sip of tea. 'We just wait now, Angie. My friend's coming, and I even baked a cake to mark the occasion. You need to get dressed and make yourself presentable because we have a lot to do today. I know you can hear me.'

A twitch in the curtain punctuated the point. She was in and listening.

'I made a cake, just for you, last night. Noel rang me, told me what happened. Do you really think that the old you would have done something like that? You think that would have been okay, before all this happened? You loved a man, Ang. A bad one, in the end. Been there myself, back in the day. Does that mean every-thing's done with?'

She turned around on the step, crossing her feet under her. She was dressed for the occasion, comfy, warm tracksuit bottoms and a thick sweater, combined with her fur-lined boots. She looked very different to her usual boho, jingly self, but she knew that today was a day to be serious, to get tough. She leaned against the bricks, sideways on from the door, and drank her tea. She kept seeing a shadow pass by the door, and she knew that Angie was in there, checking what she was doing. 'I'm not going anywhere, Ang, so open the door and come talk to me!'

No response. She delved into her handbag, bringing out an apple and a paperback, all rolled in the innards of a blanket. She wrapped the blanket around herself and tucking into the apple, pulled the bookmark out of her book and settled down to read.

'You'd like this one, very romantic. A lonely woman meets the perfect guy, but she's already engaged to a man, and he is supposed to be just her friend. She wants to live her own life, but her parents keep fighting and then she starts to fall for Mr Perfect.' She laughed to herself at a passage. 'It's good, funny. The fiancé is a bit of an idiot, but we've all been a bit blind. Let's hope the poor sod doesn't marry him, eh? Like we did?'

A car pulled up, and Jean looked and waved to the driver. 'My friend is here now. You ready to open the door, let us in?'

A woman got out of the black BMW that she had just parked outside and reached back into the car to grab a black leather folder and a brown handbag. Locking the car, the friendly-looking, dark-haired woman click clacked up the path, holding her hand out to Jean when she got to her. Jean pulled herself up, packing her things away in her bag.

'Jean, I hope you know what you are doing. This could backfire, make things worse.'

Jean hugged the woman to her. 'Lisa honey, things can't get any worse. We have to try.'

Lisa nodded, her professional face switching on. 'Okay, let's begin then.'

The two women looked at each other, took a deep breath, and knocked on the door again.

* * *

Sheila's house was in full party flow now. Summer was sitting in the garden on a long bench, chatting to Noel's grandparents, who were dressed up in thick, woolly coats, hats and scarves. Sheila was milling around everyone, her face lit up, not just by the garden lights and the light from the house, but from inside. She was radiant, in her element, and Summer couldn't help but think of her own mother. Would they have lived like this now if her dad hadn't left? Would they have been in Mum's garden, family and friends all around, Noel by her side? Her mum the happy hostess she used to be, taking care of everyone? Dad in the corner sneaking peeks at the football match coverage, or manning the BBQ, passing around the beers, making cocktails for the ladies while he laughed his deep, rumbling laugh? Would she have been happy now? Would she feel like she had started her life?

She looked across at Noel, who was talking to one of the guests, and felt the bubble of desire and excitement in the pit of her belly. Their afternoon together had been amazing, and now she was at a party. She kept counting the blessings of her weekend, mentally photographing every moment to pore over later. She was going to savour every moment.

* * *

Pulling up to the house, well, the street really, felt like tightening a noose around her own neck. The closer she got, the more she felt strangled, constricted, fighting for breath. Noel hadn't been easy to convince, but she knew that she needed to do this on her own, so he had reluctantly acquiesced. They'd said goodbye midway between the shops, and she could still feel the warmth of his lips on hers as she braved the cold. There was a definite snap in the air today, and she wasn't totally convinced it was all down to the weather. In fact, if her mother wasn't housebound, she might have put her down for a bit of naked weather summoning, to show the wrath of her *and* the gods. She walked past the car parked outside, opened the gate and, taking a deep breath, walked up the path. The house looked exactly the same as usual, but there were lights on. Again, because she probably needed the light to make the voodoo dolls of her daughter. She went to put her key in the lock and the door opened.

'Hiya love, come on in!' Jean reached for her and pulled her through the door and into the house in one swift movement. Next was a boob-crushing hug. 'Oh, you do look good Summer! You look so... rested!'

Jean, bless her. The woman was a veritable feast of tact and positivity. Rested was obviously code for *slept for once and doesn't look like the usual level of roadkill*. She was right, though; Summer did feel better. She felt different somehow. She'd had her eyes opened this weekend, and it made her current situation all the more depressing. 'Er... thanks Jean, where's Mum?' She pulled away from her friend, looking around here, but saw nothing but the usual old house. She mouthed *why are you here?* but Jean just laughed.

'Ah, your mum's in the lounge, darling, speaking to my friend. Cup of tea? I'm just bleaching your mugs, but I saved a couple.' She walked off to the kitchen, leaving Summer staring at the closed living room door. She could hear muffled voices from inside, but they were calm and collected. She walked into the kitchen and was immediately hit with a familiar smell. The smell of the office. Hardly surprising, given that Jean's cleaning caddy from work was on the kitchen top. She was busy making tea, the sink full of hot steaming water.

'I had to throw a couple that I couldn't save, but I'll pick up a couple of new ones when I go to the shops.'

Summer waved her away blindly, sinking into one of the breakfast bar stools that was now clean and looking as shiny as a new pin. 'No, it's fine. I can buy them. So... how?'

Jean looked her in the eye, glancing at the door, leaning in. 'Noel told me what happened. I just couldn't be leaving it any longer. I know you have your ways, but...' her voice cracked, 'the Angie I knew would have rather died than hurt her daughter, in any way. It's time, Summer darling. It's time I stepped in to help now.' She raised her finger in the air. 'Now, yes, yes I know, you don't want me sticking me big oar i—'

'Thank you,' Summer stopped her. 'Thanks Jean.'

'Er... yes. Right!' Jean jabbed her finger forcefully, for effect if nothing else. 'Good, glad you understand!'

Summer hopped down from her stool and swept round the counter, grabbing Jean in a huge hug. Jean hugged her back just as fiercely. 'I'm sorry. I didn't know it was this bad.'

'I didn't want to tell you, really. I was scared she might have to go somewhere or go to hospital.'

'I know,' Jean smoothed her back, patting her like a baby to be burped after a big feed. 'Anyway, how was your trip away? Anything interesting to tell me?' She made a little thrusting motion, pulling away and working her fists like they were holding ski poles.

'Jean!' Summer laughed. 'Come on, I can't tell you that!'

Jean snorted. 'Of course you bloody well can! At my age, I live for this stuff!'

Summer thought of her time away with Noel. Laughing with his family, washing up with his mother, laughing with his uncle and dad's best friends. Lying in the dark together, talking, touching, kissing...

'All I can say,' she replied with a smile. 'Is that there were certainly fireworks.'

Jean had made two pots of tea, and they had cleaned the kitchen down together, scrubbing every long-encrusted stain from the floor, every bit of errant food hiding and breeding behind the fridge. Jean had wanted to start on the cupboards but Summer knew that her mother would never be on board. They were just debating what, if anything, they could get rid of without her knowing when the lounge door opened.

'Jean, you ready?' the female voice called. Jean patted Summer on the shoulder, picking up her caddy and steam mop.

'Yes love, I'm in here.' She headed to the door, and a few seconds later and a bit of shuffling, and the front door closed behind them. Silence. She could hear the two women walking off, knew every step along the path, the slight squeak and creak of the front gate, and then the car started up, moving off. She listened for movement, for something being thrown, or an angry voice, but nothing came. She walked slowly towards the lounge and saw her mother there, lying down on the sofa, a bundle of tissues in her hand.

'Mum?' She ventured. 'You okay?'

She was staring into space but Summer saw the flinch of her shoulders when Angie heard her name. She was in there, somewhere. 'Mum?' she tried again. No response this time at all and eventually, her eyes began to close. Summer stood there in the doorway like a naughty child out of bed, watching her mother fall into an exhausted sleep. Only then did she move her aching body to cover her with a blanket before heading to bed herself. After the last couple of days, it seemed that both Hastings women were in need of a good night's sleep.

* * *

Avril bounded into the shop, full of energy as usual. 'Saturday, finally!' She threw her coat off and hung it on the pegs in the corner.

'Good week at school, eh?' Noel joked, earning him an eye roll and a look that left him in no doubt she wished it would inflict pain on him.

'Yeah, of course it was! I not only have idiots for peers; I also have the worst teachers in the world!' She started ranting on about double maths and punishment for something called flossing, all the while sorting out the stock levels in the shop and straightening up the displays. If she didn't speak, she would be the best possible employee ever. If he could clone her, there would be a franchise of Forever Festive shops all throughout Europe, complete with their own crazy dancing elf shop assistants.

'Anyway,' she spat, coming out of the stockroom with a box full of snow globes and continuing her monologue, 'I said to him, "Mr Turner, mate, get real! When am I going to need algebra in real life? I'm not going to space!" He didn't get it. I'm a realist, nothing wrong with that!'

Noel chuckled. 'Ooh, brutal. What did he say?'

She put the box down, picking one of the pretty blue globes up and shaking it vigorously. 'Well, he said that I needed to learn algebra *and* decent manners, so I ended up in isolation all afternoon, doing the same work I avoided all lesson!'

'What did your parents say?'

Summer walked in then, a bag from the local sandwich shop in her hand. 'Breakfast time! Jean's next door so I have a while. She's moaning about my u-bend or something, got the bleach out like it's going out of fashion. Avril, sausage and bacon on white with red, right?'

Avril gasped, pouncing on Summer. 'Oh my God, you remembered!' She took the packaged sandwich and tore open the paper, ripping into it and taking a big bite. 'Oh, wow, it's amazing!' She announced through a mouthful of sausage.

'Okay, say it don't spray it!' Summer laughed, pretending to dodge out of the way. Avril faked shooting at her with the sandwich, and Summer pretended to be wounded, falling to the floor theatrically. She 'died', sticking her tongue out to one side and crossing her eyes, and then looked across at Noel. 'I got your usual too, baby.'

'Ooh, baby is it!' Avril screeched, earning a slap on the leg from Summer.

'Shut up, you,' Summer laughed, getting up and going to sit down next to Noel. She gave him her sandwich and was just opening up hers to take a bite when she saw something in the corner of her eye. A figure standing in the doorway, looking at them all, an expression of shock on their features. Noel saw that she had stopped and turned his head to see what she was looking at.

'Summer, what's wrong?'

Avril turned to look too, and a piece of chewed up sausage fell from her open mouth.

'Summer? What is it?' Noel looked at the man standing in the doorway. Something in his brain clicked but didn't register, like a car trying to turn over on a cold wintery morning. Avril and Summer both looked at him, the confusion he felt mirrored in their features.

'Why are *you* here?' Summer asked, but the man just stared back. He was tapping his hands at his sides, as if he was trying to wake himself from a bad dream.

'Summer, Avril. Go in the back,' Noel said, moving forward to block his entrance further into the shop. Whoever it was, they didn't look happy to see him.

Avril looked at Summer, her face contorted with pain. 'Summer, I'm sorry. I didn't mean for this, I just wanted...'

'Don't,' Summer said, her voice low and threatening. 'Not now.'

Noel was antsy now, his eyes pinballing around the room.

'What's going on? Who is this?' he asked, exasperated. Avril looked down at her feet and Summer didn't move. She didn't take her eyes from the man.

'It's my dad,' the two of them said in unison.

'What the hell are you doing, Avril?' There he was, her father, scolding Avril like he was her daughter too. Summer was still feeling numb, like she was frozen, watching him tell her to get her things and get home. Noel stepped forward between Avril and the man, his arms raised, his stance relaxed but ready. Summer could feel him keep looking over at her but she couldn't move. Her father was here. In this shop. Here. Alive and kicking. Not an abstract figure any more, but flesh and bone.

'Dad, I'm working. I told you I was working!'

He slapped his hand against his forehead. 'Yeah, but not here, not near...' He looked at Summer, just for a split second, and the spell was broken. His look snapped whatever string was holding her in place.

'What are you doing here?' she asked, genuinely interested in the answer. 'Mum said you moved away.'

'Avril, go get in the car.'

'No, Dad, I'm working!'

'Sir, she is due to work today. I am sure that I can get her home safe, or you could—'

'She can't work here any more,' he snapped, jabbing at the door with his short, stubby fingers. 'Now, Avril. Move it.'

'No, I want an answer, actually.' Summer stepped forward, heading towards the man. Noel moved to stand beside her but said nothing. 'What are you doing here?' She turned to Avril then, who was reluctantly pulling her backpack onto her shoulders. 'You.'

Avril opened her mouth to speak but Summer had twigged on now. 'Those days, outside the shop? You were watching us...' She shook her head at the young girl, stepping back in horror. 'You knew about him, and me? Why did you come here?'

'Come on Avril, we should go.'

'Yeah,' Summer said sarcastically, her body weaving around like an angry snake now as she bobbed around the shop, moving from foot to foot. 'You should go, play the dutiful father. She is yours, yeah? Actually yours, your blood?'

The man's features closed down, his face pinching together. A look she knew well. And relished being the cause of.

'So that's a yes. So not dead then, lying in a ditch bleeding out, or rotting away. You're fine and dandy, just raising your little princess there, while I pick up your shit! Are you kidding me?' She went to him, grabbing his hand and waggling his appendage about. He just stood there, his hand slack, his eyes on the floor.

'See,' she was off now, head gone. She was pulling at his fingers, each one in turn, wiggling and shaking each one and presenting them to the room as if they were a line of severed heads on the castle walls, deterring any contenders to the throne. 'Fingers aren't broken, and you drove here, so no excuse for not coming to see us, and calling us once in a *blue fecking moon*!' She rounded on Avril again, her body humming with anger and shock. 'What was the point in all that? Him? Me?'

Avril was stammering, her bottom lip quivering as she tried to control her emotions. 'Summer, I...'

'I trusted you, I thought we were actually becoming friends.'

'We were!' Avril stamped her foot. 'We really were. I was so happy to find you! Dad said—'

'Avril.' Ronnie's tone was low, a growl of warning. 'Not now. Car.'

'Running off, eh?' Summer snorted loudly, folding her arms, clasping her sweaty palms under her armpits. She wanted to scrub her hands. She felt dirty just touching him, the man who left and smashed all their lives apart. 'Sounds about right. I'm surprised you're still with this one, or are you working on more bastard kids?' Her face dropped. 'Oh, you already did that. Two-year-old brother, right?' She glared at Avril, who seemed to shrink before them all, her glasses dwarfing her face.

'Summer,' Noel gasped. 'Stop!'

She turned around, but didn't pay any attention to him, or his concern. She felt like she was on fire, every nerve ending wanting to sizzle and pop in her body. She felt sick, and shaky, and so very, very angry.

'No! I won't stop, but I am leaving.' She pushed past the useless lump that gave her life and went straight back to work.

'Hi, love,' Jean trilled as she bounded through the agency. Thankfully, it was empty. She headed straight for the store cupboard, slamming the door behind her.

Jean sighed, throwing her cloth back into her caddy and feeling every inch of her years in that moment. Noel crashed through the shop door, looking around like a crazy man, and she just pointed to the storeroom door. 'She's in there, but if I—'

'Summer!' Noel was already striding across the shop, tapping on the door. 'Summer, it's only me. Come out, let's talk, okay?'

Nothing. Noel knocked again. 'Summer, come on! Talk to me. Jean?' Noel turned to her, but she was already back to her cleaning. She shook her head, waggling her Dave the duster at him.

'Noel darling, when she is in there, she's either crying or plotting to kill someone. Leave her be, I say. She'll soon feel better.'

Noel shook his head, coming closer to Jean, one eye always on the closed door. 'It's not that, it's... her dad showed up.'

Jean's face dropped.

'Yep, well that was Summer's face too when she saw him. It didn't go well. Avril, my shop girl? She's his daughter.'

Jean slapped the side of her own head hard, the fluff from the duster she was holding landing in her hair. 'I knew it! I knew I felt something funny when I saw that girl; she looks like him. It's so obvious! I must have had sugar in my eyes!' She went over to the door and tapped on it herself. 'Summer, it's okay! We're all here for you honey. Will you come out?'

Nothing. Noel looked stricken. 'It's my fault. I brought her into the shop, next door. I knew that there was something she was hiding.'

The door opened and Summer was standing there, glaring at Noel, mascara and kohl streaking her face as tears slid down her cheeks, tracking her emotional meltdown. 'You knew? Seriously?'

Noel went to walk closer, his arms out palms up in surrender. 'No, Summer, I didn't know what, I just thought she was a bit of a neglected kid maybe. New baby and all.' He winced as he said the words, his eyes closing in sheer disbelief that he had said too much.

'Oh yes, a baby too, eh? Ronnie has been busy, hasn't he! Do you know what this will do to Mum? She is trying so hard, and some things are still really hard, sure, but this?' She started to cry again, wiping furiously at her face and streaking herself more. 'This will kill her Noel, and you employed her.'

'Summer, it's not his fault,' Jean chipped in. 'You can't blame anyone here but that man.'

'Oh, I do! Jean, that's all I do. Where's that got me though, eh? Does he pay the mortgage, or come and help me with Mum? Does he listen to her rants, her episodes, her terror at real life stuff?' She shook her head, a twisted expression playing across her features. 'Does he heck. He left us and walked right into a new life...'

Her voice faded as she did the math in her head. 'Avril, she's a school girl. High school, even. Which means that when he left, she was already here. Or on the way at the very least. He left his wife and daughter for another, plain and simple. I hate him so much.' She looked like she was going to faint, huffing and pulling at her clothes, before bending in half in front of them, her hands resting on her thighs as she struggled to breathe. Noel went to her side, rubbing her back, but she shrugged him off.

'Leave it Noel, just leave it. You've done enough, haven't you? Just leave me alone, all of you!'

She ran past them all, grabbing her bag on the way past, and flinging her keys on the counter. 'Lock up the shop!' she shouted over her shoulder as she barged out of the door, straight past Mrs Wimslow who had come to book her annual trip to Bronte Country. Jean gave Noel a sheepish look before ushering Mrs Winslow in with the promise of a cuppa.

'I'll handle things here,' she murmured once the lady was installed in a comfy chair with a cup of English breakfast and a plate of biscuits. 'I can book her onto it; Summer showed me ages ago. You go find her, before she doesn't have a business to run.'

Noel patted her on the shoulder and, grabbing his own shop keys, locked up and sprinted up the street to find her.

Two hours later, he admitted defeat and headed to the shops again in case she had returned. He knew the one place she wouldn't go was home. She wouldn't want Angie to find out, but something in Ronnie's demeanour had made Noel second guess just what had gone on. Why did Avril even know who Summer was, if Ronnie didn't care?

* * *

'Ssshooo,' Summer jabbed the air in front of the barman, close enough to bop him on the nose with a wobbly digit. 'I actually wasn't a bad person that day. I was stressed and harasshed.

Harassed,' she tried again, 'because basically, I turned into a teenager and then every man and his bloody dog turned into the biggest lying ashholes I have ever met. Do they care about me? No, Barry, they don't!'

'It's actually Bahram, but that's okay. Can I call you a cab?'

'Well you can,' she replied, giggling, waggling her fingers at him again with wild abandon. 'But I won't answer, cos it's not my name!'

Bahram rolled his eyes, smiled tightly, and moved to the other end of the bar to serve more normal, sober customers. Summer drained her glass of pink gin and raised her glass.

'Barry, another when you have a minute, and make it a double.' She eyed the back of the bar, her head swaying slightly and her eyes narrowing as she tried to focus. She felt someone come to the side of her, and she beckoned them closer.

'Hey, hey, what flavour crisps are they, on that display wall?' She pointed in the general direction of the back of the bar.

'Umm, sea salt and balsamic vinegar?' The man leaned in. She couldn't quite make out his face, or his body, but he smelled nice and could translate crisp packets, which was a bonus.

'Yousmellnice,' she slurred. 'Whatthehellisgoing on with these crisps? Why do people have to lie?'

The man chuckled softly, waving a hand towards the barman. 'A pint please, and whatever she's having, plus two bags of those sea salt crisps please.'

Bahram looked uncomfortable as he eyed the pair, but in all honesty, the woman, who was dressed like some kind of pop band, all colour blocks and jaunty accessories, scared him to death. He didn't need women like her shouting at him or refusing to leave. His second shift was eventful enough already.

'Aww, you'reshocute,' she simpered, trying to bat her eyes at him and managing some kind of demented face spasm. 'Thank you.'

'Todd,' the man answered from his swirly blob of a face area.

She smiled, smiling more broadly at Bahram when he gave her the glass of pink gin and the bags of crisps. 'So, are you here alone?'

Summer was about to answer, but she heard a voice from her other side.

'No, she's with me actually.' Noel. He placed a note on the bar and spoke to Bahram briefly.

'Great, Todd,' she glowered. 'Noel's here now, with hiss bloody elfveses. Ha! Great Todd, like Great Scott! Geddit?' She flicked out her elbow, connecting with his body and producing a huge 'uff' sound. 'Great Todd!' She shouted again, in a deep booming over the top British voice. 'The crisps here are too posh, I say!'

Noel picked up her handbag, which had been dropped to the floor during her enthusiastic crisp diatribe, and knelt beside her.

'Come on Summer, let me take you home.'

She looked at him, all three of him, and growled, 'I don't have a home. Don't you get that yet?' She turned around to talk to Todd, but the blob man was gone. 'Aww, Todd's gone.' She stuck out her lip like a drunk and very petulant toddler. 'Great Scott! Barry, Barry! We need to find Todd, dude, come on!'

Noel sighed and, sticking his hands underneath her on the stool, he hoisted her up and over his shoulder the best he could, even with her still waving and talking like a British Lord.

'Home James, and don't spare the horses!' She giggled, and hiccupped. 'Night, Barry, love!'

Bahram waved as congenially as he could, no doubt glad that Noel had arrived before she roped the other punters into a moonlight quest for Todd.

Noel slung her bag over his arm the best he could and stepped out of the pub into the crisp night air. 'You shouldn't just run off on your own like that, getting drunk and talking to random people.' He thought of Todd and felt his stomach flip with jealousy.

Summer, speaking from over his shoulder area somewhere, punched him in the bottom.

'Ow!' He staggered a few steps, his butt cheek stinging. 'What was that for?'

'Put me down!' Summer demanded. 'I didn't ask you to come find me, all caveman like, shaming me for having a bad day. Tell me, if I was a bloke, would you have just done what'cha did?'

He set her down on her own feet, gently holding her at her sides as she swayed and tried to focus.

'Well, no, but if you were a bloke, there is a lot of things I wouldn't have done with you.' He smirked, but it was lost on her, and he sagged. Summer, his Summer, the one that was happy and growing to love her life, was absent. Replaced by this rather inebriated, bitter version with daddy issues that he didn't fully understand.

'Summer, just tell me, okay: what can I do? I was worried, so I looked for you. I found you drunk, with some guy chatting you up. What do you want me to think? Are we together or not?'

'Not,' Summer mumbled. 'I think more not than together, don't you? I can't come to the shop any more, not with her there. You leave in January anyway, so it's just brought things forward really, that's all.' She looked at him, her expression blank.

'What?' Noel asked. 'What are you talking about? If it's about Avril, I won't employ her. I'll explain things to her. I don't want you to feel uncomfortable, but you have a sister, Summer. Aren't you at least a little happy about that? You like Avril!'

Summer pulled her handbag from his arm, pushing it onto her own shoulder after a half dozen flailing attempts. Noel's hands itched to help her, to hold her, but he held them at his sides instead, clenching them tight.

'I liked her as a Saturday girl, yeah sure! Not as a sister, and now I have another little baby linked to me too? I don't want brothers and sisters, Noel! I wanted a normal life, with both parents with me, not gone and batshit crazy!'

Noel went to go to her, but she started walking away.

'No, Noel, leave it please. Just leave it, okay? Have a nice life.' She turned and walked away, hailing a cab as she weaved slightly on the pavement in front of him.

'Summer, please wait!' He tried, but she thrust her hand back behind her, warning him not to follow her.

'Leave it Noel, go save the world! I'll be just friggin' fine.'

Noel watched her taxi drive away till she was out of sight, and then he turned and walked in the opposite direction. At this point, saving the world seemed a darn sight easier than staying and trying to convince his girlfriend to let him in, to trust him. To let him help.

15

DECEMBER

The month that Summer dreaded with every inch of her being was halfway over and she was already sick of the countless festive emails, texts, songs on the radio, happy people Christmas shopping on the high street. She hated it all and as the days passed, she found herself missing Noel more and more. Not that she would tell him that, or answer his texts, emails or funny Instagram pictures aimed at provoking a response from her on the subject of the red bearded guy.

Her mother was in therapy three times a week now with Jean's friend coming to the house, and last week, a breakthrough had occurred.

It was Sunday morning, and Summer had the day off from the shop. Before her father had turned up, she had spent it in the garden with Noel, working on getting it all finished for spring, and so she found herself sitting at the dining room table, looking out of the newly utilised patio doors, to the fence where a few weeks before, her and Noel had spent the best part of the day painting. It wasn't finished, and the last few Sundays she had spent in bed reading, or at the shop, doing the admin or just avoiding being at home for twenty-four hours with her mother. Therapy was working but it was also bringing up a lot of past issues for Angie, and sometimes, Summer found herself wanting to blurt out the story about Avril, and Ronnie, and Noel. Angie had been very curious about why Noel was suddenly never seen or talked about, but Summer had just been vague and mentioned work and being too busy to commit to a serious relationship. Every time Angie asked her, 'Seen Noel today?' was like a dart to the heart, because she *did* see Noel. She saw him everywhere, but she couldn't bring herself to speak to him. That night, when he had pulled her out of the pub, she was wasted. From the frantic texts she read from him that night, and the days after, she knew she had ended it in a drunken, emotional mood. She felt ashamed and guilty, the usual responses from a drunken night out when you don't have control but the drink demons in you do. She wanted to go to him, say sorry, ruffle his thick, black curls and tell him that she wanted him, needed him even, but she couldn't. What would be the point, for a month? All of her problems would still be there. He would still be leaving. The only difference would be the level of pain when he left. Ending it was a mistake, a knee jerk reaction, but she knew in her heart that if she went to him now, she wouldn't be able to let him go when the time came. And let him go she must.

She was sitting at the table, looking at the part finished fence, munching on her toast, when her mother came and sat down with a cup of coffee.

'I'm going to finish the fence today,' Summer declared to her. 'The junk has all gone, the grass is cut, everything's planted, we just need the fence done and the shed sorting and we're ready. We'll need some new garden furniture of course, but there's time for that yet.'

Her mother took a long, slow drink of her steaming hot coffee.

'Well, I actually wanted to go for a walk today. So, can that wait a while?'

Summer choked on the little piece of toast in her mouth, gasping a couple of times before coughing it out and shooting it across the table towards her mother. Angie pulled a face.

'Well, I wasn't quite expecting that reaction! Will you come or not?'

Summer wanted to jump from her chair and moon walk across the floor, but what she actually did was give her mother a slight nod and shrug. 'Sure, I'll come.'

It was freezing cold outside, but Angie's last coat purchase still fit her and they both bundled up in warm boots and sweaters, donning coats and the same nervous expressions. There was thankfully no ice, but the biting wind when they opened the front door told them that it was indeed winter. Angie went as white as the snowdrops along the front path as they opened the front door and looked outside. The street was thankfully quiet, most people preparing their roasts, getting ready to sit on the sofa in last night's PJs and watch their favourite soap omnibus. Sunday was a wonderful nothing day to many, a family day that encouraged them to chill out, forget about work and enjoy their time off. Angie looked as though she had been sentenced to the gallows.

Summer reached for her mother's glove-clad hand. 'You ready?' she asked, taking a step outside. Her mother didn't say anything, just looked at her and matched her step. Summer turned and locked the door with her free hand, and they gently, slowly, started to take a step down the path, like skittish brides heading down the aisle. One, together. Two, together. Angie's hand gripped hers tight, and she gave it a little encouraging squeeze.

'Keep going, Mum,' she said, and they kept walking, one step at a time towards the gate.

* * *

Ronnie was used to the women in his life giving him grief, but his daughter Avril had the capacity to finish him off for good. Since that day in the shop, she had been a full-on, pink, sparkly nightmare. He gripped his steering wheel tight, telling himself that she would soon get over it. The same nonsense he had been trying to convince himself of for the last few weeks.

'Are you listening Dad? It's so stupid! Mum doesn't mind, she's already said, so why not? Why even tell me I had a sister if I wasn't ever going to see her?'

'Avril, for God's sake love, give it a rest, will ya!' He pulled into the car park, slamming his little van into a space. 'We've come to get your brother's nappies. Can you just stop it about the job? If there's something you want, you can work with me, get some cash. I don't know why you needed that job anyway.'

Avril tutted loudly. 'Err, duh, my sister? A Christmas shop? Independence? That enough for ya?'

Ronnie sighed, turning the key and killing the engine. 'Av, we can't keep talking about this. I promised Summer's mum that I wouldn't bother her, so that means you too. You saw how she reacted. She doesn't want to know us.'

Avril banged her fist on the dashboard, startling Ronnie.

'Hey!' He scolded. 'Pack that in, now. I know you're mad, but it's better this way. Believe me.' He sagged down in his seat, looking out of the window at the sea front, where the water was sparkling with the little bit of sunlight shining through the gloom.

'Well, I *am* mad. If Mum took me and Billy away, would you leave us too?'

Ronnie turned to his daughter, the shock of her words hitting home. 'Do you think I'd do that?' He looked straight into the scrunched-up face of his middle child, and was once again struck by how much she was like Summer. Seeing her again that day, all grown up, running her own business, it had half killed him. She hated him, and he didn't blame her. He regretted so much, and now his other daughter was looking at him in just the same way. Mistrusting, angry. The look of adoration that she had once had, which Summer had once had, was gone. Would it happen to baby Billy too, once he was old enough to know the truth? Would his little gurgles and coos turn to accusations and the look of a disappointed child?

'Avril, I love you and Billy so much. I love Summer too, and I know you might not believe that, but I do. Her mother and I, we were great, but sometimes, people change. I don't know what it was really, but I just set eyes on your mother and that was that.'

Avril folded her legs up, slinging her dirty trainers up on the dashboard. Normally, he would have told her off, but he didn't dare today.

'Well, it's rubbish. All you and Mum talk about is Billy, and I get bored with all the bouncing baby boy stuff. I got 97 per cent on my exam the other day at school, and Billy farted and laughed at himself. Guess which got more attention?'

Ronnie laughed a little, but it turned to ashes of death in his throat with one glare from his offspring. Wow, she really did remind him of Summer.

'I'm not kidding! Mum did a whole Facebook post on it and put nothing about my exam! What should I do? Pass wind to get a bit of praise? Please. I know why Summer's so mad now; you get a new kid and the other ones just aren't important any more.'

Ronnie got out of the car, slamming his door and heading to the shops. He heard Avril's door slamming shut behind him, but he kept walking. He needed a minute. Amazing how someone you love can say the worst things, the very thing that cuts your feet out from under you. He kept walking, pulling out his list of items that his wife Holly had asked for. He was just about to turn to see if Avril was still there, skulking and scowling behind him, when he heard a voice he never thought he would hear again.

On the corner, looking pale and a little frail, was Angie. 'Ron?'

He stopped and watched as she came walking over to him, slowly, so very slowly. He could feel Avril come and stand beside him, and he was grateful that she hadn't completely abandoned him. Of course, people used to attend public hangings as a bit of a day out with the fam, so the jury was still out.

'Hi Angie, Summer,' he said softly. Summer looked as horrified as he felt and seemed to be holding Angie up. 'How are you?'

Angie took a step forward and punched him. Full pelt, clenched fist, right in the face. He felt his nose crumple, saw the spray of blood erupt from his face onto the pavement, heard the collective gasps of his daughters as Angie stood over him, pointing.

'How am I! Ronnie Hastings, I hate you! You took my life, and I let you!' She let out a scream like a banshee, and dived straight on him, her fists windmilling into his body.

'Mum!' Summer shouted, pulling her mother off her father. 'Stop!'

'No!' Angie screamed, her face contorted with the force of her fury. 'My therapist told me that getting angry is good!' She almost had a smile on her face as she ground her knee into his private parts, making him scream too.

'Dad, say sorry!' Avril shouted, all the time trying to pull her father out from underneath an irate Angie. 'Just say sorry to them!'

'I'm sorry!' Ronnie shouted meekly. 'I'm really sorry!'

'Mum, stop it! Get off!'

'Sorry, are you? Sorry? I'll give you sorry, you waste of skin. You ruined my life!!'

'Mum!'

'Dad!'

'Get her off him!' Avril shouted at Summer, aware of the small crowd gathering around them now. 'Summer!'

'What?' Summer growled. 'He deserves this anyway! He *did* ruin her life, and mine!' She tried to yank her mother off her father again, but she was glued to him. 'I actually hate him too!' After a minute, she gave him a little kick too. 'And that made me feel a little better.'

Avril was furious. 'Kicking a man while he's down – nice work, sister!' She jeered at her, pulling her tongue out. Summer rolled her eyes.

'I'm not your sister, and you have a bloody perfect life, so just shut up!'

'Make me!' Avril shouted, slapping her sister in the face. Summer reared back, dropping the hold on her mother, who just kept trying to murder her dad on the kerb.

'You little witch! You hit me!'

Avril started to cry. 'I know, I'm so sorry! I just wanted to meet you, and now look at us.' She broke into a full-on teenage wail, and Summer stopped feeling angry. Reaching towards each other, the two sisters hugged each other, both crying and telling each other how sorry they were.

'Dad told me where you worked, and I knew I shouldn't, but I just wanted to see you.' Still hugging her sister, Summer turned to look at her parents, who were now both laying on the floor, spent and bleeding.

'You knew where I worked?' she asked her father, and he nodded. One look at her mother, and she knew he was telling her the truth. 'Mum, what's going on?'

* * *

Half an hour later, they were all sitting in Angie's front room. Angie had run off into the kitchen as soon as Ronnie had driven them home, and she hadn't said a word since her outburst. Summer and Avril had both sat in the back seat, feeling very much like the quiet children in the back of the car, aware that their parents were in a fight. Avril had nudged her at one point, and Summer had reached for her hand, holding it in her lap. She'd been so angry but when they were both there, pulling apart their parents, seeing Avril cry had made her wake up. It was happening again. Another little girl feeling lonely and upset because of the car crash that was Angie and Ronnie's marriage. She thought of how Avril had her own family, yet she had still wanted to seek her out, to know her. Would she have done the same, had she known? A few months ago, she would have laughed at the very notion. Now though, after Noel, she wasn't so sure.

'What's your mum's name?' Summer asked now, sitting across from her father and Avril in one of the armchairs.

'Holly,' Avril said with a smile. 'And my brother is called Billy. William really, but that's not very cool for a baby. Baby Billy sounds well better.'

'Holly?' Summer checked, thinking how ironic that she had a festive name. 'Really?'

'Yeah,' Avril laughed. 'Holly and Noel, eh! So Christmassy!' She looked at Summer's flinching face and her smile dropped. 'Sorry, I forgot.'

Ronnie looked at the floor, and the awkward silence descended upon the room again.

'Tea,' Angie announced, bringing through a tray with a teapot, mugs, sugar, a jug of milk and a small pack of ginger biscuits. 'Biscuit, anyone?'

'I hate ginger biscuits,' Ronnie grumbled, holding the ice pack wrapped in a tea towel against his nose.

'I know,' Angie said brightly. 'Always have them in.'

He tried and failed to give her a funny look, her returning look being enough to freeze him solid on the spot.

'So,' Avril spoke next, her mouth half full of ginger biscuit. 'You've been out then? That's good.'

Angie and Summer, both looking like little socially awkward bookends now in the matching armchairs, looked at each other in horror.

'I'm a kid, but I'm not daft either; I know you don't go out of the house. Are you getting better now?'

Summer opened her mouth to shut her sister down, but Angie beat her to it. 'Yes, actually I think I am feeling a little better. Punching your father helped a lot.'

Ronnie spluttered. 'Aye, well it didn't help me. I think my nose is broken!'

'Oh, shut up,' Angie spat back. 'You broke your nose when you were seventeen doing back-alley fights. Don't try and reinvent the wheel, Ron; don't forget I know you. You broke my heart, so a bloody wonky nostril is the least you can expect.'

Ronnie looked panicked at the thought of no longer having symmetrical nasal features. Summer turned to Avril, desperate to get this over with, stop the tension.

'So, your mum's Holly, and you have baby Billy. Where do you live?'

'Here,' she said simply. 'In Brid, the other end like, but not too far. Have you always lived in this house?'

'Yep,' Summer poured herself a cup of tea, needing something to do with her hands at least to stop her from wringing them together. 'Always. Tea?'

'Please, two sugars.' Avril leaned forward. 'Are they going to talk, or not?' she whispered. Summer shrugged, handing her a brew and standing with hers. 'Do you want to see the garden that we've... I've been doing?'

Avril was on her feet in a flash, beating Summer to the patio doors.

'Yep, won't be long Dad!'

The two sisters grabbed their coats and headed out into the garden, sliding the doors closed behind them. The living room fell quiet, the ticking of a distant clock somewhere the only indication of life.

'So, you finally got your boy then?' Angie snipped. 'Bet that made your day.'

'Stop Angie, just stop.' Ronnie gingerly pulled away the ice pack and was relieved to see that the bleeding had slowed down to a tiny drip. 'This martyr routine is getting rather old, don't you think?'

'Huh!' Angie folded her arms in disgust. 'Martyr, am I? Really!'

'Yes, you are a bit. I never once said anything but how sorry I was. I fell in love Ang; I just fell in love. I couldn't help it, and you must admit, we weren't right for each other. Not really. I was too messy, too loud for you most of the time.'

Angie shook her head. 'I don't remember it like that. I remember being the main breadwinner, looking after the house and Summer, and you doing what you could, but we were happy. Till you messed it up. I've got nothing now Ron, nothing.'

She half expected Ron to apologise; she could almost taste how she would feel when his words washed over her. What she had really wanted for ages. Him to admit how much he messed up.

'Do you know what, Angie?' He poured himself a mug of tea and added too much sugar. Angie's teeth hurt just watching him. 'I'm not the baddie in this story. I fell in love, I cocked up, sure. I hurt you and Summer, but you know as well as I do that I didn't leave. You pushed me out. I tried for months to speak to you, but you pushed me out with your threats, the school phoning me telling me I was banned from the premises, missing my daughter's parents evenings, the lot. I chipped in with bills, I offered more help. I even offered to help with Summer's college, or university, whatever she wanted. I could have helped her with her business, but oh no, you would rather her, and everybody else in this godforsaken place, think that I am the one with a scarlet A on my forehead. I cheated on you, yes. I got another woman pregnant, and when that baby came, I left. I had to. I was trying to do my best.'

Angie was clenching and unclenching her fists, her face going through a rainbow of indignant expressions. 'I had everything, and you tanked it! Don't you get it? I had a reputation around here. I loved my job, my life. Do you realise what it's like to be the jilted woman?'

'Holly was spat on by one of your little buddies, do you know that? They spat on her in the street for being a tramp when she had Avril right there in the pram with her. Do you think that's right, do you? They did nothing wrong. I lied to everyone, in the beginning. I only came clean when she was pregnant, and by then I was in love with her anyway. I have two innocent kids at home, Ang. Can you say you did your best by Summer? People talk. I know you're a recluse. Do you think it's right, you checking out of life and leaving Summer on her own? I could have been there, but oh no, you threatened to ruin me, and my family. What could I do?'

'Tramp is right,' she muttered. 'Holly Atkinson was always a bitch if you ask me.'

'Well I didn't, and she only has nice things to say about you, despite the fact that you kept my daughter from me. Well, no more, Angie; you're done with all that. I always told Avril about her big sister, and wouldn't you know it, she's bloody braver than me! She had the balls to come and find her, to get to know her, and I am bloody proud of her. Summer is my family too, so get used to it. If Summer wants to know me, I am here.'

'I do want to know you,' a voice said from behind him. Summer was in the dining area, Avril in tow. 'I do, but it will take a bit of time.'

Ronnie nodded, smiling. 'I'll wait forever, Summer; just let me know when you're ready.' He delved into his jacket pocket and dug out a business card. 'I work here, and our house is next door. Up to you, love.'

Summer stepped forward and took the card.

'Come on Dad, I think we'd better go. Billy needs nappies, remember?'

Ronnie nodded, not taking his eyes off his eldest. 'Okay. You look good, Summer. You turned into a very beautiful woman. I know it's not down to me, but I am very proud of you.'

Summer didn't answer; she had all her focus on trying to keep her tears in. She couldn't have spoken if she had tried, and his rant at her mother was still rattling around in her head on repeat.

'Bye, sis,' Avril gave her a squeeze. 'Do me a favour: speak to Noel, okay? I want my job back, and you need him. He makes you a bit nicer to be around.'

Summer laughed, hugging her sister as a stream of silent tears fell down her face. 'You're so annoying, slug,' she whispered into her ear. 'Love you Av.'

Avril squeezed her tighter. 'Love you too, Mrs Grinch.'

Ronnie and Avril headed out, and Summer closed the door behind them, sagging behind it and running her fingers over and over the embossed business card her dad had given her. *My dad. My dad. My dad wants to be my dad. I have a sister, and a baby brother, and a stepmother. I have family.* She couldn't wait to tell Noel. *Oh. Noel.*

Her heart sank again, and she headed back into the living room, pushing the card into her skirt pocket.

'That man will never set foot in this house ever again,' Angie spat from the sofa. 'I mean it; he is dead to us.'

Summer looked at her mother, sat folded up on the sofa, her arms under the backs of her legs, her whole body rocking gently to try to take back some control from the demons that were swirling around her, unseen. She wasn't the bright and shiny woman of yesterday, and at that moment, Summer realised something. She never would be again. That woman was gone. What was left was broken, beaten down, and they were both lying to themselves.

'Mum,' she said, sitting down on the sofa next to her. 'You kept my dad from me, can't you see? I had a sister, and now a brother, and you left me on my own, thinking I wasn't enough, that we weren't enough. Why didn't you just tell me the truth? Why did no-one tell me the truth?'

Angie didn't answer her; she just kept rocking, shaking her head and whispering to herself. Summer took her mother in her arms and held her.

'Mum, whatever happens, you're still my wonderful mother. That will never change, okay? This has to stop. It all just has to stop.' She laid her mother down on the sofa and went to call Jean.

They needed the therapist there, to try to help Angie come to terms with today, and how things were going to change.

16

Christmas Eve, and Summer was at the shop, setting out a mass email schedule for Boxing Day. Boxing Day was when the Christmas revellers would wake up, full of cheese, booze, fat and regret, and want to grab a bargain or a cheap break to escape the dull, grey January. Or have something to look forward to while they pounded the discount gym membership to get the beach bod on the go.

Jean had called in with Jim and the children and Summer had never seen her as happy. Who knew, a nipple cake and a need for a cuppa had led to two lonely and sad people finding each other, and being happy together. Jim couldn't stop looking at Jean, and she couldn't resist an opportunity to touch him, whether it was a piece of lint on his sleeve, or a peck on the cheek. The children were doing well, settling in to their new home with Granddad and the kind lady with the mean cat next door. Kyle and Alex were typical boys, running their cars along the carpeting, Isobel still a little shell shocked around strangers, Bradley Bear tucked tight in her arms. Summer went into her cupboard and brought out three wrapped up presents: a mixture of chocolate, books and pencils and crayons for them all. She'd even bought baby Billy a few little bits, not being able to resist once she started buying.

'Here you go, kids: the elves left these here for you because I begged them to let me play Santa, just this once!'

The kids all ran to her, taking the presents and whooping and shrieking at each other.

'What do you say?' Granddad Jim prompted happily, his eyes filled with love for his young charges. It wasn't easy, but with support and counselling for the children, things were looking brighter. They'd been to lay flowers for their mother and were all booked in next door to see Santa. Noel had hired a guy and was offering a chat with Santa cheaper than the competitors around, doing it for the joy and not the profit. Needless to say, the shop had been swamped every day, and he had been kept gratefully busy. Well, Summer was grateful, because she was terrified about seeing him again. She knew Avril had gone back there on weekend – they had kept in touch – but Summer had begged her not to tell him anything.

'Thank ooo!' Isobel said from behind Bradley Bear. The boys snatched theirs up, throwing their arms around Summer and then running away like little squirrels to shake the boxes and discuss the possible contents.

'So,' Jean said, her eyes narrowing as she focused on her friend. Jim faded away, taking the kids out of the shop and round to Forever Festive. 'That's a Granddad moment, Santa. I have time for a cuppa. My friend said that the therapy is still going, though she obviously won't tell me more. How's your mother, after everything?'

Summer went to flick the kettle on, and they both leaned against the counter top, waiting for the water to boil.

'She's okay. She has her bad days, but she's doing things, you know. She had some homework, she had to write to some old friends and post the letters. Tell them what she could bear to tell and explain why she checked out of the world. Now, every day she goes to the gate and gets the post. Yesterday, she baked some buns and took some in a box for the postman. She actually talked to him and got the post straight from him.'

Jean smiled and nodded encouragingly. 'Good, I'm glad. What about your dad?'

Summer spooned coffee into each of their favourite mugs, getting the milk out of the fridge and adding sweetener for them both. She couldn't help but smile as she thought of her dad running his little junk shop at the other side of town. She had been to visit him a few times, and he had even turned up with lunch for both her and Avril on Saturdays, bringing baby Billy with him. The baby was a little mini me of him, and had Avril's laugh, and she loved him so.

'Billy's so cute,' she fawned to Jean. 'I never thought I would love a brother, but I do. He's adorable. Holly's lovely too, although things were a bit awkward at first.'

Truth was, the first time she had summoned up the courage to take Ronnie up on a tea invitation, Holly had answered the door and dissolved into fits of tears.

'She felt so bad that they hadn't tried to see me more, or help with Mum, but they didn't know how bad it was, and Mum didn't even let them try, to be fair. She still hates him with a passion, but she likes Avril.'

Avril had been round a few times now, mostly after school when Summer was still at work. The cheeky bugger had started inviting herself for tea, but Summer was thrilled when she found her mother baking a Victoria Sandwich, in preparation for her coming.

'They keep each other company, truth be told. My mum is teaching her how to sew. They don't talk about family stuff of course, but still, it's good.'

Jean was in awe. 'That's all great, Summer, but what about you?'

The kettle clicked off, and she poured the hot water into the mugs. 'What about me? I told you, things are getting better. Dad even gave me a box full of Christmas cards, birthday cards. He kept them all for me over the years. Mum sent back what he posted to me so he kept them all. It's a bit weird, but it's a bit of therapy for me too. I get it now, more than I did.'

Jean was still not appeased. 'That's all nice, Summer, but again, what about you? Angie is getting help, you have your dad, the truth is out, but what has changed for you, really?'

Summer passed her the mug and smugly opened her mouth to tell her dear friend and work colleague all the ways in which her life had changed for the better, and how happy she was.

'I'm miserable,' she uttered. *What? No, you're not!* 'I didn't mean to say that. I am happy. I just...'

'You miss Noel, and you want to have your own life.' Jean took a sip of her coffee, the steam rising and fogging up the glasses that sat on her forehead. 'You are allowed, Summer, to have what you want.' She thought of her and Jim, and the partners and children they had loved and lost. 'Life is bloody short, and brutal. What makes any of us get up in the morning is the chance of happiness, of love, of living our lives how we want to. You're still young; you need to fight for what you want now.'

She heard the shrieks of laughter coming through the joint wall and tipped her head in that direction.

'Hear that? Happiness. Those kids have had the worst year of their lives, yet here they are, laughing with Santa, happy and excited. It's the stuff of life, Summer, embrace it.'

Summer hugged her friend, careful not to spill their drinks. 'I do love you, Jean. Thanks so much for being the mum I didn't have.'

Jean took a long moment to reply, and when she did, it was a strangled little whisper. 'I couldn't be more proud, or love you any more, if you were my own daughter. Fight for him, love. Take a chance.'

The door burst open, and in ran the boys, followed by Jim and little Isobel. The little lad's faces dropped when they saw the two women, sobbing and holding each other tight.

Kyle, the more confident of the two, came and threw his arms around them both, around their legs. 'Don't cry! Santa will bring you a present too.'

Alex nudged him, covering his mouth with his hands. 'Only if they've been really good!' he corrected.

When the boys had finally started to come down from their sugar high, and Isobel was falling asleep in Jim's arms, they all went home to have hot chocolate and read stories in their PJs, ready for Santa in the morning. Summer could have closed today, but in truth, she wanted to see the people next door coming in and out, happy about the holiday, buying last-minute gifts. She had even sold a couple of day trips and a fair few Paris trips, mostly to harassed-looking men racing round the shops with wrapping paper, screaming things at each other like, 'What the hell is a bath bomb?' and, 'Who is Jo Malone when she's at home, and why does she charge forty pounds for a bit of smelly wax?'

She didn't shudder at the mere thought of Christmas, which was a first. Holly and Jean had both extended invites for Christmas dinner, but the thought of leaving her mother at home to spend the day with her father and his family didn't sit right with her, and she wanted the children to have their first Christmas in their new home and not have any strangers there who might not be the best company. Her mother was going to do a little Christmas dinner, and she found herself looking forward to the day. She'd bought her mother a new patio set for Christmas, with a stack of new paperbacks to read in the garden, so she couldn't wait to see her face.

It was nearly five when the door went.

'I got it! I hope it fits now!' Avril came dashing through the door, a clothes bag hanging over one shoulder, a shoe box in the other. 'They didn't have many left.' She handed her sister a wad of notes. 'Dad's outside. I need to get back, he paid, and he says not to argue, and good luck.'

She had opened her mouth to do just that but smiled and stopped herself. Her dad wanted to help, so she should let him. She took the bag and box from her sister and gave her a squeeze. 'Thanks, Av. You got your gifts, right?'

Avril nodded. 'Yep, Jim dropped them off a while ago. Sure you won't come tomorrow?'

Summer shook her head. 'Not this year. Maybe next, you never know.'

Avril nodded. 'Softly softly, catchy monkey—'

'As Dad says!' They said in unison, giving each other another hug.

'Bugger off now, I have to get changed.' Summer gave her a gentle shove, pushing a little box into her hand. 'This is for you too.'

Avril gasped, looking at the box. 'A nose ring. You didn't!'

'No, I didn't!' she laughed. 'Ronnie would never let that happen and you know it.'

Avril pouted and opened the box. On the black velvet, a little silver chain sat with a half heart on a pendant. It read, *Sisters*.

'Wow,' Avril exclaimed, taking it out of the box and giving it to Summer to put on for her. 'I love it, but where's the other half?'

Summer lifted up the collar of her blouse and showed Avril the other half that read, *Together*. 'Just a little something, from me to you,' Summer said breezily, putting the necklace around her sister's neck and clicking closed the clasp. 'Something to strangle you with when you're a pain.'

Avril went to poke her, but missed, Summer dodging it and

jabbing her back. 'Go on now, give our brother a kiss from me, okay?'

Avril picked up the box and headed for the door. 'Okay, but I want photos, and details, okay? WhatsApp me later!'

Summer waved her off, the bubbling tension in her stomach rising as she eyed the bag and shoe box. 'Right,' she said to the empty shop as she flicked the sign to closed, 'time to go.'

* * *

Noel had been run ragged over the past few weeks with his Santa's grotto sessions. He had Avril back, which was great, but he hadn't seen Summer beyond the odd glance through the window or passing each other on the beach before work. She never spoke to him or acknowledged his presence but he knew she was aware of him. He was aware of her all day long. He saw her face in his bed at the B&B, her hair ruffled, lips bruised from him kissing her, touching her. He thought of her at work, just through the wall, smiling at customers, chatting to them as she played with her hair in that little way she had. The way she nibbled her pen tops and her bottom lip when she was concentrating, or stressed. The way she felt in his arms, and the look she gave him on the last day they were together. Ronnie was in her life, he knew that they had been seeing each other, and it made him glad, but why was she keeping away from him? He knew she had a lot on, and he was leaving, but he couldn't believe that they had ended. Not like that, especially.

He was due to drive up to his Mum's after work, to spend Christmas with his family. His mum was delighted and judging from the social media videos and pictures the people back home had been posting, she'd gone all out, which meant that her house would be like Lapland and Disney all rolled into one. He just had to lock up and be on his way. He had a little stop to make first.

The shop bell went, and he groaned from the back. He'd forgotten to lock the door.

'Sorry,' he called out, walking through to the main shop floor. 'I'm closed actually, but if you need something I can—'

'Hi.'

'Hi,' Noel replied. 'Can I help you?'

The person walked forward awkwardly, and Noel glanced down at her feet. 'Wow, nice er... feet.'

The feet wiggled from side to side. 'Thanks. I've actually come because I have been called a few things lately, and I thought I would come to an expert for some help.'

Noel's lip twitched, but he took a few steps closer. 'Really? What exactly is the problem?'

'Well,' Summer said, her face painted bright green, her whole body encased in a rather fluffy Grinch costume, complete with huge, long, green feet. 'I've been called a Grinch, and told I have no Christmas spirit.'

Noel nodded his head, rubbing his fingers down his chin in deep consideration. 'Well, that is terrible. Have you seen a doctor?'

The Grinch nodded, taking another two steps closer, so close that her 'toes' brushed against his trainers. 'I have, and he said it's because I met someone lovely, and kind, and I broke him, and pushed him away.'

'And got him attacked by a waffle-stealing rodent with wings,' he added, his lips pursing at the memory.

'And that, and a few other things that I really regret.' She looked at him, taking him in. He looked a little thinner, a little more tired than usual.

'You regret them, but it doesn't change much, does it? I'm still leaving, Summer, you still don't really trust me.'

'I know. I'm not perfect, I know that. I've been awful to you. My life is complicated, I know, and that's not your life.'

'It was never about that, Summer! None of that was your fault.'

'Do you miss me?' she blurted, suddenly finding herself hopeful that he was pining for her like she was for him. 'At all? Or am I too late? Do you want to try again?'

He looked at her for a long moment, and then turned and walked into the back, leaving her standing there, all in green, her face paint melting with her nerves.

She stood there awhile, feeling bereft. She'd tried, finally, but it was too late. Here she was, standing in a Christmas costume, in a festive shop, on Christmas Eve, getting pied by the only man she had ever had feelings for. If she didn't need therapy before, this would be her cue to start. She started to turn to leave, at the last minute placing a tiny box tied with ribbon on the counter.

'I do want to try again.'

She turned around and he was striding over to her, a present in his arms. 'I just wanted to get this. It's for you.'

She took the present but didn't open it. 'You really do want to try again?'

He grinned. 'Summer, I never wanted to stop, but after our fight, I replied to the charity I worked for. I took the job. I leave on the fifteenth. I've given Mrs Simpson notice.'

Summer's heart stopped for a beat or two, clunking, slowing and then pounding back into action. 'So, we have nearly three weeks. We'll just have to make the most of it.'

Noel came closer and pulled her fluffy body closer. 'Deal,' he beamed, pulling her in for a deep kiss. When they finally came up for air, he had a green tinge around his lips, making her laugh.

'You've been Grinched,' she quipped, rubbing it off with her gloved hand.

'I certainly have,' he replied goofily. 'Worth it too. I missed you. Open your present?'

She remembered the little box and ran over to grab it. 'I got you one too. It's just something silly.'

She handed it to him, and he walked her over to the armchair and fireplace, sitting her down in the chair so she was sandwiched in with him, half on his lap. He couldn't resist grabbing her and kissing her again, and this time when they pulled apart, they held each other tight.

'You look a bit tired.' She took her gloves off and ran her fingers along his face, smoothing his eye bags. 'You've lost weight too.'

He dropped a kiss on her green nose. 'What can I say? I *really* missed you.'

She looked into his big, brown eyes and vowed never to hurt him again. She would treat him like a rare butterfly. She would love him and look after him, and when it was time to go, she would let him fly away to make some other corner of the world kinder, more beautiful.

'No more. Shall we open on three?'

They both counted to two and then ripped into their parcels, each loudly declaring the other a cheat. Noel opened his little box, and nestled on a bed of shredded paper was a perfectly smooth stone from the beach, in the shape of a heart.

'I told you it was daft,' she said sheepishly. 'I've had it a while. I saw it on our beach one morning and I thought of you.'

'I love it,' he said, genuinely. Their beach. They really were more alike than she thought. 'Open yours.'

Hers was somewhat larger: a shiny gift box under the wrapping paper. Opening the lid, she pulled out a huge jar with an airtight, sealable lid. In the bottom was a layer of sand.

'It's from our beach. It's so you can collect the sands of all the beaches in the world you'll visit one day.'

She looked at the jar, turning it over and over in her hands.

'It's stupid, isn't it?' He mumbled, mistaking her silence for disappointment. 'It was just something small, that's all.'

'I love it,' she said, kissing away his doubts. 'It's wonderful. You'll have to send me some from your travels too.' She kissed him again, and he pushed away the feeling of dread he felt at leaving her. They had three weeks, almost. It was enough. It had to be.

17

Angie was just starting the day when there was a knock at the door. She sighed, eager to get some breakfast and sit and read the paper. The paper that was now delivered to her doorstep every morning by a paperboy kid from the estate. Cute little thing he was, on his bike. She'd ignored him for years, but the day before, she had left a box of buns out with a note thanking him for being so nice. It was the kind of thing that 'old Angie' would have done, but in therapy, they were sifting through 'old Angie' and trying to recognise what behaviours were healthy, and which weren't. Baking buns for the paperboy was a good behaviour, so that was her homework. Maybe it was him, knocking to say thanks. Or Summer, maybe she had forgotten something. It was the day that Noel left the country, so she hadn't been home for many nights since Christmas.

Opening the door, Avril was standing there.

'Er, Avril? Why aren't you at school?'

Avril was standing there in her uniform, a large envelope in her hand. 'It's okay, my parents know. I've come to see you, actually. We need to talk, now.' She came bundling into the house, heading upstairs to Summer's room.

Angie, still clad in her dressing gown, was taken aback to say the least. 'About what? What's wrong?' She followed Avril into the bedroom, where she found her dragging a suitcase out from under the bed. Opening it, Angie was shocked to see it was half packed, clothes and bikinis there with the labels all still on.

'What's all this?'

Avril thrust the envelope at her. 'Read that, and then help me, okay? We need to get to the airport.'

Angie's eyes bulged, and she half fell onto the suitcase.

'Angie, Angie, come on, pull it together, okay? I have a lift, but we still need to move.'

Angie looked again into the case and pulled out a little red booklet. 'Her passport,' she said numbly. 'She's had her own passport all this time.'

Avril gave her a little hug, taking the passport and checking the dates. 'Phew, I thought it would be ready, but I just needed to check.' She looked at Angie, who was sitting there flapping her mouth like a fish out of water as she slowly read the contents of the envelope. 'Do you understand?' Avril pressed, in between running to the bathroom to grab toiletries and throwing random bits of underwear into the case.

She put everything back into the envelope and nodded slowly. 'I get it. Okay, what's the plan?'

Avril looked at her, a devilish grin on her face that made Angie think of her own daughter. 'Well, you might need a vodka or two, but hang in there.'

* * *

The last three weeks had been amazing. They'd spent every waking minute that they could together. Boxing Day at his mum's house, when Noel missed her so much on Christmas Day that he drove his mum's car to come back and kidnap her. New Year's Eve early bird at their little restaurant just the two of them, the three of them all ringing in the New Year wrapped in blankets, drinking champagne in mugs in the garden. Angie loved her patio furniture, and loved to sit out, even in the freezing cold. Day by day, she was growing. Setbacks still happened, and some days the black dog still grabbed her by the throat, but she was healing, a little. Ronnie and Angie had even spoken, when they had to, sure, but it fell short of GBH, which was always a step forward.

They'd had nights at the B&B, and stolen nights when Noel had shimmied up the drainpipe to her bedroom, careful not to wake Angie. They'd christened both shops, and Summer's cupboard (that one didn't go too well, what with Jean walking in on them and complaining about the naked bottom prints on the furniture). They'd collected sand from beaches along the coastline and had searched every one for another heart pebble. They'd seen baby Billy, and Jean and Jim playing with the kids in Jim's big, happy house. They'd crammed a lifetime of firsts into those few months. First kiss, first fight. First breakfast in bed. First time she realised that she loved him so much that she would never be the same when he left.

Today, all that screamed in Summer's head was all the lasts. This morning, they had woken up at the B&B together for the last time. The last time she would wake in his arms, his legs wrapped around hers, as though his body was trying to absorb hers into his so they could be together. Last breakfast. Last walk on the beach. Last, last, last. She wanted to stop them all, to stop him, to stop the world. Why, when she finally had all she wanted, all she had longed for, why did she have to lose it? Why did others get their happy ending and not her? She wanted to scream, to have a tantrum. In this moment, she understood her mother more than ever. The way she felt now, walking into the airport with Noel's fingers wrapped around hers, with his warm body pressed against hers. She got it. After he left, she could happily go to sleep forever, hide from the world, check out from caring, from trying. None of it seemed to matter. Who would she tell it to, if she had a good day at work? He was the voice in her head and she was losing him.

They came to a stop, and he said nothing, lost in his own thoughts of happy endings and bad timing. The weight of unsaid things hung in the air between them like a thick curtain, separating them from each other.

This is it. He's leaving. This is it. Say it. Say something.

It went around and around in her head, circles of inner monologue swirling around in her brain. She felt like she was going to pass out, but she stood there, a happy smile plastered across her face, all set to wave him off with a cheerful hug.

They held hands in silence, his backpack on his shoulders, thumb stroking hers in lazy circles as he always did. *I will miss that thumb*, she thought to herself and almost sobbed at the mere thought of his thumb, and his hands, being thousands of miles away from her, helping people, building things, whilst she went back to her work, her life. A single tear fell down her cheek, and she brushed it away quickly with her other hand. She wasn't going to fall apart here; she would wait till she got back home. Jim was waiting in his car for her and she knew she had to hang on till she was firmly back into her old life, her old room, now full of memories, to fall apart. She would sob on the bed that smelled of him now. Until the smell faded, then she would be alone again.

'I think it's my check in time now,' he said softly, turning to face her. 'I'd better go.' He was looking down at her with a look that broke her already fragile heart that bit further. His eyes were bloodshot, and he looked tired from their late night. His hair even looked less springy than usual, and she reached up and ran her fingers through it.

'You look tired,' she ran her fingers down the sides of his face, down his chin and brushed her fingers along his luscious lips. He kissed them.

'It was worth it. Summer, I...'

She shushed him with her fingers, and then replaced them with her lips. He grabbed her and pulled her into his arms, lifting her up.

'Don't say anything,' she whispered against his mouth.

'But, I have to, I...'

She kissed him again, till he pulled away, looking deep into her eyes.

'Summer—'

'I think I might know what you're going to say,' she uttered quietly, 'unless you are saying thanks, and bye forever.' Her face dropped a little. 'You're not, are you?' She pretended to punch him, poking him in the ribs, making him laugh.

'No, I'm not saying that. Never that, Summer.'

'Then I know what you are going to say, and I can't bear it, Noel. Please, don't. Not now.' He searched her face, and she looked up at him, memorising his features to save in her head forever.

'Summer, I don't want to not say this. I don't want to walk away from you and regret one second of our time together. So far,' he added. 'Because I am not letting you go easy.' He drew her closer. 'I love you, Summer Hastings. I have done since the first moment you bounded into my life with your kung-fu, tree-kicking ways.'

She laughed. 'You did not, you thought I was annoying.'

'Annoyingly lovely, and I did. I love you so much, Summer.'

She started to cry then, and he brushed her tears away with his thumbs. 'I told you before,' she whispered, her voice cracking. 'You are far too positive. Especially when you are being Mr Full-On Christmas.'

He smiled sadly and kissed her again. They could hear a slight commotion behind them, but they didn't break away. Neither of them could break away first. The whole airport could fall down around them, and they would still keep kissing. They knew, once this embrace ended, he would be leaving. The devastation could wait one more minute. She needed the minute. She needed to keep her mouth busy kissing the man she loved, before she slipped up and said it back.

'Summer!'

'Noel!'

'Summer Hastings!'

They kept kissing, oblivious till they heard it. A voice, familiar, loud and alien in this environment.

'Summer!'

They both turned and looked at the airport doors. Running through them, screaming at the pair, was Avril, holding hands with Angie. Avril was more dragging Angie, who looked very pale and sweaty, but both pairs of eyes were focused on them. Just behind them, dragging a suitcase, was Ronnie.

'Mum! Dad!' Summer dashed to her. 'What...? Er... how the hell? Why? What's wrong? Not the baby?'

Ronnie came to a panting stop, and Angie took the suitcase from him, gripping it tight as she leaned on it.

'Thank you, Ronnie,' she said, as cordially as she could muster, her eyes darting around the huge space. 'For the lift too.'

Ronnie mumbled something about it being okay, and Summer and Noel looked agog at the pair.

Avril threw her arms around Noel, rolling her eyes at them both. 'These two are like wooden puppets when they get together. Thank God you haven't gone yet!' She nudged an ashen Angie, who jerked at the movement, looking around her as though she had just landed on a new planet. 'See, I told you we'd make it!'

Summer wrapped her arms around her mother. 'Are you okay? What are you doing here?'

Avril took her backpack off her shoulders, and Summer noticed it wasn't her usual pink, sparkly affair. Her little sister thrust it into her arms, Angie thrusting the case forward as best she could in shaky hands. Ronnie, after deliberating for an age, held out his arm for her to lean on. Angie eyed it suspiciously for what seemed like another age, before reluctantly slipping her arm through his.

'Here, I packed what I could find. We can send the rest on.'

Summer looked at Noel, who looked just as confused as she did. 'What the hell are you talking about?'

Angie stepped forward and pushed something into her hands. 'Love, it's time for you to start your life. I made some mistakes—'

'We both did,' Ronnie added, 'but we love you, girl. You've done us proud, you really 'ave.'

Summer looked at the little folder in her hands. In it was her passport, plane tickets, and a bank statement. 'Mum? have you been looking in my room?'

Avril tittered, clapping her hands together like Mr Burns. 'No silly, it was me! This is my idea.' Ronnie cleared his throat, and she pulled a face at him. 'Okay, nearly all my idea. I'm thirsty, anyway; it's knackering doing all this running about. Noel, get me a drink?'

Avril and Noel wandered off, her little sister waving her arms around at Noel, chatting enthusiastically. Looking at Noel, she noticed he was looking at Avril, open mouthed.

Angie put her hands around the folder, clasping her clammy, shaky hands over her only child's. 'Avril came to my house. She told me everything, how selfish I was being, how unhappy you had been all those years, with me. She's a smart kid. Annoying, but smart.'

Summer was looking at her mother, feeling as though she was dreaming, seeing her in a setting other than her house or the local streets. She was really here, in the airport, hijacking her goodbye. 'Mum, no, it wasn't your fault.'

Her mum wiped a tear away. 'It wasn't yours either, but I guess I chose to punish you somehow. Keep you close to me, but I shouldn't have. I should have pushed you out into the world so you could live your life just how you want to live it and not worry about a twisted old woman like me. I want you to get on that plane and live your life.' She hugged her tight to her. 'I love you, Summer. Thank you for everything.'

Summer looked over her mother's shoulder, gripping her tight. Noel and Avril were standing together now. Noel mouthed *come with me* at her and her heart skipped a beat in her chest. Her mother pulled back and started to open the folder properly.

'Jean and I sorted the tickets, and she is sorting out cover for the shop. I am going to learn the business too and do what I can from home. I am going to work on going to the shop, but Jean says she will keep an eye on things. Apparently, Holly is a dab hand with a computer too. We'll all pitch in. Your passport is here, and luckily you don't need any jabs, although you might need to get things checked when you land. This bank account has a bank card with it; you just need to activate it.'

Summer looked from her face to the folder, rapid fire, trying to make sense of the last ten minutes. 'But Mum, this account had been open for years. There's such a lot of money here. How did you do it?'

'I didn't,' she replied, looking at Ronnie almost kindly. 'When I stopped your father seeing you, he started it.'

Ronnie stepped forward, holding out his hand. Summer took it. 'I was going to save it for your birthday, but when Avril told me about Noel leaving, well, I thought it was a good a time as any. It's your money love, every birthday and Christmas, Easter, every time you got a school award, or an award at work. I have my spies, duck, I kept an eye on you as best I could. This is years of being my daughter, all in money. Go and get on that plane, start living how you want to. We'll all still be here when you get back.'

Summer looked at the account paperwork and threw her arms around her father. 'Thanks Dad. Look after everyone, won't you.'

Ronnie hugged her tight back. 'I will love, I promise. Keep in touch.'

'Ring every day, at least,' Angie added, linking her arm back through Ronnie's for support.

'I can't just go now though, what about you? Who's going to look after you?'

Avril and Noel came forward and the tannoy for Noel's flight was called. 'We have to go, Summer, or we'll miss the flight.' He took the bag and the folder from her and looked at her questioningly. 'You coming?'

Avril started to push her towards the departure lounge. 'Go, come on, get gone. We have things covered. It's only for three months, not forever. You'll be back!'

Summer looked at her mother, who nodded encouragingly. 'She's right, you have to go!'

Noel took her hand in his, and she looked across at him. 'You heard them, Summer. I don't want to pressure you, but we can do this, together. Worst case scenario, we come home early, but at least let's try.' He turned to face her, and everything melted into the background. The noise, the people, they all faded away, winking out like stars in the night. Right then, it was just the two of them, standing in an empty, silent lounge.

'You didn't know about this, did you?'

Noel shook his head slowly, a wry smile on his face. 'No, but I love your little sister for helping. Your mother left the house and came all the way here, with your dad, for this. Imagine the drama that could have exploded, with those three in a confined space moving at speed. It would be rude to waste that effort. Come with me. It's three months, let's go for it. I want you with me. I always did. I always do want you with me, Summer. This is it for me.' He dropped another slow, seductive kiss on her lips. 'I told you, us Pritchetts have weak hearts, but we love hard and forever.'

Summer looked at the man who had crashed into her life, riled her up, helped her, took her shouting and screaming fits, and introduced her to his family. He had laid his life wide open for her and shook her very existence in the process. She'd been dragged out of her comfort zone, dealt with her demons, and now, she had family. So much more family than she ever would have hoped for, and they were all here for her today. Just as she had tried to be for them.

'You sure you're up for this?'

He took her hands in his and squeezed them in his. 'Baby, I never wanted to leave without you. If I could have stuffed you in my pocket, you'd already be in there, covered in lint.'

'Lovely,' Summer laughed.

Noel didn't answer. He was looking at her as though he was terrified that she would disappear.

The tannoy sounded again, announcing the gate was open for the flight.

'Now or never,' Noel said. 'You coming?'

Summer looked back at her mother, father and sister, who were stood looking at them both, arm in arm. 'I love you, Noel Pritchett. Even with your godawful Christmas obsession. I will follow you anywhere.' She stood on her tiptoes and kissed him. He pulled away just enough to speak against her mouth.

'Did you just say you loved me, Summer Hastings?'

She kissed him again. 'Yeah, yeah, like you didn't know.'

He pulled back, stroking the sides of her face and rubbing his nose against hers, Eskimo style. 'Knowing and hearing it are two different things, and you are a bloody stubborn bugger.'

She looked at him, and once again marvelled at this man, who came into her life and changed it forever. 'Let's start our lives then, eh?'

Noel just smiled and took her hand in his. 'Let's go.'

* * *

Two weeks later, Angie woke up and looked at the closed curtains in her bedroom. She remembered buying them. She had bought the material and run up the curtains herself, putting in the soft cotton lining. Sat at her machine one Saturday afternoon, the patio doors to the garden open, bringing with it the smell of sweet peas and sunshine. She had made a pot of tea in her favourite fox teapot, and it sat steaming next to her favourite china mug. She had sat at that table all afternoon, enjoying the peace of her beautiful home, her husband out at work, their daughter out with him, helping him to run his usual weekend market stall. Two peas in a pod, they were, the pair of them. She had the perfect life.

Angie looked at the curtains now and saw them for what they were. Faded, old. Out of fashion, out of step. Sitting up in bed, she looked around her bedroom. Nothing had changed. She had the same wallpaper, the same wardrobe with the wonky door. The wardrobe only half filled because she hadn't even thought to use the space he left. She hadn't even kicked him out of her bedroom really. The photo of them on their wedding day still sat in the bedside table drawer, where it had sat since the day he left. Everything was the same: depressing, muted, dull. She threw back the covers, and walking over to the window, she yanked the curtains open wide. It was time to start the day.

Heading downstairs, she looked around her house through new eyes. Over the last couple of weeks, she had been slowly cleaning, kicking out the dust and dirt from her home, but she hadn't thrown a thing away. She had kept the shrine of her old life intact, just blasted off the grime. Her therapist had been helping her even more since Summer left, and her and Noel had kept in near daily contact, sending her videos and emails and photos of their work, the little hut they had been sleeping in, the children they were helping. She sat and pored over every little nugget of information her daughter sent her, feeding her need for her child through the happy smiles in the photos and the laughter in the videos. Young, happy and in love. Her daughter was finally free, and out there doing what she wanted to do. The business was holding its own, and she had checked in from time to time, but it couldn't last. She needed to start work; it wasn't fair to Summer that her income was so low due to the house costs and the wages for the cover. She walked to the patio doors and looked out at her garden. It was neat now, and tidy, the beds all put to sleep and ready for spring. It looked so pretty, so hopeful now. A promise of things to come.

Walking over to the telephone, she looked in her address book and dialled a number. It was time for her fresh start.

'Is that Home Sure Estate Agents? I would like to put my house on the market.' Listening to the man on the other end, she smiled to herself. It was time for new adventures, a home of her own that she could drink tea and sew curtains in. A house full of laughter and light, with no ghosts of the past clanking their chains. It was time to start living and fill her own jar with beach sand.

ACKNOWLEDGMENTS

This book has been a real labour of love, and I am very proud of how the story came together. I love Bridlington, so visiting and researching with my family was a lot of fun, and I hope I have done it justice.

The idea of *Summer Hates Christmas* came to me just like that – with a title. I had a thought about a girl who was always sunny, always bright, switched on. Wearing the colours of the rainbow, and I wondered what the dark was in her story. We all have it within us. Loneliness hits people in many different ways, and there is nothing quite so sad as someone suffering. I hope that reading this will make people happy and lift that mood. Reading does for me, and that's a precious gift to have.

As ever, huge thanks to Emily Ruston and the amazing power-house team that is Boldwood. I love you all, thank you!

Big thanks to all my writer friends for your support and friend-ship. It's an isolating job, but with you guys at the end of the phone, it's much better.

Thanks to my family, who as ever keep me so busy I can barely write anything half the time, but I wouldn't have it any other way. Love you.

My biggest thanks go to my readers, who keep coming back and reading my stories, reviewing, sharing the love, coming to book signings, getting in touch on social media. I love to chat to readers, so do get in touch and say hello!

P.S. No seagulls were harmed in the making of this book. The one-legged seagull is thriving, and Avril now feeds him daily. Ronnie is working on a pigeon splint, patent pending.

ABOUT THE AUTHOR

Rachel Dove lives in leafy West Yorkshire with her family, and rescue animals Tilly the cat and Darcy the dog (named after Mr Darcy, of course!). A former teacher specialising in Autism, ADHD and SpLDs, she is passionate about changing the system and raising awareness/acceptance. She loves a good rom-com, and the beach!

Sign up to Rachel Dove's mailing list here for news, competitions and updates on future books.

Visit Rachel's website: www.racheldovebooks.co.uk

Follow Rachel on social media:

twitter.com/writerdove

instagram.com/writerdove

facebook.com/racheldoveauthor

tiktok.com/@writerdove

ALSO BY RACHEL DOVE

Ten Dates

Summer Hates Christmas

Mr Right Next Door

Boldwood

Boldwood Books is an award-winning fiction publishing company seeking out the best stories from around the world.

Find out more at www.boldwoodbooks.com

Join our reader community for brilliant books, competitions and offers!

**Follow us
@BoldwoodBooks
@TheBoldBookClub**

Sign up to our weekly deals newsletter

https://bit.ly/BoldwoodBNewsletter

Milton Keynes UK
Ingram Content Group UK Ltd.
UKHW041319170823
427024UK00001B/3

9 781804 836262